Shoestring

an Adventure in the Florida Keys

by

Barbara D. Hall
and
Jon C. Hall

AuthorHouse™
1663 Liberty Drive, Suite 200
Bloomington, IN 47403
www.authorhouse.com
Phone: 1-800-839-8640

First published by AuthorHouse 10/27/2008

ISBN: 978-1-4389-0513-6 (sc)

Printed in the United States of America
Bloomington, Indiana

This book is printed on acid-free paper.

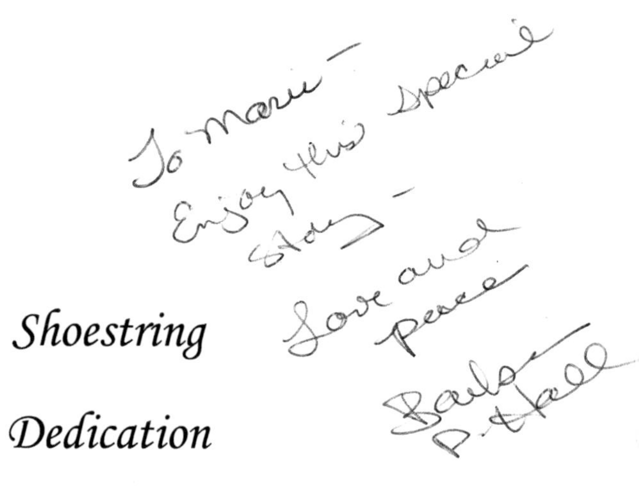

Shoestring

Dedication

I dedicate this book to my oldest brother,
in honor of all the tall tales and stories he told during his life, his kind
and gentle spirit and his sharp intellect.
I thank him, with mixed emotions,
for the journey he gifted me on his passing
and the legacy he left for me to
complete.

The journey has opened the door for me to meet
many wonderful new people and
visit places I never would have found without this gift.
I have received treasures for the mind, spirit and
most importantly, inspiring me to go
beyond *Reality* to discover a new life.

Barbara D. Hall

May 2008

Shoestring

Acknowledgements

I would like to personally thank my sister Barbara D. Hall who continually encouraged me to take a pen in hand and put my stories down on paper. The origins of this story begin with our childhood trips to the Florida Keys. For these adventures and experiences, I thank our father Russell Stewart Hall. Again, much appreciation and thanks go to my sister, whose untiring efforts and support in being a sounding board made this book a reality both in the ideas and assistance in writing this manuscript. Without her continued support and belief in my abilities, this book would not have been possible.

Jon C. Hall

I would like to commend my brother Jon C. Hall for his untiring persistence in writing the preliminary drafts of this manuscript. His natural ability for story telling and unending creativity always held me captivated when he began spinning his tales. Sadly, Jon only finished the first very rough draft of this manuscript, leaving me the monumental task of finishing the story, developing the characters and completing the dog work of editing the final manuscript. I am pleased to have the honor of finishing the final manuscript and seeing the book published. Again, I wish to share one more of my brother's tales with the reader.

I thank my father, Russell S. Hall for his unwavering support for both Jon and I in our endeavors to complete this manuscript and our other three works, *BOKURU, Adam's Eve,* and *Sadie's Secret.* His objective support is greatly appreciated. Special thanks go to Hannelore Hahn, founder of IWWG for her vision in creation of "the magic" at Skidmore, and the inspiration of each and all workshop directors. Special thanks go to my guide who took me for a visit to the Mud Keys, who also has requested to remain anonymous. Photographs for the front cover were taken by Barbara D. Hall on her visits to Florida and the Florida Keys.

Barbara D. Hall

Shoestring

Introduction

For many years now, I have visited the state of Florida, as a child camping with my parents and two older brothers and as an adult visiting my oldest brother who moved to his favorite state, Florida. The beginnings of this story come from our experiences camping in Florida over Christmas vacation as children and revisiting our favorite campgrounds as adults. Unfortunately, Jon passed before finishing this story and manuscript, passing an unexpected legacy for me to complete. This book is the fourth and final of the collaborative efforts with my oldest brother, marking the fulfillment of the promise I made to him to complete the manuscripts if anything happened to him. The journey began when he suffered a brain stem stroke and came to live with me. I never expected to become a writer of fiction and non-fiction books. The journey expanded for me as a full time effort on his passing and finding his encouraging words in the "five blue file folders." Look for our story in my upcoming memoir, *A Stroke of Genius.*

Shoestring is the story of Steve Andrew's journey from Coconut Grove to Key West in his sailboat, through the backcountry of the Florida Keys. On his journey, Steve discovers a desperate villain is tracking him to recover a stash of gold hidden on his sailboat. On this journey, Steve meets various natives and natural inhabitants of the Keys and finds a new life and vision.

The story of ***Shoestring*** is set in the backcountry of the Florida Keys. The authors explore the conflicts of man and the environment on the flora and fauna in our Garden of Eden. An underlying theme of the story becomes how the protagonist deals with the discovery of his love and respect for the treasures in the Florida Keys through his friend, Shoestring who saves his life more than one time and in more than one way.

Barbara Hall

Table of Contents

Shoestring

Prologue

Like many stories that leave a lasting impression, the tale of Shoestring is a personal one. First spoken around the warm glow of an evening campfire along the shore of old Key West, I remember its every detail, for I was the one to whom it was told. I was in awe that evening, a wide-eyed child sitting beneath a canopy of coconut palms that swayed gently in the warm tropical breeze, while the lights of shrimp boats out in the Gulf Stream drifted silently by on the horizon.

For me, the innocence of youth so often absorbed by the fairytales and myths of prior generations paled before this remarkable narrative, and my personal age of wonder focused on a plain, ordinary bird with a name. Little did I realize then that in the end, this story was as much my own as it was of the one who told it. I share it now, because it's message is more relevant than it was when first spoken those many years ago. Of course, for me, the story is deeply emotional for the man who first told it to me was my father.

Lisa Andrews

Chapter One

An Unmarried Man

The law office of Arthur, Williams, Santini, Gold and Eppstein was situated on the 45th floor of the Seminole Building on Brickell Avenue in Miami, just south of the Miami River. As the morning sun rose over a cloudless sky, bright orange and red rays reflected off the water in Biscayne Bay, filling the lobby with bright checkerboard patches of light and shade. Two men dressed in expensive business suits crossed the lobby from the ground floor restaurant to the elevator. As the elevator door closed, the taller of the two men pressed the button for the 45th floor. The elevator whisked the two passengers upwards.

"One more floor," the shorter man remarked casually to his companion.

"Ah, yes, the Penthouse," responded the taller man nodding toward the console light as it blinked on.

"You know, Larry, I can't help feeling sorry for this poor sap."

"Yeah, Detective Rodriguez said our two perps got everything. They cleaned him out. I suppose they'll disbar him, too."

"Well, if he works in this building, he can take the hit. Anyone working here pulls in big bucks. That's the game here or they'd be somewhere else."

"Actually, we're just meeting here. He's a sole practitioner. Rodriguez told me his office is located down the street in another building. Only the two of them worked in the office, leaving her solo when he went out of town. It's a shame, but at least we're onto them sooner this time."

"You mean he left her to work alone? No checks and balances? Isn't that like leaving a fox in charge of the hen house?"

"Sure, but he thought he had a foxy lady, not a fox. Besides, they were married."

"That's right. I forgot about the marriage, the new twist. So maybe it's more like a fox in model's clothing."

"You got it. Rodriguez says the vic was in Orlando when they made their move. When he called her to check in, the fox had blown the coop."

"She emptied all his escrow and trust accounts. I'd like to haul them in before we leave town."

"Me, too. I'd like to stop these two."

"Maria is, what, twenty-four?"

"Closer to twenty-seven. He's around thirty-eight. I don't have any other information about him right now, only what Rodriguez told me on the phone."

"He does fit the whale profile."

"Yes, since he's older he should have known better. He's got nearly twelve years on her."

"She's a real looker from what I heard."

"Yeah, that's why she's the bait. That's the standard pattern-- lawyer falls for pretty office secretary, always a looker."

"This case isn't the first time an attorney was suckered in by a pretty face, drops his guard, and wham, it's over before he knows what hit him. They've had a raft of cases like this down here recently."

"Yeah, maybe, but we're only involved in one, this one."

The elevator stopped and the door opened facing the dark wood paneled lobby of the law office.

"Good morning gentlemen," the receptionist greeted the two men.

"Morning," the taller man responded as he handed her his business card. "I'm Larry Stokes, Investigator from the DA's Office in Las Vegas. This is David Bishop from the DA's office in Denver. We're here for the Andrew's case."

She pressed a buzzer. "The others are waiting for you in Conference Room C. Miriam, Mr. Eppstein's secretary will show you in. Mr. Eppstein is Mr. Andrew's advisor."

A moment later, a young Spanish woman arrived.

"Miriam, these gentlemen are here for the Andrew's meeting."

"Please, follow me," Miriam directed.

Conference Room C faced Biscayne Bay. The walls in the room shimmered with sparkling streams of light reflecting off the water. The beige colored vertical blinds were partially closed to soften the glare, focusing bright parallel bands of light across the walls and ceiling. Ten soft leather upholstered chairs neatly circled a massive mahogany conference table. Four of the chairs were occupied.

"Welcome, gentlemen, we were waiting for you," a white haired gentleman at the head of the table greeted them. As he rose from his chair, his tan suit jacket opened to reveal a small paunch around his middle. Nodding, he introduced himself. "I'm Tom Fieldstone, District Investigator from the Florida Bar. Mr. Andrews invited me to sit in on this meeting." He peered at the attendees over the top of his wire-rimmed bifocals. "Please, gentlemen, have a seat."

The men shook hands briefly and each selected a seat at the table.

"Good morning, gentlemen," the man at the far end of the table spoke as he learned forward, unbuttoning his suit jacket. "We've met on the phone. I'm Special Agent Brian Bellows from the FBI's South Florida District. This is Detective Arturo Rodriguez with the White Collar Crime Division, Miami-Dade Metro on my left. I understand you've all met by telephone."

Detective Rodriguez rose from his chair and shook hands with each of the other gentlemen.

"The gentleman here with the telephone on his ear is Mr. Andrews," continued Agent Bellows with a slight grimace.

On hearing his name, Steve ended his conversation and reached across the table to greet the new arrivals. "Gentlemen, thank you for coming this morning. Help yourself to a cup of coffee and Danish," he pointed to the spread on the credenza behind Agent Bellows. "Please, call me Steve."

"The victim," added David Bishop nodding toward Steve.

"Unfortunately," Steve smiled meekly.

"Just call me David."

"I don't know about you, David, but we just had breakfast in the restaurant downstairs. I couldn't look at another cup of coffee," complained Detective Stokes, "Thanks anyway."

David Bishop nodded in agreement.

Steve removed a stack of report folders from his briefcase. He passed a folder to each of the attendees. When he finished, he closed his briefcase and placed it on the floor beside his chair. "I compiled this report yesterday to give you my perspective on this case. If you need more copies, I have a few extra. The report is divided into sections. The first section contains my resume, a history of my practice, and a list of my regular clients. I provided a brief personal sketch of my background to give you an understanding of who I am and how I got into this mess."

"You've put a lot of time into this," commented Agent Bellows as he thumbed through his copy.

"I wanted to anticipate any questions. It's a Grim story, perhaps a tragedy, but all true," Steve continued. "My parents met in college at Mid-America University outside Cleveland. Neither family had a lot of money, so they both commuted to classes. With a bright future in front of them, they married after graduation. Dad completed a double E."

"What's a double E?" Bellows asked.

"Electrical Engineering. Brocton Electrical hired him immediately out of school. They were an electrical contractor for the aeronautical industry in California doing work for the government on military airplanes. When the war ended, Brocton floundered and failed so Dad lost his job. I was three at the time and they were hesitant to have more children. With the instability of Dad's career, I ended up without siblings. Dad moved into consumer electronics and away from military avionics, then lost his job again. By that time I was in high school and Ma became the sole provider for the family. Electric General closed the Cleveland plant and moved to Mexico. So, that was it. Dad never worked again, by then his skills were obsolete. We scraped by on Ma's income as a secretary and what was left of the family savings."

"This all sounds tough, but I don't understand why you are telling us this," Bellows observed.

"Unfortunately, putting this together and facing the facts was tough. I was suckered in because of my background. I knew I had to go to college to make something of myself. So, to help the family, I worked a daytime job and went to college at night. I had no social life and my friends melted away. We had nothing in common. At first I worked in a grocery store where I became the union steward and department manager. My mother warned me against young women who she perceived as husband hunters, so I didn't date. My sexual awakenings began with the cashiers in the grocery store and others in the stores in the mall. The differences between me and these young women in culture and social background was as deep as the Grand Canyon, so I avoided serious relationships until I finished my law degree."

"You're trying to tell us something?" Bellows asked.

"Yes, why I fell for Maria. Since she vanished with my escrow and trust funds, I've been thinking about it a lot. My lack of social skills through high school and college made me vulnerable to the attention of such a beautiful woman. I never suspected that she was lying to me or setting me up to rip me off."

"She's a looker, that's for sure," Stokes commented.

"She fit my dream. I pictured being a successful lawyer married to a beautiful, sexy woman, have a family and all that. I wanted the American Dream to make up for the struggle I'd had as a young man."

"How did you get here from Cleveland?" Dave Bishop asked.

"One of my friends in law school came from a wealthy Ft. Lauderdale family. He invited me to visit here on spring break. I'd never been to Florida. I loved it. I was tired of the cold and snow, and the palm trees fit my vision of success. I wondered, why wait for retirement? I applied for a job with an abstract company in Cincinnati. When I got the job, I started saving to move to Florida. After working there for about five years, an opportunity to transfer to their Ft. Lauderdale office opened up. I applied for the transfer and they selected me over several other candidates. As you can see on my resume, I worked for them for another five years. I left when one of the partners set up a real estate division on Key Biscayne. He asked me to cover their legal matters. I worked with most of the owners and contractors on Key Biscayne and became the major attorney for the area. One of the contractors picked up the building where Maria was living. I handled the leases and contracts for them. My boss invested heavily in the building. When his health took a down turn, he offered to back me financially to take over his share. The opportunity was like winning the lottery. The building had four condominium units, all of which were undervalued. I estimated they would reap fortuitous profits in five or six years when the current residents moved out. Maria was living in one of the units when we met. The first time I saw her, I was smitten. Old country Italians call it being struck by 'the lightning bolt.' You know the rest."

"So you're not a partner in this firm?" asked Larry Stokes.

"No, my office is down the street a few blocks. Eric and I have a working relationship, so he offered use of the conference room today."

"Well, this is some story," Bellows commented.

"That's the sum of it. I wanted you to understand why I became involved in this whole mess. The second section in the report contains a narrative on how I met Maria and a description of her responsibilities in my office."

"This second section is very interesting," David Bishop commented after perusing the materials for a few moments. "I'd like to study it more thoroughly."

Steve watched as the others continued to thumb through the report. "The report is confidential, for use in this investigation only. The third section describes the case in detail, including copies of the front and back of the stolen checks."

"Are all of the checks accounted for?" asked Rodriguez.

"Yes. They carefully organized their plan, using four different entities and four different banks."

"I'm assuming none of the missing money came from your own personal funds," commented Agent Bellows.

"No. Maria was thorough. She knew all the accounts and authorized the release of client escrow and trust accounts. I included a list of the affected clients, a written authorization for you to do a credit and background check on me and, in the final section, photographs of Maria. They're all I have. I took them with a one shot camera so they're grainy. I'm not a great photographer. For the report, I scanned the originals. Unfortunately, the originals are not so good either."

"Do you have the originals with you?" asked Agent Bellows.

"Sure, in my briefcase."

"I'd like to see them. The copies are too fuzzy, maybe the originals are better," commented Detective Bishop.

"Certainly," Steve opened his briefcase and removed a stack of photographs held together with a rubber band. He slid them across the table. David Bishop removed the rubber band, separated the top few and passed the remainder to Larry Stokes. After reviewing the pictures, they exchanged stacks. No one spoke as they studied the pictures.

"She's the one," David Bishop spoke first, looking over at Agent Bellows. There was an air of finality in his voice.

"You're sure?" Bellows asked.

"No doubt about it," Bishop reaffirmed.

"How about you, Larry?" asked Agent Bellows.

"I agree. She's the one we took into custody in Las Vegas. We released her when the victim refused to press charges."

"Since I've never met her, I have to rely on your assessment," Agent Bellows responded. "You and Bishop are the only ones of us to actually have met her, besides Andrews." He paused for a moment as he perused the material in the folders, stopping to read scattered sections.

"Your story of marital betrayal touches me," Stokes continued. "Believe me, your situation is not unique. You paid a big price to obtain your legal education. I can't imagine what you're going through."

"Anyway, the photos will help us make a positive identification," Bellows added.

Steve looked away from the table, his jaw tightened. Regaining his composure, he turned back towards the men, speaking firmly, "I called this meeting to go on record officially that I will cooperate in every way I can. I want to prevent this from happening to anyone else."

"Just so everyone understands, I'm here on invitation. The Bar has not received a complaint or any report filed against Mr. Andrews as of this date. Mr. Andrews invited me to be a representative here as an observer. We have no plans to audit his escrow or trust accounts for at least another eight months. Again, no one has ever filed a complaint with the Florida Bar against Mr. Andrews."

"Thank you. That's important to know. We haven't pressed charges against Mr. Andrews, either. Our goal is to apprehend Carlos and Maria," Bellows informed the men.

"We brought some photographs of our own, Mr. Andrews. Can you identify the young woman in the photo in the upper left corner of page one?" Larry Stokes slid an open three ring binder across the table to Steve. "Most of these are originals. Leave the prints in the plastic sleeve."

Steve studied the photo intensely. "No, I don't recognize the lady in the photo."

"Sorry, our photos are about as good as yours. When we blow them up, sometimes the fuzzy figures help identify the subjects," Stokes commented.

"No," he said studying the photo carefully. "I definitely don't know her." Steve put the binder down on the table. "I've never seen this person before. I don't know who she is."

"Don't apologize. That photo is a test. Try the next ones, on the last page. They appear to be two different individuals with red hair. The other two photographs were taken when she dyed her hair blond. They're all the same woman."

"You're kidding," Steve looked closer at the pictures. "The differences are astonishing."

"A wig, Mr. Andrews, and different make up. She's a master of disguise," Detective Bishop explained. "All of the pictures are the same person with different wigs and make up."

"The ones on this page are Maria?" Steve mustered slowly. "It's her, all Maria? They're all Maria. She's phenomenal, a real chameleon."

"His wife?" asked Detective Stokes, glancing over at David Bishop.

"Yes," Steve whispered almost incoherently.

"Good," Detective Bishop sighed, relieved. "How about the rest of the pictures on the other pages? Maria?"

"Any doubt about the identity of the subject in any of these pictures?" Agent Stokes asked.

"Absolutely, they're all Maria. Remember, we've been married for nearly a year. They're all Maria."

"Let's try one more. Turn the page. There's another, the FBI Wanted poster. The picture may be a bit fuzzy. It was taken about three years before you met her," Bellows offered the poster to Steve.

Steve studied the photo on the Wanted poster, "That's her, too," his voice quivered as he read the bold print at the top of the page.

"Can you read the name under the picture on the poster?" asked Detective Stokes.

"Yes, Maria Suarez." Steve's voice was filled with sadness.

"There's a second name printed there as well. Do you recognize that name?" Stokes pressed Steve again.

"The alias? No, I've never seen that name. She never used that name around me."

"I see," Larry continued, staring momentarily at Steve and then glancing at Agent Bellows. Bishop continued, "On the next page, check the photo of a new subject in the upper left. Can you tell us about the man in this snapshot?"

"I can't help you with this one. He doesn't look familiar," Steve responded.

"Okay, how about the one on the right."

"Carlos. That's Carlos. Maria's brother." Steve looked up from the pictures.

Stokes continued showing Steve photos, allowing him time to absorb the information. "Carlos? Carlos is Maria's brother?"

"Steve, here's a copy of an FBI Wanted poster with pictures of both, a man and a woman," Larry Stokes retrieved a letter sized poster board from his briefcase and slid it across the table to Steve. "Take a good look."

"Yes, I see the pictures. The last names for the man and woman are the same. I recognize them. They're Maria and Carlos."

"Both listed with the last name, Santiago," Larry Stokes spoke with heavy conviction.

"Yes, I see that on the poster." Steve's gaze remained on the poster, his eyes moving back and forth across the images. "They're brother and sister."

"The next page doesn't have any photos," Stokes stated factually. "You've helped us so maybe we can help make sense of this embarrassing situation."

"Help me?" Steve asked as he picked up the page Larry Stokes handed him. "This is written in Spanish. I don't read or understand Spanish. What does it say?"

"Do you remember the names on the Wanted Poster?" asked Stokes.

"Yes, Santiago. I believe it was Santiago," Steve answered politely.

"Santiago is correct," informed Stokes. "This is the photocopy of a marriage certificate from a little village up in the mountains outside Caracas, Venezuela. It's dated seven years ago, memorializing the ceremony between a man named Carlos Santiago and a woman named Maria Suarez."

Steve sat silently, staring at Stokes.

"What he is saying, Andrews, is that you are not as married as you think you are. In fact, you're seven years too late to be legally married to Maria," Detective Bishop spoke sternly.

"What? How can this be? Maria, married to Carlos? She told me he was her brother," Steve protested, sinking lower into his chair. He suddenly felt very tired. His body sagged as he began to grasp the degree to which Maria had betrayed him. "Maria is married to Carlos? Carlos is Maria's husband?"

"Look, Carlos masterminded everything and Maria followed his instructions," Bellows added.

"Yes, but she's involved in it. She's part of it. It doesn't matter if he planned it and she followed directions. In the eyes of the law, she's equally as responsible as he. There's no denying the truth. Maria is an accomplice." Steve began to get testy and agitated, stuffing his feelings down.

"Carlos took her off the streets of a poor back country village and brought her to The Big City of Caracas, where he trained her. When Carlos was confident she was ready, he brought her to the States," Detective Stoles continued.

"And a life mired in crime," Agent Bellows added.

"Precisely. She might have escaped his control, but we hypothesize the Grant Case was the one that bound her to Carlos," said Detective Stokes.

"The Grant Case? I might as well hear the whole ball of tar." Steve sat quietly as the group of men told him things about Maria he never suspected. With each story, his spirits sank lower, as if he were stabbed in the heart with a barbed spear.

"Yes, the Grant Case, Stanley Grant. Steve, Stanley Grant died." Stokes paused. "This case is a perfect example of their MO. Carlos came up with the plans and the locations and Maria always served as the bait."

"Bait? That beautiful woman, my wife, was bait?" Steve was beginning to waiver between anger and remorse, his emotions a confused mix of sadness and horror.

"I don't have to tell you, men are drawn to her like bees to honey. She worked the cocktail lounges, latching onto the first whale from out of town drinking alone and maybe a little lonely." Stokes watched Steve's face carefully as he revealed Maria's duplicity.

"A whale? What is a whale? I'm sure you're not talking about one of the denizens of the deep."

"Sorry, in Vegas lingo a whale is a mark from out of town, a guy alone with a big wad of money, looking for a good time. Maria's role was to pick up the whale or mark, and steer him away from the bar to either his hotel room or hers where she mixed a special drink for him. We hadn't identified the drug until we encountered the late Mr. Grant," Stokes explained.

"Drug? Late Mr. Grant?"

"Horse tranquilizer, really powerful, jail-time stuff," Stokes added.

"What? Maria did what?" Steve was incredulous. His normally controlled expression cracked with his eyes widening and his lips moving nervously.

"Unfortunately she mixed in too much powder and Mr. Grant became permanently tranquilized," Stokes explained.

"When diluted, it would knock anyone out almost immediately for a good eight hours. However, the important part is that when the victim woke up, he didn't remember a thing. The events several hours prior to the ingestion of the drug were totally erased. They wouldn't even remember having met Maria. They'd wake up with an empty wallet and a major portion of their ego missing," Bishop explained.

"Tell Mr. Andrews about Don Charles, too," suggested Detective Stokes, grinning slightly.

David Bishop went on, chuckling slightly, "We see a lot in this business. Mr. Charles takes the prize. He imagined himself as quite the ladies man. His wife thought he was at a convention in California, but he showed up skiing in Colorado. Carlos and Maria followed the same MO, but with a humorous twist."

"Oh, how so? This isn't funny to me," Steve commiserated with the imagined victims.

"They cleaned him out of everything. When I say everything, I mean everything. They took all of his clothing, even the blanket off the hotel bed, loaded up his rental car and drove away."

"Shocking. Maria did this?"

"The next afternoon, when Mr. Charles woke up, he was stark naked, wrapped in a bed sheet. Can you imagine trying to explain how all this happened to your wife? Needless to say, Mrs. Charles was not too happy. She had to wire money to the hotel so he could buy a shirt and pants, shoes and socks to get home. I'd love to have heard that conversation. Seems he had been making side junkets regularly without his wife's knowledge when he went out of town on business," Bishop continued filling in the details.

"It's hard to believe that really happened." Steve was astonished.

"I digress. The Grant incident became important because he died. Maria misjudged and added too much tranquilizer. The State's Attorney in Vegas wants to press for murder one. Since Maria administered the drug, that put Carlos in total control of her. He threatened to turn her in," Stokes explained.

"So that's how he kept her working for him. I'm convinced she wanted to break away," Bishop added.

"The Grant case is weak. The State failed to produce evidence tying them to the tranquilizer and failed to find any witnesses. She doesn't know our case is weak. Murder one may not stick. Carlos used his knowledge of her role in the case to control her," Stokes continued.

"If you know they did it, why wouldn't the murder charge stick?" asked Steve.

"Well, the complicating factor is that Mr. Grant was not well. Unknown to Carlos and Maria, Mr. Grant had received an artificial heart a few years prior to his death. To prove the cause of death was the tranquilizer and not a problem with the device could be tricky for the coroner. A good defense attorney would have a field day. The truth is that a plea bargain for manslaughter is a realistic possibility. If Maria knew she could beat the murder one charges, she may have broken away from Carlos long ago, and we wouldn't be here today," Stokes commented.

"How long ago did you marry Maria?" asked Bellows.

"About ten months. The exact date is in your folder."

"I'll give you credit," commented Stokes. "You're good. They couldn't separate you from your money without her going through a wedding ceremony. This is a new twist."

"Speaking of being here today," Bellows continued. "Although these other cases are interesting, the FBI is here only because of the Carey case."

"There's more?" Steve moaned.

"Yes, they used the same MO except it went wrong. They kidnapped the victim, taking him across state lines at gun point," Bellows filled in the details.

"Maria was involved in a kidnapping? I can't believe my Maria could ever be involved in these horror stories."

"Your Maria mixed a little tranquilizer drink for her target, only to discover he didn't drink," Bellows informed Steve.

"So what happened?"

"She had to call in the cavalry."

"Carlos?"

"The one and only. He thought he could salvage the situation by taking the mark hostage and holding him for ransom, but that failed. Mr. Carey had no immediate relatives to meet their demands. Anyway, he escaped, but not until they had taken him across state lines, a hundred miles from where they started. That incident made the action a federal offense and brought our office into the picture," Bellows frowned.

"I see." Steve shook his head back and forth, leaning his forehead on his left hand with his elbow on the table.

"Now you know you're a free man. Your marriage is not legal," Detective Rodriguez informed Steve.

Steve's spirits had fallen to the lowest ebb as all the color drained from his face. "Guess you're correct," Steve responded sadly. "I really care for her, Maria. I love her."

"Sorry Andrews. We all thank you for helping us today. We appreciate your cooperation. I hope you find some solace in that you're not legally married to this woman. We're sorry to have to tell you about her dark side, but that's part of our job." Rodriguez spoke apologetically.

"You have certainly opened my eyes. I don't have any choice but to help you apprehend her and Carlos."

"I'm not sure when we'll pay a little visit to the address you gave us for Carlos in Miami Beach, perhaps this afternoon. Assuming we make an arrest, we'll need you to ID them. Because they're both so good at disguises, we anticipate difficulty with the line-ups. We have fingerprints for Carlos, but so far none for Maria. We don't have any evidence to implicated her directly yet," Bellows informed them.

"You're going after Carlos this afternoon?"

"Yes, as soon as we can make the arrest, the better for everyone," Bellows responded enthusiastically.

"I was hoping to take off for a few days."

"Take off?" Detective Rodriguez sounded concerned.

"I signed a contract to sell my sailboat to a buyer in Key West. As part of the deal, I agreed to deliver the boat."

"That's a long trip by boat down the Keys. I have a trailer, wouldn't you rather motor it down on land? It's quicker," Bellows offered.

"You don't understand. I want to do this. I don't really want to sell my boat. I have to. Besides, it's a 26-foot sailboat. It's too big to trailer without taking down the rigging and the mast, and too expensive to hire a yard to do it. I don't have a cradle to secure it on a trailer nor the money to pay someone else to do it. For me it will be easier to sail it down the Keys to Key West. Besides, I want one last cruise on it."

"It's about 150 miles to Key West. If you make 5 miles an hour and spend eight hours a day sailing, it will take you a good four days to reach Key West," Bellows estimated.

"Actually, estimating the distance from the charts, I calculated closer to 180 miles by water. It's not a direct shot. So, realistically, I estimated six days with good weather."

"That won't work. We need you here," Bellows objected.

"Not a problem. I'll come ashore each evening to call in. If you need me, I can always leave the boat at a marina and fly back to Miami from either Marathon or Key West."

"Why do you need to come ashore? Don't you have a cell phone or VHF radio on board? Can't you just check in periodically from the boat?" Bellows asked.

"Maria took my cell phone and my VHF radio isn't working. Besides, it's not a good idea to make phone calls over the radio. You'd have to broadcast your credit card information. Eric has agreed to cover my office while I'm gone. I'll need to check in daily on the status of my cases. If I come in too late at night, I'll call him in the morning. He can keep you advised."

"That's not ideal, but it might work. Don't go anywhere this afternoon or tomorrow in case we wrap this case up today," Bellows demanded of Steve.

"Before you guys get all warm and cozy, I object," Rodriguez butted in. "We have an open investigation with a lot of money missing. Everyone is a suspect including Andrews until we rule him or her out. Mr. Andrews is a suspect until he's eliminated by substantiated facts. A few years ago we had a similar case where an attorney claimed his secretary ran off with his money."

"I remember that case. I didn't handle it, but I was aware of it," Tom Fieldstone interjected.

"Actually, the attorney was in cahoots with the secretary. They embezzled the money and converted it into gold coins. They chartered a boat out of Mexico," Rodriguez continued.

"This case is different. No one has contacted us with a complaint. The funds were taken from a title company, not a trust account. As I recall, the guy in the other case led the good life down in Key West for a while," Fieldstone continued.

"Precisely. He buddied up to the Mayor, the Sheriff and the State's Attorney. When he was caught, the news media had a field day, especially when they discovered he and the Sheriff had regular dinner engagements," Rodriguez summarized the details of the case. "We don't want to repeat an embarrassing incident, especially when the circumstances appear so similar. How do we know Mr. Andrews doesn't plan to run off with Maria and the money, leaving Carlos behind?" he asked the group.

The men were silent. A flash of lights on the console and buzz from the receptionist's desk broke the silence. Steve tapped the intercom button on.

"Yes?"

The receptionist's voice responded, "Mr. Andrews, please."

"Yes," Steve repeated into the speaker.

"This is Miriam. A fax just came in for you. Do you want me to bring it in?"

"Yes, immediately."

Miriam appeared in the doorway and handed several documents to Steve. After checking the pages, he handed them to Tom Fieldstone.

"These are close enough," Steve commented as Tom Fieldstone read them slowly.

After a minute, Fieldstone looked up and spoke. "You know, Mr. Andrews put up his personal property against the missing funds and informed the clients affected. In reviewing these documents, all have accepted the agreement providing his property as collateral to cover the missing funds. This means, in real terms, they have no loss. Since there is no claim or complaint against Mr. Andrews filed with the State Bar Association, we have no basis to audit his accounts. The official position of the Bar is that we have no basis to open a disciplinary investigation of Mr. Andrews. These letters are executory, so I'm going to request Mr. Andrews confirm them in writing when everything has taken place as indicated. Other than that, gentleman, the Bar has no further interest in this matter. On the face of these documents, Detective Rodriguez, Mr. Andrews preventive actions make this case quite different from the one two years ago."

"Interesting," Bellows commented, looking over at Detective Rodriguez. Rodriguez said nothing. "Apparently there is no reason for us to press charges against you. You have been most helpful in our investigation. We won't take up any more of your time until we apprehend either Carlos or Maria, or both of them. Then we will need you to identify them positively for us."

"Before you leave, Agent Bellows, I'd like to introduce you to Eric. His office is down the hall. I've prepared a detailed sail plan estimating when I'll be calling in and where I'll come ashore to check in with him." Steve informed them.

"I'll coordinate," Bellows volunteered. "That is, if everyone else agrees," he looked toward Detective Rodriguez.

"Okay, I'll go along with it," Rodriguez conceded, "but you'd better avoid the Monroe County Sheriff while you're in the Keys. He's still smarting over the other incident two years ago. If you ask me, he's likely to haul you in on charges of vagrancy or something equally as vague to show he's doing his job."

"Is he a sailor?" asked Bellows.

"No, I'm sure he isn't," replied Rodriguez. "He's into motorcycles, big time. He runs the local motorcycle club and takes advantage of the frequent weekend rides and gatherings up and down the Keys."

"Ok, Andrews. Follow Rodriguez's advice. Stay off shore as much as you can. That way you can avoid the local authorities and stay clear of Carlos, too," Bellows recommended.

"I will. Actually, I prefer sleeping on board rather than in a motel. I'll come ashore daily to call in and pick up provisions. So, gentlemen, I gather we have an agreement and I'm free to take the boat to Key West?"

"Good, yes. We've covered everything for now. We'll do our part to find these two before they do any more harm. Ok, Andrews, let's go meet Eric."

Chapter Two

A Simple Choice

For hours, Steve waited in the bar at the Coconut Grove Yacht Club for Agent Bellows to call. The call never came. When he arrived, he had delivered a copy of his sail plan to the commodore's office. Before he left Miami, he had also dropped off a copy of his plan for Eric, marked with his anticipated stops on copies of the marine chart from his Chart Kit. After checking and rechecking the weather reports, he waited for the predicted storm front to blow through before going out to his boat. The worst part of the storm had hit the harbor a little after 8:00 PM. The initial dark clouds and winds were severe. Frequent rumbles of thunder and flashes of lightning disturbed the usual tranquility of the harbor. Once the earlier angry clouds had passed, the rain remained heavy for a couple of hours as the wind settled down to a steady, manageable blow out of the northwest, perfect for heading down the bay. Steve anticipated by morning the wind would shift out of the north, bringing a strong, steady cold front for two to three days. Eventually the wind would clock around, turn east and lose intensity, warming up again. Winter weather in southern Florida was broken by frequent fronts blowing in a fairly predictable cooling and warming cycle.

Finally, around 11:00 PM, when the worst of the front had passed over, Steve gave up waiting for Agent Bellows' phone call. He left the bar to catch the last tender run for the evening. Scattered storm clouds continued to deliver light intermittent showers as gusty winds traced across the harbor on the way to the Gulf Stream and off into the Atlantic. Darkness and rain limited his visibility as he buttoned up his foul weather jacket. With the aid of glimmering harbor lights, he motored out of the harbor. Peering through the light mist, he located the channel markers leading to the open bay. Due to the weather, he decided not to put up the main sail. Sailing solo at night was not the time to leave the cockpit to raise the main, besides he could control his roller-furling jib from the cockpit. He released the jib sheets, knowing that the jib would provide enough sail power to cross the bay. Cranking the jib in and out according to the strength of the wind, he glided down the bay away from Coconut Grove. Once out of the channel, he had turned the engine off, enjoying the sounds of the boat slicing through the gentle chop of the following waves and listening to the main halyard clanking against the mast. He sighed, relishing being at the helm again, feeling the wind blow across his face and jacket. As the familiar glow of the distant lights from downtown Miami faded into the darkness behind him, he noted how much light there still remained from the moon and stars above as night enveloped him.

To stay on track with his sail plan, he must reach Jewfish Creek by noon the next day. The small drawbridge at Jewfish Creek crossed US Highway 1 where the Keys met the Florida mainland. His first challenge was to find the markers for the Intercoastal channel at Black Bank. Without a radio, if he ran aground and missed the passage, help would be a long time coming if he needed assistance. Although narrow, the passage was well marked with reflectors fixed on the channel markers. Steve followed his compass course to make the first channel marker.

The soft glow light on the compass mounted on the bulkhead provided his primary navigation instrument. The steady breeze and intermittent brushes of raindrops streaked gently across his face. The Intercoastal channel was several miles ahead, providing the only passageway through Black Bank. Black Bank was a long, muddy bank stretching across the bay, dividing it in half. The only way to reach the lower bay was to pass through this channel. If he missed the channel, he would run aground in the soft mud. Running aground without a working radio could set his schedule off if he had to wait until daylight for help.

Steve's first scheduled stop was to be at Jewfish Creek Marina. The marina was situated on the far side of the US Highway 1 drawbridge, before entering the Florida Keys. He had marked the marina on the charts as the first stop to call Eric. To keep his planned timetable, he needed to make up for the hours he had spent in the yacht club bar waiting for Agent Bellows' call. He had many miles to cover before dawn.

Steve was concerned about making the channel at Black Bank, but was even more apprehensive about the longer narrow channel near Card Sound Bridge. As he sailed swiftly down the bay, he decided not to attempt the Card Sound passage until the weather cleared and he had daylight. In addition, the stress of the past few days was catching up with him. He felt drained mentally and physically. Knowing that exhaustion was a sailor's greatest enemy, he modified his plan to anchor in the lee of Black Bank once he had passed through Black Bank Channel. A few hours at anchor would allow him to rest while the remainder of the weather passed into the Gulf Stream. Daylight would allow him to successfully follow the ribbon-like Intercoastal Waterway as it narrowed near the Card Sound Bridge. Since he was not as familiar with the lower bay, he opted to wait for daylight.

Shortly, using his flashlight, he picked up the channel marker reflecting back a bright beam of light, confirming his course. Within thirty minutes he had passed into the channel. He headed *Seaseeker* into the wind, loosened the jib sheet and furled in the sail. He started the engine and thrust the motor into gear. With low visibility and intermittent moonlight, he rounded the last channel mark and turned close to the north end of the bank where the water depth readings on the Fathometer started to decrease. Although he was not sheltered from the wind, the bank blunted the force of the choppy waves following him down the bay.

Even in the darkness and misty rain, Steve could see the eelgrass breaking the surface along the outcrop of the mud bank. Since it was low tide, the windward side of the bank would provide protection from the wave action. Despite anchoring in the middle of Biscayne Bay, Black Bank would provide protection from the waves while he rested.

Seaseeker's primary anchor was a twelve-pound Danforth mounted on the bow. The Danforth anchor is most commonly used for the size of his boat. Although the Danforth was easy to handle, he did not want to take the time go forward to set the anchor. The Danforth's two pointed flukes, when properly set, dig deep into the bottom, producing far more holding power than any similar sized anchor. As he mulled his situation over, he decided he was too tired to play out the chain and anchor line. Anxious to go below to rest under a warm blanket, he dismissed taking reasonable precautions as too much work under the prevailing conditions. He convinced himself that, for a few hours, he would be safe without setting the Danforth. He also dismissed the knowledge that sailboats tend to swing at anchor. Even when anchored properly, under certain conditions, swinging could cause the anchor to break free. Steve carried a second smaller mushroom anchor stored in the lazarette he used occasionally to stabilize the boat. In contrast to the Danforth, the smaller anchor had little to no holding power and would not prevent the boat from swinging in a brisk wind. Steve retrieved the mushroom anchor from the lazarette and dropped it over the side. He walked the anchor line to the bow of the boat and secured it to the bow cleat.

He knew the mushroom anchor would not hold all night but convinced himself it would hold for a few hours. Even if the boat dragged a short distance, he would not be in any danger. After all, no one else would be out in the middle of Biscayne Bay late on a weekday evening in bad weather. He watched the anchor line briefly. When he was confident the anchor appeared to be holding, he slipped below out of the rain and wind. Removing his foul weather gear, he collapsed onto the closest bunk, pulled up the comforter and snuggled under its warmth. He fitfully mulled over the conversations with the detectives and Agent Bellows at the meeting in Eric's office, chastising himself. How could he have been so wrong about Maria? How had he missed her deception? Why hadn't he detected the true relationship between Maria and Carlos? How could he have been so gullible? His heart ached remembering his feelings for her and felt the stabbing pain remembering her deception. Confused, hurt and tired, Steve drifted into a fitful state of semi-consciousness. With his physical activities terminated for the day, his mind took over playing havoc with his emotions.

He shuddered agonizing over the terrible mistake in judgment he had made in trusting Maria and what it had cost him. How could he ever recover the money he lost? How could he ever get over her? He still had strong feelings for her. Waves of anger, disappointment and affection raged war inside his head. Hadn't he decided to sell the boat, his passion when Maria announced she was not a sailor and refused to join him on the boat? He was willing to make any sacrifice for the success of his marriage. Sadly, since he had not wanted to sail alone, or spend his leisure time without her, he agreed to sell the boat. Fortunately, he had found a buyer in Key West. Because the offer appeared timely in view of his current financial crisis, he had readily signed the sales contract. With Maria out of the picture, even if the buyer let him out of the contract, Steve still needed to sell the boat. Maria had cost him everything, his practice, his reputation, his investments and savings, but deep down, he resented having to sell the boat more than everything else. He did not want to give up his sailboat. To him, the boat represented his peace, tranquility, and escape from the constant stresses of his legal practice. He loved being outdoors experiencing the continually changing conditions of wind, weather and observing nature's creatures. Being out on the water soothed his soul and rejuvenated his spirits. Recognizing the sale of his boat was his greatest loss after Maria, he tried to picture his life without his favorite escape from reality. With conflicting thoughts running through his exhausted mind and body, Steve fell into a deep sleep.

Chapter Three

A Tap in Time

Most sailors sleep lightly attuned to the motion of their boat and the sound of the waves lapping against the hull, particularly when they are the sole crewmember. Steve woke suddenly and sat bolt upright in his bunk. In the darkness, an annoying sound above his head at the porthole window had startled him awake.

There it was again. Tap. Tap. Tap. Realizing he had heard the sound before, like an object hitting a windowpane, the sound repeated. Tap. Tap. Tap.

He shrugged the drowsiness out of his eyes, noting daylight was beginning to lighten the haze of the low-lying clouds surrounding the boat. He was annoyed that the strange tapping sound had startled him awake. As he swung his legs over the side of the bunk, he could see an eerie yellow light infusing the fog, penetrating the mist and reflecting off the white cabin walls. The light illuminated the cabin with an ominous yellow glow.

At the back of his consciousness, he thought he detected the motion of a black blur slide across the porthole window. His heightened senses told him something was outside on the starboard deck. Between the strange yellow light and sensation of something on deck, his skin began to crawl with fear.

A second later, he heard the unmistakable, deep throbbing pulse of the cylinders of a large diesel engine, not very far away. The sound screamed at his senses that something was wrong, terribly wrong.

Without taking the time to dress, Steve bolted up the companionway ladder, skipping steps, sliding open the hatch, and climbing out into the cockpit. The worst of the weather had passed, improving visibility. Looking in the direction of the sound, he saw, looming out of the darkness, the massive hull of a fuel barge, pushed by a huge two-story tugboat. Judging the speed and distance between the tug and his sailboat, Steve estimated there were only a few crucial minutes before the barge would plow into *Seaseeker* broadside, crushing the fragile fiberglass hull into tiny bits beneath its massive hulk. Steve instantly recognized the familiar outline of the fuel barge and tug on the way to the Stock Island power plant, providing all the power for Key West. He reminded himself that the rig also passed through Black Bank Channel on its way south. As fear penetrated his body, he could not believe he had forgotten about commercial traffic traveling along the Intercoastal Waterway. Every pleasure boater in Biscayne Bay gave this rig a respectfully wide berth.

The huge searchlight mounted on the tug powerhouse scanned the opposite side of the channel for the last marker on the south side. Steve realized that no one on board the tug had seen his boat adrift in the channel to the north and if they had, there was no way to alter its course due to the momentum of the tug and barge in the water. Steve and *Seaseeker* were in a collision course with the tug and barge.

Steve stumbled to the stern of *Seaseeker,* quickly switched the ignition key on, and pushed the ignition button. As he heard the engine kick into life, in one motion, he thrust the engine into gear, pushed the throttle as far forward as it would go, and leaned on the tiller. Ever so slowly at first, *Seaseeker* began to move out of the way of the ominous dark mass of the barge as it bore down on Steve in his much smaller sailboat. The passageway was narrow, but the sailboat responded more rapidly, moving at a right angle from the channel, heading away from the path of the rapidly approaching tug and tow. To avoid the impending collision, Steve had to move out of the center of the channel into the shallows toward the mud bank as fast as possible. Only at the last moment was he sure that the tug and fuel barge would pass safely by, barely a few feet from the stern of his boat. As the tug passed by with a narrow margin, he watched the powerful surge with awe and nervous relief that he had avoided meeting the force of the large, deep-set propellers churning behind the tug. Briefly, the force of the water pulled a surge back towards the tug. Steve struggled with the tiller to maintain control and direction to keep his sailboat out of the strong slipstream attempting to pull him back toward the propellers. In the flash of an eye, the danger was over.

For several moments afterwards, he sat shivering in the cockpit, quietly recuperating from his too close encounter with disaster. As he regained his composure, he watched the white stern lights of the tug retreat steadily away from him, down the channel toward Stock Island. As the rig turned and disappeared from sight on its way to Key West, the tension in his body began to subside and he began to shudder. He faintly remembered the thought that a tapping sound on the porthole window had broken his sleep. When he glanced at the window and along the deck, nothing was there.

Since he was still shaken by the near miss, he decided to stay in the protection of the mud bank until after dawn. He went forward to the bow of the boat and tugged on the anchor line. The line was hanging straight down in the water. Feeling the tension in the line, he knew the anchor was no longer hitting bottom. He pulled the mushroom anchor back on board and re-anchored using the Danforth, setting it properly. When he finished, he returned to the cabin to prepare some nourishment and a cup of hot coffee. He contemplated the incident again, mulling over and over every detail and every move he had made. He was comforted knowing his instincts and automatic responses had brought him successfully through the danger. While his coffee was brewing, he refreshed himself with a moistened washcloth, wiping the nervous sweat from his face and neck. He slipped into dry clothes. Warmed and relaxed, he stretched out on the bunk, wondering if perhaps the tapping sound he thought he had heard had saved his life, or had that been merely part of a dream?

Chapter Four

Shoestring

Steve woke at dawn as the rays of sunlight filtered through the porthole windows and reflected off the interior of the cabin. He bolted upright in his bunk, startled by the sound coming from the porthole window immediately above his head. Tap. Tap. Tap. Now he knew he had heard that sound before. He recognized the sound as the same one he had heard earlier as it resonated like an object hitting a windowpane. As he struggled to shake out of his drowsiness, Steve heard the sound repeat. Tap. Tap. Tap.

Steve twisted his body to look through the porthole window. A black blur slid across the narrow Plexiglas pane. In contrast with the evening before, he could clearly see something black on the starboard deck blocking his view.

Standing, he slid the hatch open and scrambled up the companionway to get a clear view of the deck. In spite of the bright rays from the sun, he shivered from the chill in the air. Since the storm front had passed, he knew crisp, cool weather would prevail for the remainder of his trip.

"Well, I'll be," Steve exclaimed out loud.

On the deck, standing beside the porthole window was what many of the locals referred to as a "black duck." Steve recognized the bird immediately as a common cormorant, a frequent inhabitant of the eastern shores of the US, southern Florida, and the Keys. Although not a true duck, many people confused this bird with the loon due to its appearance. Unlike true ducks, the cormorant's head was no wider than its neck, giving it an odd, comical appearance. When viewed head on, the bird resembled it's closest relative, the anhinga, also commonly found in the Florida Keys. The characteristic structure of the anhinga's neck led to its nickname, "snake bird." The cormorant, with its curved, hook-shaped bill distinguished it from the anhinga's sharply pointed dagger bill. Adding to the unusual demeanor of this bird, a piece of seaweed dangled from its curled beak.

"I'll be damned, a black duck. Did you wake me last night, just in time to save my life?"

The duck did not answer. With its head cocked slightly to the side, the bird stared back at Steve.

"Everyone else has a guardian angel. I get a duck. You look hungry. Stay there. I'll get you something to eat. That's the least I can do to return the favor." Not wanting to disturb the bird, Steve backed down into the cabin and rummaged through his food stores until he found a can of sardines. "Perfect," he announced as he pried the can open. Removing two of the oily fish, he placed them on a small plastic plate, and returned to the cockpit.

The bird had not moved. Steve eased along the deck toward the bird. As he drew closer, the bird turned and waddled away toward the bow of the boat, still carrying the seaweed in its beak. Steve placed the plate on the deck below the porthole window and slipped back into the cockpit. Although the bird appeared not to fear him, it maintained a safe distance between them.

Once Steve returned to the cockpit, the bird waddled back to the porthole window, dropped the seaweed and peered at the sardines. Without wasting any motion, the duck picked up one of the sardines; front end first and promptly swallowed it whole. The bird looked back at Steve, paused, then repeated the process, consuming the second sardine. Once finished, the duck looked at Steve, turned and waddled to the bow of the boat where it stood like a sentry on duty. Silently, the duck began vibrating its throat and spread its wings out to dry. The outline of the black bird made a stark contrast against the large red-orange orb of the sun rising on the horizon.

"You are a strange bird. Look, I've got some housekeeping to do and I've got to make some breakfast. If you're still hungry, tap on the window. I have more sardines left in the can. They'll go bad if you don't eat them all. Oh, and don't poop on my deck, I have enough to do."

The bird remained at the bow facing into the chilly wind. Steve slipped back into the cabin and gathered his wet clothing from the previous evening. "This cool wind will dry these out in a hurry," he muttered. He hung everything, including his wet sneakers, over the lifelines along the stern. He carefully tied the shoelaces of each sneaker to secure them to the rail. With the sun warming up, his clothes would dry quickly.

Returning to the cabin, he scrambled two eggs and reheated his coffee. Detecting motion in the cockpit out of the corner of his eye, he looked up to see the duck waddle along the deck towards his sneakers swinging in response to the breeze. Fascinated, he watched the duck approach the first sneaker, grasp the shoelace with its beak and pull until the knot untied. The sneaker dropped to the deck and rolled onto the cockpit floor. Without pausing, the bird addressed the second shoe, pulled on a loose shoelace until the knot gave way and the second sneaker dropped, hitting the deck. This time the sneaker fell, rolling in the opposite direction, falling over the side and splashing into the bay.

"Hey, wait a minute," Steve hollered as he scrambled up the companionway steps. "That's my shoe. I need it." Steve's loud protestations frightened the bird. With the noise and commotion, the duck flew away. When he reached the stern, Steve leaned under the lifelines and peered into the water. His sneaker was resting on the bottom in five feet of water. Steve cursed the duck as he shed his warm clothing and jumped into the water to retrieve his sneaker.

That was enough excitement for one morning Steve decided. After returning to the boat with his shoe, drying off, and finishing his now cold scrambled eggs, he pulled up the anchor and set sail. Running under the power of the jib he glided down the Intercoastal Waterway. Forty minutes later, he passed under the Card Sound Bridge and by noon he had crossed Barnes Sound. As he approached the entrance to the Jewfish Creek Channel, he loosened the jib sheets and rolled up the large Genoa. He would have to motor using his diesel engine now for the entire journey through the channel to the marina. Because the channel was narrow and wound around through the mangroves to the drawbridge at US Highway 1, he would not be able to sail during this section of the trip. The marina was located on the other side of the bridge and was his first stop to call to Eric.

He started his engine and steered the boat toward the narrow entrance to the channel. Watching the bow of his boat slice through the water, the cormorant returned and slowly dropped onto the bow, once again standing in position as sentry on *Seaseeker*. The bird had followed him for nearly thirty miles down the bay

Steve thought silently, "This is unusual behavior for a wild bird." Out loud, he directed his thoughts to the bird, "You're back. If you're going to hang around, you need to have a name." Steve paused to think for the best, most appropriate name for this persistent bird. "I think I'll call you 'Shoestring,' because of your propensity for shoelaces. I've never heard of a bird doing that before. An unusual bird merits an unusual name."

The bird paid no heed to the fact that it now had a name. Shoestring stood on the bow, facing the direction they were headed, oblivious to anything that Steve said or did.

Chapter Five

Encounter at Jewfish Creek

After passing through the open drawbridge, Steve eased *Seaseeker* up to the marina dock and secured the boat. Surprisingly, Shoestring had remained at his post on the bow during the whole distance through the channel. Even when Steve approached the bow at the dock, Shoestring did not fly off. Instead, holding his ground, Shoestring waddled a short distance back from the bow along the port deck where he remained until Steve finished securing the bowline. Once Steve moved away from the boat, Shoestring waddled back to the bow, reclaiming his post.

Steve placed the weatherboard over the companionway and closed the lock over the hasp. Before leaving the boat, he slid the remaining sardines onto the plastic plate and placed it on the deck by the cabin. Steve could see the pay phone mounted outside the bait and tackle shop next to the dock. He chuckled out loud at the pseudo-tropical cabana surrounding the pay phone. A medium sized plastic coconut palm shaded the phone booth from the heat of the noontime sun. Eric had agreed to accept collect calls, which he would repay when he returned to Miami. He dropped the empty sardine can into a trashcan as he picked up the receiver. The dial tone sounded; the phone was working. So far, his plan was working.

As he dialed Eric's number, he glanced sideways toward the highway, beyond the drawbridge. His heart skipped a beat as he caught movement. Parked on the berm of the southbound lane, he saw a yellow Hummer, exactly like the one Carlos drove. Strangely, the driver was leaning across the front fender onto the hood, peering directly at Steve through a pair of binoculars. Steve looked away pretending not to see the observer. Curiously, as he turned back to the phone booth, he caught the image of a second vehicle parked along the berm of the southbound lane, farther north on the landside of the bridge. What made Steve take another surreptitious glance was not the dark colored four-door sedan, but the fact someone outside that vehicle was also peering through binoculars. However, this man in the second vehicle was watching the occupant of the yellow Hummer. To Steve, the scenario appeared ridiculous, reminiscent of a Keystone cops caper. Why was someone watching him and then, why would someone so obviously watch the driver of the Hummer?

With shaking hands, Steve finished dialing Eric's office. The phone rang over six times.

"Hello, Steve?"

"Yes, Eric, it's me. I'm glad you're there."

"Right on. Where are you now?"

"Check the charts. I'm on target at the first mark at Jewfish Creek. I'm calling from a payphone at the marina on the Key Largo side of the highway bridge. I've made it to the beginning of the Keys."

"Great, I see the mark. Congratulations, so far you're on schedule."

"Look, Eric, something's wrong. Some guy in a yellow Hummer is watching me from the highway bridge through binoculars. I swear it's Carlos."

"Geez. That can't be. Carlos and Maria are on their way out of the country."

"Says who?"

"Says you. That's what you told me, Steve."

"That's what Bellows and the government agents predicted, but I swear that's Carlos' Hummer parked by the highway."

"Can you see the license plate?"

"No, not from here. The car is parked parallel to me. I can't see the back."

"What about his face?"

"No. He's hunkered down on the hood. His face is hidden behind the binoculars. Besides, he's too far away even if he lowered the binoculars."

"He could be a bird watcher."

"Yeah, right, but I'm no bird. He's looking directly at me."

"That could be your imagination. There are a lot of yellow Hummers in southern Florida."

"Sure, but I didn't tell you about the other car. There's another guy watching the guy in the Hummer."

"Another car?"

"Yes, I see two more guys in a dark colored sedan. The passenger in the sedan has his binoculars focused on the guy in the Hummer."

"Another bird watcher?"

"Now you're being funny. I know what I see, Eric, and they're not watching birds."

"Geez. Steve, I don't know. You're there and I'm here. Pretend you don't see them."

"I am. I'm minding my own business."

"Good. Can you hide out there, somewhere?"

"Hide? Not really. A boat on a dock is not easy to hide. Even on the water, there isn't anywhere to hide."

"Can you get out of sight for a while? I'll call Agent Bellows to see if he knows anything."

"Good idea. I can do that. Did they raid Carlos' apartment yet?"

"I haven't heard. Hole in there while I call Bellows."

"I'm next to a bait and tackle shop. I'll go inside for a while."

"Good, hang around for half an hour or so. If I find out anything, I'll call you back. The number came up on my caller ID. Will you hear the phone ring if I call back?"

"Sure, the phone is next to a screen the door and there's no air conditioning. I'll hear the phone."

"If I have any news, I'll call back. If you don't hear from me in half an hour and they're still there, call me back."

"What if they leave?"

"Then you're okay, they're birdwatchers. Stick to your schedule. Call me tonight at your next stop. Hmm, there it is on the chart. I plan to work late, probably 'til around 9:00. If you miss me tonight, call me first thing in the morning. I should be in by 8:00. Are they still there?"

"Yes, nothing has changed."

"Good luck."

"Bye for now."

Steve placed the phone in the receiver and entered the bait and tackle shop.

Chapter Six

A Bird's Tale

A cozy clutter of every conceivable item a fisherman could ever need or want decorated the inside of the bait and tackle shop. Racks containing a variety of fishing rods and reels, lures, shiners, poppers and bobbers filled the western wall. The drawers below contained spools of various weights of fishing line and drawers labeled with sinker weights. In the middle of the shop, several racks ran the length of the store, filled with snacks and miscellaneous grocery and toiletry items and another with boating supplies and hardware. A small, heavy wood table covered with a green and white-checkered tablecloth was nestled under a window in the far corner. Four captains' chairs with cushions matching the tablecloth surrounded the table. A coffee maker sat at the back edge of the table with a full pot of coffee. Steve's mouth watered for a cup as he drew in the welcome aroma of fresh brewed coffee. A big, burly, bearded man stood behind the counter. His well-worn blue jeans, faded sweatshirt, and weathered captain's hat bespoke years of outdoor activity.

"Mornin,'" the man greeted Steve.

"Good morning," Steve smiled back, nodding slightly as he closed the screen door behind him. How was he going to spend half an hour in this small shop doing nothing with this man watching his every move?

"M'name's Will Turner, but everyone 'round here calls me Cap'n Bill," he spoke smoothly with a heavy Scottish lilt.

"Steve Andrews, here," Steve volunteered, holding out his right hand. Cap'n Bill grasped Steve's outstretched hand firmly.

"Anythin' I can help ye with t'day?"

"No, thanks. I'm just looking. Actually, I'm killing time waiting for a call on the pay phone outside. I'm sure I'll find something in here for my trip."

"Be me guest. That yer boat on the dock?"

"Yes, the Essex 26."

"I know the Essex. Old man Stanton's been working on those boats over in Tavernier for years. They're perfect for the water here in the Keys. Shallow draft's an asset so ye kin pull into any lagoon or inlet and not go aground."

"Mine's an older model, about 15 years old. I bought it in Ft. Lauderdale and kept it in Coconut Grove."

"Where ye headed, mate? Haven't seen ye here before."

"Key West. I'm running my boat down there to deliver it to the new owner. I just sold it to a guy in Key West."

"Steppin' up to a bigger boat, mon?"

"No, not sure what I'm gonna do. My wife doesn't like the four s's: sea, sand, sun or sailing."

"Sorry. I understand," Cap'n Bill shook his head knowingly. "Still, I wouldn't head down to Key West without crew. Boating's no fun unless someone else comes along, plus it's safer, especially with our sudden afternoon squalls. Better to have extra hands if ye get in a bind. Helpin' hands make a big difference."

"I agree but I was caught short at the last minute. None of my sailing buddies could shake loose to help. I could have used help last night. I tired fast with the bad weather so I anchored off Black Bank."

"Tell me about it," Cap'n Bill motioned for Steve to sit at the table. "If there's something to be learned, I'll share it with me customers. We all can learn from someone else's mistakes."

Relieved to have someone to help pass the time, Steve chose a chair facing Cap'n Bill. What could he lose to tell his story? The pay phone was silent. He had the time to tell the tale of his near miss with the fuel barge.

When he finished, Cap'n Bill spouted, "That's some story, Andrews. Have a cup of coffee on me." Pouring coffee into a small Styrofoam cup from the pot on the table, he handed it to Steve. "Cream or sugar?"

"Black is fine. Thanks." Steve inhaled the rich aroma and took a sip.

Bill poured a second cup of coffee. Taking a slow sip, he placed the cup down on the table. "What kind of anchor do ye have?"

"A twelve pound Danforth."

"Chain?"

"Sure, twelve feet of 5/8"."

"How 'bout yer rode?"

"A hundred seventy five feet."

"Hell, Andrews, ye got the right ground tackle. Why the hell didn't ye use it? There was no reason to drift if ye'd anchored proper like."

"I was exhausted, wet and cold and it was late. All I wanted was to rest for a couple of hours."

"A sailor's nightmare."

"I didn't expect anybody else out there so late in such bad weather."

"Hell, I wouldn't rule in yer favor on this one. Commercial traffic ignores time and weather. They just plow on. Big rigs don't have to look out for anybody in their way."

"So I found out."

"Yer whole incident happened because ye failed to anchor properly. An undersized mushroom on a short line is fine for bass fishing in a dinghy on Lake Okeechobee on a lazy summer afternoon, not in bad weather on the Intercoastal in a 26 foot sailboat."

"I admit it wasn't the best decision I ever made."

"Smart? A damned fool mistake, if ye ask me. Andrews, ye nearly lost yer life, and yer boat. Forgive me my outspokenness. Well, let's look at what ye did do right afore we condemn ye for what ye did wrong."

"I didn't do anything right." Steve hung his head.

"Maybe not, let's take a look. Ye sailed down Biscayne Bay past Black Bank to hole up for the night. That decision was good; the conditions were bad so ye decided to ride out the storm at anchor and start back up when conditions improved and ye rested up a piece. That was good thinking."

"I wasn't familiar with the lower bay down to Card Sound. I didn't want to try to find that channel in the dark and rain."

"Okay, that was a good decision. Next, ye picked the only protection around, Black Bank. Oh, Black Bank won't protect ye from the wind, but snugged up on the lee side, the mud bank will shelter ye from the waves. Hell, even if the tide came all the way in, ye'd be fine. The tidal difference can't be more than eighteen inches out there. Even at low tide, there's plenty of water close to the Intercoastal. That was good thinking."

"Seemed like a good spot to me."

"Black Bank's secluded and the bottom there has good, hard mud for anchoring. No one would hassle ye out there and there's plenty of room to move around when the boat swings."

"That's why I carry the mushroom. Sometimes I use it to steady the stern."

"Out there ye wouldn't be bothered by sand flies, mosquitoes, or no-see-'ums, even in the summer when there's no wind. As I see it, yer problems began when ye yielded to the sailor's nightmare, fatigue. We all know fatigue impairs yer judgment. Hell, all ye had to do was trip your Danforth and back yer boat into the mud. Yer mistake was grabbing the wrong anchor. Otherwise, I see good seamanship."

"Thanks. I knew I'd drift some, but I forgot about commercial traffic, like the Key West oil barge."

"Of course the mushroom didn't hold and ye drifted into the middle of the channel. Ah yes, and suddenly ye wake up in time to scramble to the cockpit, start yer engine and avoid the oncoming barge. That rig has to displace at least forty tons fully loaded. Hell, that barge would crush any fiberglass boat like an eggshell."

Steve shuddered.

Cap'n Bill paused to sip his coffee. He stared back at Steve. "Ye know what really bothers me about this whole affair, Andrews?"

"You mean my stupidity?"

"No, not yer bad anchoring decision, but getting too tired, every boater's enemy. An occasional lapse of good judgment under stress and exhaustion on the water can end up deadly."

"I made a stupid decision, but the bird saved me. You forgot the bird." Upset at the omission, Steve demanded Cap'n Bill acknowledge the bird.

"Ah yes, the bird. That concerns me, mate, yer conviction that some stupid bird saved yer life by tapping on yer porthole window. Ye claim a bird woke ye up just in time to avoid the collision, saving yer life and yer boat."

"Yes, that's what happened." Steve put his coffee down, glaring at Cap'n Bill.

Cap'n Bill scowled, "And ye don't think the sounds of a big rig and its bright search light shining through yer porthole window had a thing to do with it?"

"I'm sure. The bird tapping on my window woke me."

"Seems to me yer discounting the sounds and smells and lights of a four ton tug powered with 2000 horse power diesels pushing a forty ton barge a few feet from yer boat. A rig like that don't just creep up on ye. Andrews, I'm familiar with those rigs. Seen 'em many times. They do a bang up job announcing their arrival everywhere they go. Ye come in here and try to tell me some bird acted like a guardian angel, saw yer predicament, and swooped down to save yer life? Hogwash, Andrews. Hogwash." Cap'n Bill shook his head and slapped his hand on the table. Steve's body jerked in response to the sudden noise.

Cap'n Bill waited for the effect of his words to sink in, then reaching across the table, pulled a napkin out of the dispenser. Smoothing the folded napkin flat, he removed a pen from his shirt pocket and drew a circle about the size of a dime on the napkin. He studied the circle for a moment, then blacked in the center. Steve watched silently, his brow furrowed.

"There ye have it, mate. Ye see it, don't ye?" Cap'n Bill leaned back in his chair, satisfied as he folded his arms across his chest.

Steve peered at the dark circle. He didn't know what to say. He squinted at the drawing on the napkin as the wrinkles on his forehead deepened. "It looks like a large dot to me."

"Bigger than a dime, smaller than a quarter."

"Yes, but..."He had no idea what Cap'n Bill was trying to demonstrate about the boat, the fuel rig, or the napkin.

Cap'n Bill glared back at Steve's puzzled expression. "Instinct," he spouted pointing to the dark circle on the napkin. "The brain of a bird, Andrews. Me sketch may not be exact, but it's close enough, don't ye think?"

"Yes," Steve responded automatically, relieved to know what the circle represented.

"Ever see a bird faced straight on? Ever looked one eyeball to eyeball?"

"Never got that close."

"No room in there for cognitive thought. Bird brains are all instinct and genetics. Ye know, inherited behavior. No room inside a bird's head for anything else."

"You make a strong point," Steve eyed the drawing.

"Look at that dot, no room for gray matter. Birds are hard wired, no cognitive ability. Know what yer missing?"

"What?"

"Ye self…Picture this: Here's this tug and barge bearing down on ye in the middle of the night in a thunder squall. With seconds to spare, ye scramble out on the deck, size up the situation, start up yer engine, put it in gear, and steer yer way clear. Hell, the average person would panic or freeze and would have been lost in the crush. Yer a real cool customer, mate. Anyone can get themselves into trouble, but it takes a cool head and good seamanship to get yerself out, especially what ye did last night." Cap'n Bill was silent. There wasn't much more to add. "Ye sell yerself short, Andrews. Yer mystery bird didn't save yer life, ye saved yer own soul. Ye want some more coffee? It's on me. I'm glad yer alive." Cap'n Bill poured more coffee into both cups. "After hearing yer story, I'd need something stiffer than a cup of coffee to settle me nerves, but it's too early in the mornin'."

"No, thanks. I'm fine. I don't think I could drink another sip."

As Cap'n Bill passed by the open screen door, he glanced out at the dock, "That yer boat out there?"

"Yes, *Seaseeker*."

Both men gazed through the screen door. Cap'n Bill paused, shook his head from side to side. "That yer bird?"

"Oh, yes. That's him, at his station on the bow, just like I said. He's followed me all the way down from Black Bank."

"Ye didn't tell me yer bird was a cormorant. Hell, mate, that's Shoestring. I know that bird."

"Shoestring? That's the same name I gave him this morning." Steve's eyes grew wider.

"Hell, everyone calls that bird Shoestring. He sure makes a nuisance of himself trying to untie every shoelace he crosses. He's been hanging around here off and on for months."

"That's amazing. We call him the same name."

Cap'n Bill returned to his post behind the counter and rummaged around underneath before he returned to the table. He carried a small, green leather covered book and a folded pair of bifocals back to the table. He refilled both cups with coffee before sitting down. Putting on his bifocals, he began to thumb through the book.

Steve noted the title of the book, "Birds of the South."

Finding his page, Cap'n Bill spoke: "Here's what the book says about yer feathered friend. I been wanting to look him up for some time. Ah, here he is, they call him a double crested cormorant." He peered over the top of the book at Steve, dropping it slightly.

"Shoestring? Are you talking about Shoestring?"

"The book says cormorants measure nearly thirty-six inches tall, standing upright; they are black with a slender body, long neck and an orange, sharp hooked beak."

"That's Shoestring. Why do they call it double crested? I've never seen crests on a cormorant. Shoestring doesn't have them."

"The book says cormorants have two tufts of short feathers on the top of their head. I've never seen them either. The book says they're supposed to be there," Cap'n Bill continued to read silently, flipping to the next page. "I'm sure we have the right bird. Only two other types of cormorants are found in the US and neither one inhabits the Keys. This one, the double crested cormorant, inhabits the entire US coastline."

"The description sounds like Shoestring."

"According to this book, the bird grunts like a pig," Cap'n Bill chuckled and continued to read to Steve.

"Shoestring hasn't made a sound, other than tapping on my porthole window."

"The silent type. Hell, I'm sure we have the right bird, Andrews. Yer bird looks like the picture right here." Cap'n Bill turned the picture toward Steve.

"What else does your book say?"

"His Latin name is *Phalacrocorax auritus.* I can't even pronounce it right."

"That's a fancy name. Does the book tell you what that means?"

"It's Latin for *sea crow.*"

"Sea crow? That makes sense. They're so common."

"The next paragraph says the cormorant usually perches on tree branches and posts."

"And the bow of my boat."

"I think Shoestring is partially tame."

"I wouldn't use the word tame. Shoestring won't let me touch him, let alone get near him. When I get too close, he either waddles or flies away. He likes to be around people, but only at a respectable distance."

"The book says cormorants dive to feed on the bottom, usually in shallow water to catch small fish and minnows."

"Add sardines, too. I've been feeding him sardines. He wastes no time, swallows them down promptly."

"When I first came to South Florida, I confused the cormorant with the anhinga. Locals call the anhinga 'snake bird,' from its long neck and thin head. Ye can tell them apart by the bills. The cormorant's bill is stocky and curled. The anhinga has a straight, thin-pointed one to spear its pray. Oh here, they do share one thing in common…"

"What's that?"

"They speak the same language, grunts, like pigs. Oh, it says they nest near each other, but don't interbreed."

"Shoestring seems oblivious to his own kind," commented Steve.

"According to the book, anhinga's and cormorants share another thing. They both perch to spread their wings wide open to dry in the sun."

"Why do they do that?"

"Neither bird has oil glands like real ducks. When they dive, their feathers get water logged so they need to hang them out to dry, so to speak." With that comment, Cap'n Bill snapped the book closed and looked up at Steve. "That's all they wrote about yer bird."

"Thanks. You've told me more than I wanted to know."

"I think it's more interesting in what it doesn't say."

"How so?"

"Like how a cormorant can rescue people in a dangerous situation, saving some hapless fool from his own folly. In fact, the book says nothing about the intellectual capacity of any bird. I suspect the book doesn't say anything about that because there isn't anything to say."

"Well, I know what happened to me last night."

"Ah, but ye never actually saw the bird until this morning."

"That's true."

"Instinct serves nature's creatures well, mate. The problem is humans meddle in what took millions of years for nature to perfect, making crazy things happen. When the birds imprint on humans instead of their parents, the natural order for the birds is all messed up."

"We humans do make a mess of our own personal relationships, why not birds and animals, too?"

"Well, since ye got here ye call Shoestring a *he*. How do ye know he isn't a *she*?"

"Only the birds know for sure, we don't."

"Seems strange ye picked one sex over the other," Cap'n Bill sipped his coffee and watched Steve's face for a reaction.

"Yes, I did automatically assume Shoestring is a *he*."

"Know what I think?"

"Go on, I'm listening."

"In my opinion, ye couldn't accept a female of any species saving ye. It's psychic."

"I never thought about it."

"Hell, if ye don't know, neither do I. We all do the same thing. We all refer to that bird as *he* and there isn't a one of us that can explain why. What the hell, mate, it's an arbitrary call. Let's just pretend he's a *he* and let it go at that. Ye have to admit it's interesting to conjure how our brains work."

"Sure is and we don't have a clue. Hmm, would I be as accepting if the bird that saved me was female? *She* tapped on my porthole window? Was it because *she* was attracted to me rather than a friendly warrior on a mercy mission? All I know is I wouldn't be here today if it weren't for Shoestring."

"I heard a story floating around Jewfish Creek about yer bird. Interested?"

"Really? A story about Shoestring? Sure, I'd like to hear it."

"I just work here. I'm supposed to charge a buck for a cup of coffee and I've filled our cups three times. Hell, most of the time, no one shows up so I throw it away. So, we might as well finish this pot. Ye seem to have time on yer hands."

"Thanks. I can't drink another cup, but tell me the story." Steve tipped his empty cup, checking the contents on the bottom and setting the cup back down on the table.

"Ok, on one condition, don't quote me. I don't know if it's true or not." Bill refilled both cups, ignoring Steve's reply.

"Okay. I'll bite. I'm curious."

Bill took a big gulp of coffee, then cleared his throat. "I'm not much at telling stories but here goes. Some years ago, a retired couple named Svenson, that kept a farm up in Wisconsin, drove down to Key Largo every winter for four to six months to get away from the snow. The Keys got in their blood. When they came down, they traveled US Highway 1 and then on the way back they crossed the Card Sound Bridge."

"Oh, I know those bridges. I passed under both this morning on my way here."

"Well, that's where it happened, at the bend, right under the bridge."

"You lost me. What happened?"

"Heart attack. The old man died at the wheel of his car. One second he was there and the next he was gone. The wife struggled to get control of the steering wheel before the car went off the bank into the water."

"Did she make it? Did she get control of the car?"

"By some miracle she stopped the car at the bend, just before the bridge. She was lucky the car didn't plunge into the canal."

"Wow, but what does that have to do with Shoestring?"

"Patience, I'm getting there. Several old houseboats were tied up along the canal near where the car stopped. Another woman, we called her 'Houseboat Hannah,' lived in one of them. Anyway, to make a long story short as I can, she rushed off the boat to help Bertha and the old man."

"Bertha?"

"Mrs. Svenson. The two women became good friends from the accident. Hannah felt sorry for Bertha and invited her to stay on with her. They couldn't do anything to help the old man. Bertha buried him up in Homestead and never went back to Wisconsin. They stayed on at Card Sound for two to three years. Bertha had a daughter or someone settle her affairs up North."

"That must have been traumatic for her. I guess she couldn't face driving back to Wisconsin alone."

"Hannah planned to move the houseboat to Key Largo, but somehow that never happened. Bertha had a difficult adjustment to deal with the loss of her husband; apparently they were childhood sweethearts. Gradually, she started helping the birds along the Keys."

"How did she do that? Involved with the birds on the Keys, doing what?"

"Oh, not the healthy ones flying around. She helped the injured and sick ones, the ones that needed assistance. She borrowed Hannah's skiff to check the shoreline regularly, looking for sick and injured birds, particularly after a storm. If she couldn't help them, she took them to the Seabird Rescue Station on Key Largo. If she could do something, she nursed them back to health, then released them. Helping the birds gave her life new meaning."

"That's a touching story."

"She developed quite a reputation because she was so involved with the birds. In the upper Keys, people began to call her 'Birdie.' They called day and night with sick birds that were pets as well as birds rescued from the wild. She never said no. Hannah helped until her health failed and she had to move to a nursing home, but Birdie stayed on."

"What dedication. That's admirable, but what does that have to do with Shoestring?"

"Be patient, I'm getting there. When I was fishing, I used to see her paddling around the mangroves looking for injured birds. She'd find birds with broken wings or tangled up in discarded fishing line, plastic bags or those rings from soda can six packs. Anyway, one afternoon after a big blow, she was doing one of her routine checks up at Black Mangrove Key when she found a small, brown fledgling blown out of the rookery. The nest and bird were floating in a mass of leaves and branches in the bay. Apparently, the branch where the nest was attached broke off in the storm and blew out into the bay."

"Shoestring?"

"Shoestring. She knew the parents wouldn't find him. Afraid the fledgling would starve to death, she brought him back to the houseboat. In addition to feeding it sardines when he tapped on her window, she taught him to feed off the bottom by dropping a shoe in the water and rewarding him for retrieving it. He picked the shoe up by the laces."

"That was creative. Did it work?"

Cap'n Bill chuckled. "Ye know the answer to that. Didn't ye tell me ye watched Shoestring untie yer sneakers and one dropped into the water?"

"Yes, but Shoestring didn't retrieve my shoe. I had to go get it."

"Well, that's the story. Some time later the houseboat caught fire and burned down to the waterline. Some thought a kerosene lamp tipped over and started the fire. Both ladies got out safely but when the bird returned, the houseboat was gone. The two ladies moved up to Homestead and the remains of the houseboat sank to the bottom of the canal."

"Shoestring's attraction to shoelaces gives some credence to your story."

"Only the laces. Anyway, the down side of the story is that the bird was left alone and kept going back to where the houseboat used to be. When he couldn't find the houseboat, he flew out to the Intercoastal looking for the next best substitute. When he finds one, he taps on the glass for attention or food and trades a piece of string or seaweed for a meal, just like the old lady trained him. Shoestring has strayed down here to Jewfish Creek."

"Like me."

"Like ye. But remember one thing."

"What's that?"

"Shoestring hangs around the docks for a few days, nipping at people's shoes, but he always flies back up to Card Sound and starts the cycle over again."

"That's some story."

"Yup, ye got it. That's what it is, a real story, a bird story. The bird? He's a creature of habit and training, tapping on your window for food, but watch out, after he's full, he'll waddle up and untie yer shoes. With his fixation for shoestrings, as ye know, we don't know if he's collecting nesting materials or gathering food. No shoe around is safe if it's tied with laces."

"That's my experience. Even though you can't get too close, everything's on his terms. He unties laces when you're not looking."

"He's a messed up duck, Andrews. Maybe Birdie Svenson saved him, but messing with Mother Nature screwed him up forever. Instinct, Andrews, instinct. That bird didn't save ye, ye saved yerself." Cap'n Bill picked up the two, now empty coffee cups and dropped them into the trashcan by the door. "If there's anything ye need, let me know." By the time he finished speaking, Cap'n Bill was back behind the counter.

Steve began to feel he had tarried too long, waiting for a call that failed to come. He stood and followed Cap'n Bill to the sales counter. "I'll take a dozen cans of sardines, for the bird." He guessed he had been there over an hour telling bird tales. Perhaps he had overstayed his welcome. More importantly, the pay phone outside had remained silent. Eric had not called back.

Steve grinned back at Cap'n Bill as he peeled a few bills from a wad he retrieved from his pocket. "Thanks for the stories, the coffee and the sardines." Picking the bag up off the counter, he turned and headed out the door.

"Thank ye for the company, mate. Careful about the weather and yer anchor on yer trip down the backcountry."

Still concerned about the yellow Hummer and the dark sedan, Steve glanced in the direction where he had last seen them. The yellow Hummer was gone from the south end of the bridge and the sedan was missing from the north. Both vehicles, passengers, drivers and binoculars were gone, leaving an uneasy space in his mind. As he focused his attention on *Seaseeker*, he observed that Shoestring also was gone. The blood in his cheeks reddened with embarrassment. He had just purchased a dozen cans of sardines for Shoestring and the bird was gone.

Cap'n Bill was right. Shoestring was heading back to Card Sound to find his next ride down the Intercoastal Waterway.

Chapter Seven

Hurricane Express

Except in extreme conditions, powerboats are much simpler to handle than sailboats. After turning on the engine, the captain steers his boat in the direction he wants to go, shifts into gear and pushes the throttle forward. Without much ado, he'll arrive at his destination far sooner than the sailor. In contrast, the sailor has to evaluate the wind, weather and water conditions before pulling up the anchor and setting the sails. Sometimes weather prevents the sailor from reaching his destination, or brings challenging conditions to overcome to succeed. If the wind and current come out of the intended destination, the sailor may not even attempt the course, or fall back on his auxiliary engine. To reach his destination, the sailor must plot a course, tack back and forth across the wind, often in a zigzag fashion to reach his goal. Occasionally, the sailor must drop his sails and use his engine, particularly in close harbors or channels and when experiencing opposing wind and currents. For the sailor, nature's forces cannot be ignored.

Standing on the dock watching the early morning sun warm the air, Steve dismissed the events of the previous day at Jewfish Creek, forgetting Carlos and the federal agents tracking him. He focused his attention on the weather conditions. In the protected channel of Jewfish Creek, the wind had little effect. However, another hundred yards down the channel, the wind was blowing steadily at twenty knots in Blackwater Sound. The wind had churned up the bottom making the water a muddy brown, even in the channel. Out in Blackwater Sound, the wind had whipped the choppy water up into two-foot whitecaps. Once entering the bay, he would be at the mercy of the full force of the wind and chop of the waves.

Preparing for the weather ahead, he formulated his plan for leaving the protected channel. When Steve had purchased *Seaseeker*, she came equipped with a roller-furling jib, easily controlled from the cockpit. Roller furling eliminated the need to leave the cockpit to crank the main sail up. Having control of the size of the jib from the cockpit, he could unfurl the sail and adjust the amount of sail exposed to the wind while remaining at the helm, handling the boat efficiently and safely without crew and eliminating the need to raise the main sail.

Crossing the three miles in Blackwater Sound would be swift in this weather. Once he reached the opposite side of the sound, he would furl in the sail and motor through the winding mangrove lined channel of Dusenbury Creek. The far end of the creek opened up into Tarpon Basin, which was also not wide enough to sail. He would continue to motor through Tarpon Basin and through the mangroves along Grouper Creek's channel. Then, after sailing across Buttonwood Sound, he would motor through the Swash Key passage to his next stop, the Hurricane Express on Federal Highway at the southwestern end of Key Largo. From the water, Hurricane Express could be easily seen in the middle of Community Harbor.

Once underway, he sailed easily across Buttonwood Sound and furled in the Genoa before approaching the creek through Boggy Key. As soon as he had furled in the sail, he discovered Cap'n Bill was wrong. Shoestring returned to his position at the bow, gently gliding down onto the clear deck.

Steve chuckled. "Shoestring. You're back. Glad to see you." Steve stood at attention with a mock salute as his first mate landed, minding his own business. "Nice to have you aboard." In retrospect, Cap'n Bill was wrong. Shoestring had not flown back up to Card Sound but had returned to his post on *Seaseeker*. Steve felt embarrassed, not that he was talking to a bird, but at his own euphoria that the black duck had rejoined him. Steve muttered softly under his breath, "A strange companion for a lawyer."

Standing at attention, Shoestring remained silent, ignoring Steve's greeting. For Steve, Shoestring's appearance triggered visions of marine pilots on the large commercial cruise ships as they passed through Government Cut in Miami, mimicking their officious demeanor as they supervised their vessel's passage through the busy channel. The bird turned head into the wind until they entered Dusenbury Creek where they were protected from its continuous force. Repeatedly when the wind crossed the bow, Shoestring turned and pointed his head into the wind. Like other birds, Shoestring protected his feathers from damage by acting as nature's wind vane. With Shoestring on duty, Steve had a readily visible wind vane.

When Steve unfurled the jib while crossing Buttonwood Sound, Shoestring relinquished his position to the power of the sail, reappearing when he furled the sail before approaching the motel dock. Shoestring waddled down the deck along the cabin avoiding Steve as he tied the bowline to the dock cleat. When Steve had finished securing the boat to the dock, Shoestring resumed his station at the bow. As Steve stepped onto the dock to make his call to Eric, he looked back to see Shoestring at attention, like a sentry on guard.

Even though he was averaging around four knots an hour, Steve recalculated the time it would take to reach Key West. He had been far too aggressive in estimating the distance he could accomplish in one day. In reality, his course was taking much longer than he had originally estimated. He attributed the difference to the necessity of winding through the mangroves and around the flats, unable to travel in a straight line. Unfortunately, he had reached the motel after dark. Multi-colored lights surrounded the roof of the cabana by the pool, providing dim lighting as he traversed the ramp to shore. Approaching the motel, he became apprehensive when the nerves at the back of his neck and his arms prickled automatically. Even though he saw nothing to trigger his internal alarms, he instinctively sensed some unseen danger. He could clearly see the cabana, the pool and the two-story motel at the far end of the dock. Perhaps he was remembering the incident with Carlos at Jewfish Creek. Anticipating an adversarial confrontation, he pictured Carlos trailing him, with the feds trailing

Carlos. The whole scenario made little sense to him. Maria and Carlos should already be out of the state, if not the country, with the bulk of his money. Steve stopped and looked at the bird standing at attention at the bow of his boat. "Well, my friend, no matter what, I think she really loved me. You're the only one that believes me." He stood quietly watching Shoestring then turned and shuffled up the ramp to the motel.

Steve found a pay phone around the corner of the cabana, mounted on the wall. Still feeling an ominous chill, he paused to survey the back of the motel before dialing Eric's number. Scanning the people in the area, he spotted the bartender. A muscular young man in his early twenties sporting a deep bronze tan and sun-bleached hair was cleaning the bar glasses. His attention was riveted on the football game projected on the television screen suspended in the center of the cabana beams behind the bar. Two middle-aged men deeply engrossed in a heated conversation sat at the far end of the bar, while three older men and two women were playing cards at a candle lit table between the pool and the cabana. Steve could hear the rise and fall of their voices, even though he couldn't distinguish the words. Assuring himself that Carlos was not behind the motel stalking him, seated at the bar, nor sitting at one of the tables scattered around the pool, he dialed Eric's number.

As soon as the phone rang, Eric picked up the receiver. Eric was waiting at the phone, anxious to receive his call.

"Steve?"

"Yes, it's me."

"Great. Where are you?"

"Below Buttonwood Sound, see the mark on the chart?"

"Okay. Got it. I see your mark. Are you sitting or standing?"

"I'm standing. Why?"

"Are you in a safe place?"

"I'm at a pay phone behind the cabana at The Hurricane Express Resort. Why? You're scaring me."

"Okay, I've got the motel name. Look, Agent Bellows wants you to be careful from now on. Can you see your boat?"

"No, it's around the corner and down the dock. If the phone cord was longer I could see it. Why?"

"Don't let the boat out of your sight. Bellows advised for you to check carefully each time you come ashore to be sure Carlos isn't around."

"The dock is empty right now. The bartender's in the cabana with several people sitting at the bar and at tables by the pool. No one else is here. Why the mystery?"

"Bellows is worried about your safety, and secondly, about your boat."

"The boat? Why the boat?"

"Wait, I'll start at the beginning."

"Please do."

"They raided Carlos' apartment yesterday afternoon. No one was there except the old lady."

"His mother?"

"No, turns out she's the landlady, not his mother. She sublet part of her apartment to Carlos for a little cash on the side."

"Oh, I thought she was his mother."

"No, she told them the whole story."

"What story?"

"I have bad news. I don't know how you're going to feel about this." Eric hesitated before he blurted out quickly, "They found Maria there, she's in the hospital."

"The hospital! Where, what happened? She was fine when I saw her last." Steve couldn't hide his feelings. His hands began to shake as his fingers squeezed the phone tighter.

"Slow down. Apparently, she and Carlos had a fight. We don't know if she tripped or was pushed, but she fell down the stairs."

"Oh, no," said Steve, surprised at the intensity of his feelings, considering her betrayal and deceit. He realized his feelings for her were not so easily turned off. "Is she alright?"

"To be honest, she's in bad shape, Steve. I don't have any more information from the hospital. I couldn't get much since I'm not a relative. She was unconscious when the ambulance arrived and was badly bruised from the fall. I'll find out more tomorrow from Bellows. Anyway, the old lady said they fought over your money, or I should say, the gold."

"The gold? I didn't have any gold."

"Gold, Steve. They changed your money into gold coins and bullion using a dealer somewhere in Miami. You know, Krugerands, Canadian Maple leafs, standard gold currency so your money couldn't be traced."

"That makes sense. They were smart. Changed to gold, you're right, no one could trace the money."

"Precisely, but listen to this. This is bizarre. Agent Bellows says the old lady told him Maria protested she couldn't go through with the deal with Carlos. She told Carlos she gave the gold back to you."

"To me? That's preposterous. I don't know anything about the money or the gold. This is all news to me. I thought both of them would be long gone into the sunset, with my clients' money."

"We did, too. The old lady heard Maria claim she stashed the gold on your boat. In the hospital, Maria told Bellows under questioning she planned to leave Carlos and go back to her village in Venezuela, without Carlos."

"You're kidding."

"'Fraid not."

"So I did see Carlos this morning at Jewfish Creek. That was his Hummer."

"Apparently so, Bellows confirmed it."

"He was being followed, too. By the feds."

"You've got it. They found his Hummer abandoned in a mall parking lot on Key Largo. They were hanging around at Jewfish Creek because they didn't want him to try anything. Now they figure he's after the gold on your boat."

"But there is no gold on my boat."

"We know that. You know that. But Carlos doesn't know that. He thinks there's a whole lot of gold coins worth a whole lot of money stashed on your boat."

"Okay. So Carlos was at Jewfish Creek this morning behind the binoculars. This means he's seriously tracking me."

"Bellows confirmed the license plates this morning. Carlos was watching you like a hawk. He's tracking you down the Keys. While you're taking the boat down by water, he's tracking you by land. He wants that gold back."

"Geez. That's all I need to know."

"That's why I cautioned you to watch your boat at all times. He's after his gold. Bellows says Carlos sees it as his gold, stolen, fair and square. The way Carlos thinks, you have his gold and he wants it back."

"Man, that's all I need, some wacko desperado tracking me. Is he dangerous? He doesn't have a gun does he?" Steve's voice quivered and his body began to shake.

"That's why you've got to watch your boat. He's after that gold and we're sure he's desperate to get it back. We don't know for sure whether he's armed or not, but we all know he's not the three piece suit type."

"Okay, I understand, but try to find out more information about Carlos for me, okay? Will the feds stay on his trail?"

"Yes. They want to pick up Carlos as soon as they can, so Bellows wanted me to warn you."

"So Carlos sees me as 'Midas Man' and is looking for an opportunity to steal the gold back."

"Something like that, but it's not funny. Look, for what it's worth, Bellows thinks Maria told Carlos you have the gold to deflect his attention away from her. He's convinced that Maria used you to get Carlos off her back. Unfortunately, Carlos believes her story. That's why he's following you down the Keys, looking for the opportunity to get his gold back. We don't think he knows your itinerary. He was at Jewfish Creek because everyone has to go through Jewfish Creek."

"That's true. At least what I saw at the bridge makes sense now."

"Agent Bellows wanted you to know everything we know. Sorry, I had to wait for your call."

"Do you think Carlos knows I'm going all the way to Key West?"

"How could he? Only you and I knew your plans until the meeting two days ago."

"Sure, you're right. There aren't any connections between Carlos and any of the attendees at the meeting. Maria knew I was selling the boat, but I don't think she knew when or where. Carlos must have found out about my trip from someone else, maybe at the yacht club in Coconut Grove."

"Bellows says their psychologist profiled Carlos as a dry land type. We anticipate he'll leave you alone while you're in open water. He'll make his move on land, sometime when you come ashore. That's why Bellows told me to warn you to be careful until they have him in custody."

"You mean they're going to do more than stand around and watch him attempt to steal from me?"

"When you were back at Jewfish Creek, the agents hadn't confirmed the license plates on the Hummer. In fact, they didn't know they were following Carlos until they confirmed the plates. Right now, they want to bring him in on charges of assault. They don't want anyone else harmed. Most likely, he's armed and dangerous. Bellows says the psychological profile for Carlos indicates he won't come in without a fight, so they want to pick the time and place, carefully."

"Hopefully sooner, not later. Okay, I'm up to date on Carlos. Since there's only one road down the Keys and he's driving a bright yellow Hummer, keeping track of him should be easy. Right now I don't see him, but he could be anywhere, in a window or behind a curtain."

"I agree. You're vulnerable. Apparently what Maria told him worked. But remember, he's not driving the Hummer anymore. He's stolen another car. We haven't been able to confirm the make and model yet."

"Great. Let's change the subject. There's nothing I can do about that. So, have you heard from my buyer? I'm not on vacation. Any word?"

"No, still no word from him. I left a message on his answering machine and talked to a young woman at La Concha Grill where he works. He isn't scheduled to work until seven o'clock tonight, so I'll try again later this evening. He's scheduled to close the joint at 2 AM."

"Good."

"Oh, about your cases, the Williams case closed today, but Old Man Strang didn't come in to sign his will."

"Keep trying. That's a complicated will. I put a lot of time on it and I'd like to see the old man sign it before he drops dead. He has a lot vested in those documents."

"I'm going to West Palm tomorrow on business, so I can make a call on Boca Savings on my way back. You've got a lot of outstanding bills for them. They owe you a bundle."

"They add up. I appreciate whatever you can do. That money would help now."

"Look, you'd better go. Agent Bellows doesn't want you to stay ashore any longer than necessary. With Carlos on the loose, it's too risky. Stay off land as much as possible, so get out of there."

"Okay, but I thought the feds were tailing Carlos."

"They are, but they lost him somewhere on Key Largo."

"I'm on Key Largo."

"That's my point. I'll tell Bellows where you are, but you've got to look out for yourself, and the best way to do that is get back out on the open water."

"There goes my hot shower and soft bed tonight."

"Don't stay at the dock long either. Stay off shore as much as possible until they have Carlos in custody."

"There isn't a protected anchorage around here. I'll have to stay out in the bay. In this weather I won't get much sleep with the wind whistling through the rigging and choppy waves rocking the boat."

"You're on your own. Oh, Bellows wanted me to tell you one more thing."

"Okay, the best for last. What is it?"

"The old lady claimed she saw Carlos had a revolver and a high-powered rifle, both are missing from his apartment, so consider Carlos armed and extremely dangerous."

"Thanks for the good news. I'm out of here. If Agent Bellows asks, I plan to anchor behind a small key along the channel for the night. It's open, so Carlos could easily pick me off with the rifle. I'm in real trouble if he has a scope on it."

"Relax. He's not after you. He's after the boat with the gold. That's why we believe he'll make his move when you come ashore. So for now, stay off shore until they nab him."

"Alienation of affection."

"What?"

"I think he's upset I stole his wife's affection when she decided to jump ship. He may be more angry at me than they suspect."

"That may be, Steve. The psychological profile shows Carlos is tenacious. Once he sets his goal, he'll stick with it. You've got to shove off."

"Cut that out."

"What?"

"Sorry, I've picked up a hitchhiker."

"You've what?"

"Oh, it's just Shoestring."

"Shoestring? Who the hell is Shoestring?"

"A black duck, a cormorant."

"Forget the duck."

"I can't. He's my crew. The damned bird's been following me since my run down from Card Sound."

"I don't care what it is. Don't let it distract you from Carlos. What are you doing, feeding it?"

"Look, I don't have time to explain. He's crew."

"Listen to some advice."

"Shoot."

"Stop feeding it. If it's wild, it'll go away. I can't believe we're talking about a duck at a time like this. You've got to get out of there. You're not safe. Carlos is stalking you."

"Okay, okay. I'm going. I'll call you tomorrow night from the next stop on the chart. It's at the end of Long Key."

"Gotcha. I see it on the chart. Be safe and stay off shore."

"Goodnight."

"G'night."

Chapter Eight

Bad News

The sun had dropped below the horizon by the time Steve eased up to the dock at the Blue Conch Motel in Matecumbe Harbor. In the fading light, he could see the fiddler crabs running along the underpinnings of the dock. A needlefish flickered across his view, just under the surface of the water. A crusting of barnacles lined the pilings. He could see the sandy bottom of the harbor stretching out to the edge of the green eel grass patches along the Intercoastal. As the sun dropped lower in the west, the sky turned from bright yellow to a shimmering gold, with pink and red highlights the closer the glowing orb dipped below the horizon.

Steve could see the payphone in an open Plexiglas cubical shaped like a shell mounted on the harbor master's shed at the end of the dock. Averaging only a little over three knots for the day, he was behind schedule. In anticipation of the oncoming darkness, he had been motoring with his running lights on for at least an hour when he picked up the marker for Matecumbe Harbor.

As soon as the boat was secured on the dock, Steve called Eric from the pay phone outside the harbormaster's office. The phone was not as private as he would have liked, but no one was around. The phone rang more than six times, so Eric was not nearby waiting for his call.

"Hello," Steve heard Eric's familiar voice.

"Hello, Eric, Steve."

"Steve, geez, am I glad to hear from you. I was beginning to get worried. I expected to hear from you earlier. Where are you?"

"Matecumbe Harbor. I know, I'm late. I can't predict my timing on the water. You know that."

"Sure. You sound tired."

"I am. There's a shower by the marina. I'm going to freshen up when we finish. I had a problem with the channel before I got here. With the twists and turns, I couldn't see where I was going so I kept bumping bottom, feeling my way in. I'm sure I scraped the paint off the hull."

"Are you safe?"

"Sure, there's no one around and not much here. I can see an office building across the street. Oh, it's actually a TV station and apartment buildings."

"Have you checked for Carlos?"

"I've been off shore all day so I doubt he could have seen me. There are only two cars parked by the building. No place here for Carlos to hide."

"Okay. Are you sitting or standing?"

Steve cringed at Eric's familiar conversation opening. "Why? What's up?" Detecting something different in Eric's voice, Steve felt goose bumps rise on his arms like chickenpox when he was six. "Standing. I'm under one of those plastic canopies that only protects the top of your head if it rains. What's wrong, tell me. More bad news?"

"Look, Steve. I don't know how to say this. I hate doing this over the telephone. I'd rather tell you in person."

"Go ahead. You don't have a choice. If it's something I need to know, shoot. I don't have time to look around for Carlos so let's do this quickly. I want to shower and get back out and anchor for the night. What is it?"

"It's bad news."

"How bad? I had a rough day on the water. I'd rather hear good news."

"Remember, I'm just the messenger. It's Maria. Steve, she's gone."

"What do you mean, gone? Where? I thought she was in the hospital?"

"Maria's gone. She passed away early this afternoon. According to Bellows, it was about an hour or so after noon."

"What? What happened? I thought she was talking to them."

"She slipped into a coma and died of complications from internal injuries. Apparently the injuries she sustained in the fall down the stairs were more serious than they anticipated, or maybe Carlos beat her up more than they suspected before she tumbled down the stairs. Bellows called me right away. I'm sorry, really sorry, Steve."

"Gone?" Steve's face paled as he stood silently trying to grasp an understanding of Eric's words. Gone. Really gone. He had heard that word used many times before but not for someone as close to him as Maria had become. Gone. Eric meant gone from the face of the earth. Her warm smile and bubbling laughter flashed across his memory. Maria was gone. In spite of what she had done, he still loved her. She was young and beautiful, too young and vibrant to be gone. The image of her figure and glowing smile remained vibrant in his memory.

A long silence fell heavily on both ends of the phone. While Eric wished he didn't have to be the one to pass the news to Steve, Steve tried to absorb the meaning of the words Eric had spoken.

"Steve? Are you there? Are you alright?" Eric broke the silence.

"I can't believe it, Eric. She was so vivacious, so full of life. She was too young to die like this. Carlos hurt her." Tears began to form in his eyes and his head began to swirl with happy memories clashing with the rage and anger directed at Carlos.

"You don't have to say or do anything, Steve. Bellows gave the hospital a copy of their marriage certificate. It's out of your hands. Your marriage to Maria isn't legal. Carlos is legally responsible for his wife."

"But she was my wife." Visions of the warm moments they shared together as husband and wife pulsed through his mind.

"Well she wasn't, not legally. Steve, you're not married to her in the eyes of the law. She's married to Carlos. What's with you? Stop acting like a lovesick puppy. It doesn't become you. Geez, Steve, she helped her husband clean out all your trust funds. Be glad you don't have to be financially responsible, too."

"You don't understand how I feel. You're right, legally, of course, but we lived as husband and wife for nearly a year. You can't change that."

"I'm not going to try. Bellows and I agree. You have to keep going to Key West. Don't even think about coming back up here. Under the circumstances there's nothing you can do. Keep going, Steve. That's the best thing you can do for yourself right now."

"Where is she?" Steve's voice was subdued and quivered. "Where will they take her? Can you find out for me? All this outdoor activity is very tiring for a workaholic attorney. She can't be gone. She's only 27."

"Steve, snap out of it. You're in the best place to sort out your feelings about her. Focus on your situation now. Focus on Carlos and delivering your sailboat to Key West. Those two things are the most important problems you have to face now. I promise to find out about her arrangements, but without Carlos, nothing much will happen. The good news is that Metro-Dade issued a warrant for his arrest. He's wanted for questioning on assault and murder charges. They've posted his picture with all the TV stations and newspapers up here."

"Did Bellows ever consider that Carlos has a brain? Maybe he's thinking. Seems like he's staying a couple steps ahead of the authorities if they haven't found him yet."

"Well, they figure he's going to hunker down for a few days and work on a new disguise. I'll talk with Bellows but it's real important for you to keep me posted on your whereabouts. With Carlos loose, the authorities are worried about you."

"Thanks, Eric. I'm not sure where I am. There aren't any signs down here by the dock. No mile markers."

"I found your mark on the chart."

"I couldn't get in there. I'm close but I don't know exactly where I am. There must be a sign out front by the road. There are only a few powerboats tied up on the dock. I can't see too much through the darkness."

"Why are you so late?"

"I tried to make Steamboat Channel across the Bay to Bowlegs and Shell Key. I thought I had a visual on the channel markers, but I came in too close. Before I knew it, I was sailing nowhere fast. I ran hard aground." Steve hung his head sheepishly as he described his dilemma.

"Geez. Was someone there to help you?

"No, I loosened all the sheets and let the wind out of the sails. I didn't want the boat to dig deeper into the sand."

"You were aground without a radio. Did you get help?"

"Well, a big cabin cruiser passed by before I realized I was aground, but they were already too far away for me to get their attention when I got stuck."

"So you were on your own. How did you get free?"

"I felt really stupid. I knew if I tried to motor off, the propeller would only churn up a trail of mud behind the boat, like a mixer. Besides, with all the environmental regs on boating down here, I didn't try. I wouldn't have generated any forward or backward motion. I was marooned in the middle of the bay, with one hand on the tiller and the bird posed like a hood ornament on a '50's car, going nowhere fast. I must have looked as stupid as I felt. I'm lucky no one was around to see it."

"So the bird found you again?"

"That dammed bird always finds me. He finds me when I'm in a pickle and the Genoa is furled. Then he just stands there on the bow, like a sentry, watching the world."

"So, now, tell me your secret. How did you get free?"

"Kedging. It's a blessing the boat weighs so little."

"Kedging? What's that? Sounds like an alcohol activity."

"Throwing the anchor overboard into the sand and pulling it back in with the anchor line, hoping you're moving the boat and not just pulling the anchor back in."

"That sounds like hard work."

"It is. As I turned the hull off the wind, I was lucky. I could use the sails to tilt the keel off the bottom. Then by kedging, I pulled the boat toward the channel. Between kedging and using the wind in the Genoa, I slowly moved the boat back into the channel. The most difficult part was turning the boat around."

"You must be exhausted."

"I am, but I didn't tell you the difficult part. I slipped into my flippers and floated the anchor on the bumpers as far into the channel as the rode allowed. After I set the anchor, I paddled back to the boat. Usually sailors use their dinghy to set the anchor, but I didn't have the time to blow mine up with daylight fading. I used all the muscle power I had."

"Geez, how long did that take?"

"Hours. A soft bed and a warm shower sound like heaven to me."

"I have more bad news. Not as bad as losing Maria, but I haven't heard from your buyer in Key West. I called him at work around 5:00 PM and he wasn't there. A co-worker said he hasn't checked in for a few days. I can't reach him at home, either. I left another message on his answering machine."

"Thanks. Keep trying. I hope this isn't a bad sign and he still wants my boat. I'm counting on him. I need the money. I don't know what I'll do if I can't find him."

"Don't worry for now. Oh, I do have some good news. I closed the Barton case for you. There are a few minor disbursements to clean up tomorrow, but the case is closed. That means you can bill them when you get back."

"Thanks again. Glad for the good news, but the legal fees belong to you. You handled most of the case."

"I'd rather wait until you get back to discuss the fees."

"Don't be silly. Go ahead and bill them. Don't get into trouble with your time logs."

"Later about the bills. I went up to West Palm today for one of my clients, so I stopped by Boca on the way back."

"Great."

"Well, don't get too excited. There's more."

"How's that? I've always had good dealings with those guys."

"They're located in the Heller building on Federal Highway, right?"

"Sure, right around the corner, off Glades Road."

"Our agreement on the deal was 30% of collections to me?"

"Yes, I thought that was fair. All you had to do was present my open bills to the senior vice president. His name is printed on the bills."

"That wasn't possible, Steve."

"Why not? I've always had good dealings with him."

"Not any more. When I called, the phone lines were disconnected. The bank's 800 number referred me to another number with a recording. Anyway, when I went to the address you gave me, they were gone."

"What do you mean they were gone? I've been dealing with them for years."

"It's not just that the people were gone, or the offices were gone, the entire building was gutted. There's only a steel frame standing on the lot."

"You're kidding. I had no idea that was in the works. Those bills add up." Steve began to feel like a lead sinker at the bottom of the ocean.

"About twelve thousand dollars, if my math is correct. That's a big hit, Steve."

"No kidding. I'm going to have to file bankruptcy. That was where Boca Peoples Savings Bank was located." Steve's face flushed as he became agitated. His money worries were building.

"I'll follow up. Maybe they've moved."

"Don't spend a lot of time on it. Concentrate on the files where there are fees you can collect."

"I promise to make some calls for you. By the way, how's the weather?"

"Great, except for the fluky winds up close to the islands. In the open bay, the winds are still strong, around fifteen knots. Nice sailing weather. NOAH predicts the wind to shift northeast and come out of the east by tomorrow. That means the wind will be behind me all day tomorrow, so I'll be fine."

"To be honest, I'm worried about your buyer. I get the impression his employer isn't too concerned that he's been out for a few days. Your buyer should be more anxious about contacting you to wrap this deal up."

"I'm not worried. He sent a fax copy of his bank statement three days before Maria took off, so I know the money's there to do the deal. Besides, he put down a substantial, non-refundable deposit after reading the marine surveyor's report. I'd like to pin down a date and time for the closing before I get to Key West."

"I'll do what I can. I don't want to hold you up anymore tonight. Get back out into deep water. Carlos could be nearby."

"Okay. I'm out of here. In case something happens, I want you to know my exact plans. I'm going back out east of Old Sweat Bank by Old Dan Bank, then southwest across the bay through the Channel Key Pass on the bearing for the Intercoastal. I shouldn't have to tack if the winds hold. The channel is marked so I should have no difficulty avoiding Grassy Key Bank."

"Okay, I see what you're doing."

"I'll stay with the course for the channel and round the Bamboo Key marker, then head for the Vaca Key channel. The next mark is my stop on Vaca Key."

"I see it."

"It's an easy run and close to the entrance to the channel, so I should be on time. I'm familiar with the stop since I stayed there a few years ago. I'll be at the Black Mangrove Resort. There are too many crab traps off shore to go around Marathon in the dark."

"Got it. Get out of there and get some sleep. Just watch out for Rachel Bank. I've heard it's treacherous."

"Right. I've heard it's famous for snagging unwary sailors. Oh, one more thing, my first mate says hello."

"Who?"

"The bird."

"He's still with you?"

"Yup, off and on. He's good company for a sailor at sea. I think the bird has imprinted me as a parent or mentor or something like that."

"Just like a duck."

"Well, not exactly. He's a cormorant, more like an anhinga than a duck."

"I thought it was a baby."

"No, he's an adult, or a young adult."

"Maybe he likes your sardines."

"I'm sure he does, but I think it's more than food. He plays with my shoelaces. A couple of times, he's brought me spares. Apparently he collects them. So I named him Shoestring. He trades them for sardines."

"That sounds weird. Are you sure you haven't had too much sun?"

"No, I always wear my hat and long sleeved khaki shirt and pants. I told you the story about the old lady who saved him the other day. Sometimes truth is stranger than fiction. I think this bird is the same one the old lady taught to dive for food by dropping shoes with laces in the water."

"Maybe."

"Do you have any more information on Carlos' guns? I'm a distance from the highway, but I'd like to know the rifle's range so I know what to do when I meet up with him. Does anyone have any information on his marksmanship?"

"If Carlos has a gun, what good would knowing his skills do? He wants his gold. Shooting you at a distance on the water would do him no good. He has to board the boat to get the gold. Remember, he wants the gold, not you."

"Yeah, my non-existent gold. He'll have to find it to take it."

"You're right. If you ask me, he'll make his move when you come ashore to gas up or go for provisions. Do you have any plans in mind?"

"Avoidance. I'm only coming in to call you or get gas or food. I don't spend the night on the dock. I come in quickly, then anchor off somewhere in the mangroves where he can't see me from the road."

"Sounds like good planning to me. No matter where you are, you're in danger until Bellows has Carlos in custody. Like Bellows said, Carlos doesn't like the water, doesn't swim so they figure he'll go after you either in Marathon or Key West."

"That sounds reasonable, but what will he do when I tell him I don't have the gold? How desperate is he? Does anyone know?"

"Well, he did hurt Maria, but she double crossed him. He'll probably threaten you."

"So what do I do when I can't produce the gold? Will he lose his temper and lash out at me? There aren't any witnesses on the water except the birds and the sharks. I'm afraid he might shoot me out of anger and frustration."

"Sorry. That's why you have to keep us informed as to where you are. His reaction is anyone's guess."

"Thanks. I'm going to sign off and take my shower. We both say goodnight."

"Bye for now, to both you and the bird."

Chapter Nine

The Black Mangrove

A row of finely fitted charter fishing boats lined the dock a short walking distance from the dock at the Black Mangrove where Steve had secured *Seaseeker.* A large group of captains, fishermen and onlookers were gathered around the fish racks where the captains hung their catch on returning to the dock.

"Look at that enormous tarpon."

"That barracuda is nothing to scoff at. It must be 30-50 pounds."

"Somebody is going to have tuna steak tonight."

"Barracuda. Yes, they are the most common fish out in the backcountry."

"Hell, most of South Florida. Bahamas, too."

"Why is that?"

"Ciguatera."

"Ciguatera. I've heard of that. That's not a pretty sickness."

"That's why you have to be careful eating barracuda. It could have the toxin and can be fatal. If you get some from your catch, you become helpless fast."

"There isn't any antitoxin. If you're lucky it will pass through."

"The Cubans have some kind of guanabana juice enema and others use a Santeria ritual with a dove and a blood letting ritual."

"We don't have either here, so you'd be in trouble."

"Other fish can carry the toxin. Grouper and jacks can be a problem, too. They pick up the poison eating off the coral reefs."

"The bigger the fish the greater the chance they have more toxin."

"Stay away from fish near the reefs. It's a big South Florida problem. You don't know where the fish have been. Some of the smaller fish are dangerous too."

"I try to be careful how I clean the fish. I consider it an autopsy. I separate the organs from the flesh."

The chatter caught Steve's attention as he passed behind the small crowd of onlookers admiring the large fish hanging on the rack by the dock. One of the charter boats had taken out an early morning fare and returned with half a dozen large fish, one of which was the six-foot barracuda the onlookers were discussing. The barracuda was so large that its tail curled on the dock. Steve tarried to listen to the banter.

"Barracudas are like sharks. They're attracted to human activities. If a big one hangs around, it's best to back off and go elsewhere. I remember a snorkeling trip we took out to Sombrero Key a few years ago. We all geared up and went over the side one by one. Even before the last one of us hit the water, the first one was headed back up the swim ladder. When I looked around, all I could see was a solid ring of barracuda surrounding the boat like a life ring, staring at us head on. We were paddling around in a clear space, small as a donut hole. All I remember seeing is their beady eyes and rows of sharp white teeth, all around me. I couldn't get out of the water fast enough. Not a single barracuda made a move into the center of the ring, but the effect of so many eyes and teeth surrounding us drove everyone back into the boat. Not a one of us could handle seeing those teeth hanging out."

"I don't think I've ever heard of a barracuda attacking humans. I think they're more curious than dangerous."

"Just don't wear anything shiny or colorful and don't swim with an open wound. That's when they'll attack a human. But I agree, I couldn't stand them lurking around in large numbers."

"I'd be afraid they would snip off a finger or toe and I'd bleed to death."

"Actually, that's not the danger. Gangrene. That's the real danger. Like sharks, they carry the bacteria in their mouths. I was attacked once."

"You were? What happened?"

"Yup. I was out off the banks hanging over the side washing my breakfast dishes. I stuck my hand over the side to wash my fork and a big one struck like a lightning bolt. It hit so fast, I never saw it 'til afterwards."

"What happened? Did you lose some fingers?"

"Had to eat my pancakes with a spoon."

"What?"

"It stole my fork right out of my hand. It must have been hiding under my hull 'cause I never saw it 'til after the strike, streaking away from my boat. It jumped when it hit the flats and I saw the fork fly out of its mouth and splash into the water. I never did get that fork back. I tried to find it by passing over the area where I thought it fell, but I never saw it again."

"You were lucky it didn't hit your hand."

"Sure was."

Steve moved on. He needed to check in with Eric. He spotted the pay phone across the parking lot, mounted outside the bait and tackle shop. When Steve dialed Eric's number, Eric answered on the first ring.

"Morning."

"Thank goodness. I was beginning to worry about you."

"I'm okay, any changes on your end? Did you hear from Bellows?"

"Yes. I have some good news, but first, where are you?"

"On Vaca Key at the charter boat dock. I'm inside the entrance to the channel, a few hundred yards from the highway bridge separating Vaca Key from Fat Deer Key. I left the boat tied up at the dock at The Black Mangrove Resort. I'm calling from the bait and tackle shop on the north side of Federal Highway."

"You're close to the airport. Did you see the mile marker in case Agent Bellows asks? That's all his people ask, 'What mile marker is he near?'"

Steve grinned. "I'm not sure. I must be near the airport. I've seen some small planes come in and drop down west of here. Tell Bellows I'm within a stone's throw of the bridge."

"Got it. You're well short of the airport. You know, you're amazing. You've hit every stop you picked. Impeccable planning."

"I've been lucky so far. I'll continue to look good as long as the weather holds."

"Have you heard the old saying?"

"What's that?"

"It never rains in the Keys in the wintertime."

"Well, we know that's not true. The weather fronts change about every ten days and the local squalls can be powerful and unpredictable."

"Well, now for the good news. Your luck is holding today. The feds identified the car Carlos is driving. He hotwired a blue Toyota Corolla with Florida plates. Whenever you stop, check for a blue Corolla."

"Sure. I haven't seen any one or anything suspicious this morning. There's a crowd on the dock, but no blue Toyota. I want to pick up a few things in the marina and then I'll be on my way. The weather is perfect today."

"I have more good news."

"Great, I like good news."

"Someone actually saw him."

"Who, Carlos?"

"The one and only."

"Where?"

"Just past Conch Key, before Duck Key. He was watching you out in the channel with a pair of binoculars."

"Bird watching again." Steve snickered.

"Don't take this so lightly. That means he's still around stalking you. He hasn't given up. Bellows thinks he's going to make his move in Marathon. It's either there or Key West. There's nothing in between."

"Bellows says they're convinced Carlos thinks I have the gold on board, but what do they think is in Carlos's mind? The Monroe County Sheriff doesn't trust me and expects I'm going to sail off to Mexico or other parts unknown. I could and no one would stop me."

"Bellows and I know you won't do that, so chill. The Monroe County Sheriff will come around eventually. He just doesn't know you yet. You can't blame him after that case where he got burned.

Bellows says he thinks Carlos expects you to bring the gold ashore for safekeeping, either in Marathon or Key West. They anticipate he'll make his move when you move the gold. That's the official read on Carlos. They expect him to make his move on the gold when it's most vulnerable."

"Then Marathon may be a dangerous place for me."

"You got it. Keep me informed exactly where you are. Remember Carlos isn't after you, he's after the gold. Bellows is concerned that he'll get violent to get the gold back. Oh, more good news, after spotting him with the binoculars, they followed him and have his location pinned down."

"Great, that is good news. Where is he? And what do I do when he asks me for the gold?"

"You've got to be quick on your feet. You'll come up with something if that happens. But don't worry about it. They expect to pick him up soon. Bellows said a motel manager at Boot Key tipped them off. They verified the plates on the stolen car in Tavernier. He parked it at the motel and it's there right now. She recognized Carlos from the news stories on TV when he checked in."

"I know Boot Key. The marina is on the ocean side of US 1. You go through downtown Marathon and cross the bridge to go onto Boot Key. When are they going to nab him?"

"Bellows says they want to surprise him, so they plan to move in tonight after midnight when he's asleep. They've categorized him as armed and dangerous, so they want to minimize the risks."

"That sounds smart, less opportunity for Carols to resist. Once they nab him that will take a big weight off my mind. Do they have a marine patrol here?"

"Probably, but I'm not sure. I'll check with Bellows. That's the idea. Your problems with Carlos should be over tonight. Too bad that won't solve all your problems. I wish it would."

"Why? What are you talking about now?"

"I'm concerned about your practice."

"Don't remind me. Receivables have been down since the middle of last year and I haven't generated any new clients for some time now."

"I remember when you were so busy you kept four legal assistants and a receptionist busy full time, and even then you couldn't keep up. Everyone envied you."

"With the real estate crunch, I've lost three major lenders in the last two years. Two went under and one merged with a larger institution I couldn't reach. Of the two developers I had as clients, one elected to hire a larger law firm for its legal work, and the other phased their business out of this area to concentrate on the west coast. I was trying to rebuild my clientele when Maria and Carlos showed up."

"There must be something you can do find a new clients."

"I've been down-sizing for the last year. When Mildred retired, I brought Maria in to replace her."

"Mildred was very good. I doubt anyone could step into her shoes."

"Mildred was the best. You get what you pay for. When she left I hired Maria. You know the rest."

"Boca owed you a bundle, and now they've disappeared."

"I've had one set back after another."

"So bringing in Maria was your idea?"

"Absolutely. I interviewed her and hired her at a lower salary since she didn't have experience as a legal assistant. Besides, with business down, I had the time to train her."

"Geez, I had a different picture of what happened."

"Ordinarily I could recover what I lost when Maria stole the trust funds, but actually Boca meant a lot more to me than regular fees."

"How did that work?"

"Boca provided me with a continuous flow of active leads on properties, usually ones with loans that were in trouble. I'd buy out the owners or one of the partners. The bank knew it was my company so there was no conflict. Most of my leads came from my clients, especially Boca. So it's not the loss of receivables on those bills that adds up, it's the loss of referrals that will hit harder. The same thing is happening all across the country right now. Real estate is taking a big hit. The politicians are taking bigger chunks out of the homeowner's pockets in taxes and the borrowers can't handle both the mortgage and the increased tax bite. Personally I've lost three other banks that have gone belly up in the mortgage crunch over the last few months. The problem is I've built my practice around a group of lenders that have all evaporated. Their losses are dragging my office down with them."

"I see. Boca is a big loss, then."

"Well, with the economy going the way it is and housing down, the quality of my work doesn't matter. Management of the banks can't do much if their borrowers can't pay the mortgage or come up with the money for the closings. We have to see what the Fed does with the interest rates and how the banks fare with their mortgage losses."

"I don't understand why this is happening now."

"In ordinary times the lender plans on their loans to refinance or be paid off every five to seven years. The way loans are amortized, the lender pulls off profits from the interest during the first few years. When mortgages stay in inventory too long, their income drops. The last ten years of a mortgage is mostly principal. That's what creates the problem."

"So it's been piling up for some time now."

"Absolutely. Boca provided the lead on the condominiums where Maria was living."

"Geez, Maria too?"

"Well, I can't do anything about my situation while I'm here on the Keys. I'll deal with it when I get back up there. Ordinarily I'd say I could recover the property I lost, but these clients represented more than regular billing. They were my future leads. In fact, where I am living now was a lead from Boca. The owner died and the place was a mess. The bank didn't want to foreclose, so they gave me the lead. I had a corporate client who invested in problem properties. He covered the initial costs. When the corporation failed, I ended up with the corporation and the property. I negotiated a buy out on the estate with very favorable terms and kept the mortgage alive until I rehabilitated the property. Then I refinanced the property and moved in with Maria."

"Is that how you ended up with those expensive condominiums on Biscayne Bay?"

"You got it. That's were I met Maria. She was living there when I went to check them out. Now, I'm not sure how I'm going to foot the bills for all these holdings. I may have to declare bankruptcy since Maria and Carlos ran off with all my escrow and trust funds."

"I could make you an offer with my firm."

"No, that won't work. I don't have the client base to cover the revenue you'd expect from me. There's too much pressure on billing for me on the inside. I don't want that right now. Thanks for the thought."

"So what do you plan to do?"

"I'm working on that. I'll probably have to move off Brickell Avenue to save rent, then build a new client base. The competition of running head to head with the rainmakers in the big firms is rough."

"Geez. Brickell is known all over the world. It's an important address to give up."

"Yes, but I don't have international clients so that's not so important. I'll rebuild out of the local market."

"Enough of this shop talk. We'll deal with it when you get back up here. Bellows wants you safely offshore until he gives the all-clear sign. Carlos has given them the slip before, he's real slick."

"I'm in good shape here. I have my sentry back on duty. I can't go wrong."

"Your sentry?"

"I'm joking. I left Shoestring standing on the bow."

"Shoestring? Oh, the bird. I can't believe that bird is still hanging around. I hope you don't think it can save you from Carlos."

"He's been my lucky charm since I left Black Bank. I think I'm imprinted for life."

"I think you feed it too many sardines."

"How'd you know? I have no idea why he stays with me. When I put the jib up, he disappears, when I furl it in, he returns. It makes no sense. I don't know what he sees in me."

"Probably a meal ticket, but, don't ask me, birds aren't my expertise. I'm a lawyer. Oh, I checked into that bank for you. I saved the bad news for last."

"Boca?"

"Yes. They're long gone. Folded and disappeared."

"Sure could have used that money now. I'm not sure why I agreed to do this boat deal when my whole life is collapsing around me. Delivering this boat to Key West when my practice has fallen apart is sheer lunacy."

"Relax and enjoy the trip. You'll put it together when you get back. You've done it before. You can do it again."

"Maybe, but I'm tired of the wheeling and dealing. I feel like I'm on the run now. I'm running from some crazy man who's stalking me for a phantom load of gold. Gold that was my law practice."

"Carlos thinks it's his gold."

"Sure. Just keep Bellows informed as to where I am. I'll anchor outside the entrance to this channel tonight as long as the mosquitoes aren't too bad. I plan to start early and call you from the trailer park on Vaca Key west of Marathon. I think it's called the Sundowner Park and Marina. I should be able to top off my fuel tank there. If I can find someone in Marathon to check my VHF radio, I'll get it fixed before I take off. It's a long trek to the next waypoint. The Sundowner's the last stop before the Seven Mile Bridge. Since it's only eight miles around, I should be there in less than three hours. If I leave at 6:00, I should be on the dock before 9:00. Then it's on to the big one."

"The big one?"

"You bet. I'll be in open water running along the Seven Mile Bridge. After Knight's Key it's nineteen miles to No Name Key off Big Pine Key."

"I'll tell Bellows you're heading to the last stop before the Seven Mile Bridge. That's around mile marker 46 or 47. I'm not sure I like your next stop. You'll be too vulnerable."

"Just have Bellows get me some cover. Knight's Key is the best stop after Marathon. Hell, it's the last stop before Key West. Once I leave Knight's Key there's no telling where or even if I'll come ashore before Key West. Look at the charts. There's no where to come in."

"Well, either Carlos will give up or he'll head off to Mexico or other points west or south."

"Still haven't heard from my buyer?"

"No."

"I'm getting nervous about the deal. It's been too long not to hear from him."

"If he flakes out on you, you have his deposit. Two grand should cover your expenses plus some for the trip."

"You're right, but I need the whole amount, not just the deposit. I don't have a choice anymore. I've got to sell the boat. I don't have the funds for storage fees down here and I don't want to own a boat at a distance especially during hurricane season."

"His home phone is still active and his boss still expects him to show up for his shift. We'll find him."

"I hope so. I have enough to worry about with Carlos on my tail."

"Well, we're winding down the Carlos affair. His capture is imminent since they know where he is. Oh, I have one last question."

"What's that?"

"Why do they call that place The Black Mangrove? I thought mangroves were red."

"You need to know more about nature to answer that question. In Florida, there are three kinds of mangroves, red, white and black. The black ones are on the high ground."

"Oh thanks, is that it?"

"Yup. I'll call you around 9:00 AM tomorrow."

"I'll be in my office. Hopefully Bellows will have Carlos in custody by then."

"Well, that's all I can think of for now. Oh, I was curious, did you take my advice and quit feeding that bird?"

"No, I don't starve good crew. It's not that simple, there's more to it than food."

"Maybe. I think you're getting attached to that bird. It's time for you to get off shore. Until they have Carlos locked up, you've got to keep moving."

"Okay. Tell Bellows I'm anchoring off the mouth of the channel tonight. They won't be able to see me from land so I should be safe."

"I hope so. Good night."

"G'night."

Chapter Ten

Last Chance

Heading toward the channel between Vaca Key and Knights Key, Steve passed several small skiffs with a single occupant standing and poling for sponges. The half dozen small skiffs fitted with outboards were scattered across the brownish green flats like dots of green against the horizon. Numerous multicolored floats marked the locations of submerged crab pots, posing a maze of obstacles for the spongers to avoid. The sponge fishermen carefully poled between the floats pulling up their golden brown prizes and dropping them into a collection container inside their boats. As he neared the entrance to Boot Key Harbor, he could smell the pungent aroma of dead, drying sponges on racks. The stench spread across the water, blown by a steady breeze skimming across the shoreline. The repulsive smell brought tears to his eyes. He wiped the uncontrollable tears with alternate sleeves. As he approached the buildings and docks circling the harbor, the stench in the air cleared.

Steve found the Last Chance Marina inside the Sundowner Trailer Park on the west end of Marathon. He had passed the ramp leading up to the Seven Mile Bridge at the edge of the trailer park where the Pigeon Key trolley service originated. A private group, the Pigeon Key Foundation and Marine Center, had taken over management of Flagler's settlement constructed for the workers who had built the railroad from Miami to Key West in the 1800's. Since this was the last safe harbor with marinas at the edge of Boot Key Harbor and before the Seven Mile Bridge, prudent sailors checked fuel, water and supplies before shoving off for the Gulf of Mexico or Hawk Channel.

The Seven Mile Bridge was exactly that, seven miles of metal and concrete spans covering open water with no civilization between Marathon and Little Duck Key at the western end of the bridge. Once he left The Last Chance Marina, Steve would need at least a day or two to reach the next marina before getting supplies again. At least, once he left Marathon and headed out into open water, he would be safe from Carlos.

After topping off his fuel and water tanks, he bought two bags of ice and a quart of fresh orange juice, stashing them in his icebox in the galley. Concerned about his non-functioning VHF radio, he checked with the marina office for an electronics technician before making his call to Eric. He wanted to repair the radio before heading deeper into the backcountry. Anticipating good news this time, he did not rush to call Eric. The marina manager gave him the business card for a technician who could repair his radio. When he called the number, he found the man worked out of another marina around the ocean side of Boot Key inside Boot Key Harbor. The technician was not expected back at the marina for another half hour or more. Steve was determined to repair the radio so he could call for help in case of an emergency in the lower keys. He decided to go directly to the marina in Boot Key Harbor, rather than wait to connect with the repairman by phone. The lower keys, beginning with Big Pine Key and No Name Key were less densely populated than the upper Keys so he was uncomfortable without a working radio. Once he left Marathon, the backcountry would leave him more isolated than he had been up to this point. Key West was the next most developed area in the lower keys, but was still nearly 50 miles beyond Marathon.

He called Eric to alert him of the change in his itinerary while he looked into getting the radio repaired.

"Eric, Good morning."

"Steve! Geez, where are you? You're calling early, is something wrong?"

"No, I'm at the Last Chance Marina, just outside Marathon. The view is great. I can see the beginning of the Seven Mile Bridge and Pigeon Key. I filled up for my run to Key West, but I'm not going to leave yet. I wanted to let you know about my change in plans before I take off for Key West. In fact, I know my mile markers. I'm between mile marker 46 and 47."

"Great. I'll call Bellows and let him know. You know how they are, always asking about mile markers. But what's going on? What change in plans?"

"You haven't linked up with my buyer yet, have you?"

"No, still no news there. I think you're going to have to track him down when you get to Key West. I'm not having any luck connecting with him or getting any new information from where he works."

"Well, I'm not comfortable heading into the backcountry without a working VHF radio. Besides, I'd have to repair it before the sale so I might as well take care of it now. That way I can use it to call you or the Coast Guard if I run into trouble."

"That's a good idea. Looks like this will set you back at least a day."

"Yes, but that's okay. I'd rather do it now. I have to swing around Knight's Key according to the people at the other marina and go into Boot Key Harbor to find the electronics technician. They claim he can fix it. He's out on a call now but they said he'll be back in about half an hour. That's just about how much time it will take me to run *Seaseeker* over there. I'll call you when I get there. Keep Bellows informed."

"Okay, I've got the picture. I can't talk long. I have a client waiting. Oh, I do have some news. Miriam was able to prod Old Man Strang to come in. He signed his will."

"Great, finally some billable hours. Not much, but that's better than the news about Boca."

"Sure is, but don't give up on the Boca people. I might have a lead on them. They can't just disappear. They'll turn up again, even if it's in the bankruptcy courts. Catch you later."

"Sure. Thanks for your help. I'll call back with an update. I won't shove off for Key West until I call you, probably after lunch."

"Just keep an eye out for Carlos, and the blue Toyota."

"Sure, will do. Talk later."

Steve hung the phone up and headed back to *Seaseeker*. Looking around the parking lot and across the street, he saw no sign of Carlos or the Toyota. As he approached the bow of the boat, Shoestring moved away from the cleat as Steve removed the dock line. As soon as he stepped into the cockpit, Shoestring returned to his customary station.

"You aren't supposed to be here. You're a bird. Why aren't you headed back up to Card Sound courting some sassy female and raising a family of your own? Why me?"

Shoestring faced into the wind. The gentle breeze flowed smoothly across his feathers.

"What good are you if you don't talk to me? I bet you wouldn't tell me if I were off course." Steve shook his head from side to side. "Why do you stick with us humans? Don't you know there's no future with us? You're not supposed to be here, don't you know that?"

Shoestring kept his beak into the wind with his wings flattened down sleek against the contour of his body, maintaining his post as sentry. His dark black feathers glowed and glimmered with streaks of gold and purple reflecting back the warm radiance of the early morning sun. Within minutes Steve started the engine, released the stern line and was on his way to Boot Key Harbor.

"Okay, mate. We're off. I've got your message. I'm on my own."

Within forty-five minutes Steve had found the marina in Boot Key Harbor and tied up at the dock. He was relieved to have the time to fix his radio. He repeated his docking procedures and Shoestring responded in his usual manner.

"Who's your friend?"

Steve, startled by the unexpected appearance of a tall, thin dark tanned woman dressed in khaki shorts and mauve tank top, turned to respond. His eyes caught the movement of her short-cropped hair blowing gently under a baseball cap as she stood by the gas pumps with her hands on her hips.

"Oh, you startled me."

"Sorry."

"No problem. My friend?"

"The bird."

"Oh, you mean Shoestring."

"Shoestring? Your bird has a name?"

Steve chuckled. "Yes, Shoestring. That crazy bird on the bow of my boat has followed me all the way down here from Card Sound."

"That's really odd. I thought cormorants were more territorial than that."

"My friend Eric says he follows me because I feed him. I admit I give him sardines in the morning, but I expect fresh fish would be more appealing to his appetite. I'm not sure why he stays with me."

"Maybe he likes your company."

"Maybe. He likes my sardines."

"That's probably the reason. We humans project human characteristics onto animals and interpret their behavior according to our reactions, even when we know there's no possibility for rational thought in the poor creatures."

"Sure, we do it all the time, with our pet dogs and cats, and even wild animals in and out of cages."

"Exactly. We humanize them. Attribute human thoughts and emotions to their actions. They don't understand right from wrong, no moral fiber. I doubt they have the depth of feelings we have."

"Wait a minute. Don't animals have feelings? I remember when one of my cats died, his partner went into a deep depression. He stopped eating and moped around the house for over a month. Then one day, he snapped out of it and returned to his bouncy self."

"Sure, they have feelings, but not like we humans do. That's what separates us from the animal kingdom."

"Oh, now we could debate that one. Some humans act like animals."

She grinned. "I can't disagree with that one, especially men."

"Let's not go there. Do you work here?"

"Yes, can I help you with something? Need fuel or water? How about some ice?"

"No, thanks. I took care of all that over at the Last Chance Marina. I called here a little bit ago and came over because I need my radio fixed. They said the technician would be here in about 45 minutes and it took me about that long to motor over."

"Oh, you're looking for Charlie. He's not back yet. He's out there helping the people on the Irwin 38." She replied pointing at a large sailboat anchored in the harbor.

"Well, are you going to be here a while? I'll wait, but I wouldn't mind some human conversation while I'm here. The bird never answers me."

"Sure. I'm Elaine. I pump the gas and run the cash register. Charlie's my husband. He does the repairs."

"I'm Steve. Nice to meet you." Steve extended his hand in greeting.

"Nice to meet you, too, and your friend, the bird."

"I've never been in here before. This harbor is really nice."

"It's always been a good shelter from a storm for lots of boats, especially since there's lots of deep water in spite of a few shallow spots, but it hasn't always been this way. Years back, people abandoned their boats when they became too expensive to repair or were wrecked beyond salvage in the storms and hurricanes. Some folks just abandoned their boats when they couldn't maintain them, and they sank. We used to have over a hundred wrecks sunk in the harbor. They presented serious underwater hazards and an eyesore until we revolted."

"I never realized how large this harbor is. A lot of boats can anchor in here with plenty of room."

"Yes, it's the best harbor in the Keys. We were real angry at how the wrecks destroyed the view and the anchorage so we fought to have them cleaned out. That was a real political battle, but it was worth it. Now we've opened up the anchorage for more boats. This harbor can accommodate a lot of cruisers. Marathon wasn't incorporated so we had to get the attention of a bunch of authorities in the county and state to help with the clean up. The bureaucracy and red tape presented a tough barrier to fund the project."

"It sure looks great now. The water is as clear in here as it is off shore."

"You have a holding tank? If you don't, you're in trouble here. We're real strict about that."

"Sure. I'm legal. You can check if you want to."

"Just might do that. We've had our share of problems here in the harbor over the years. Once we started cleaning it up, the entrepreneurs swept in and commercial businesses grew. As the Keys became more popular for fishing and cruising, more and more snowbirds showed up down here as Islamorada filled up. There were those who liked our more causal atmosphere so the population of locals and tourists grew. The locals continued to pressure the state and county to clean up the wrecks. One of the other marina owners started pulling up some of the wrecks, so he became the unofficial harbormaster. Charlie and I took a leadership role because we grew up here and wanted to see the harbor cleaned up. Without a town council or organization, we had a tough battle."

"I bet. You must be proud."

"Sure, but the more we cleaned up the harbor, the more popular it became and the word continued to spread. We developed another problem."

"What was that?"

"The water. It wasn't always this clean. There was a time the water was actually brown and we had bouts of algae and floating health hazards, if you know what I mean. Everyone knew it wasn't safe to swim in the harbor because the pollution was so bad. The visiting cruisers and live-aboards refused to use their holding tanks since there was no legal enforcement."

"I can't picture that."

"There was no control and we relied on people to use the marina's services for their pump outs. No one was responsible and no one checked if the live aboards and visiting cruisers were using their holding tanks. The pollution increased and the water continued to turn browner and more fowl."

"That must have been horrible."

"It was. But things changed when the state passed protective legislation for the water, the coral reefs and wildlife here in the Keys. We have a lot of small enterprises now supporting the harbor. There's one guy who delivers newspapers and coffee and bagels on the water and another delivers pizza."

"That's funny. I never would have thought about that."

"The craziest one was the guy that offered on-the-water pump out services."

"Really? Now that's thinking out of the box."

"Human nature being what it is always affords someone a golden opportunity. He was clever and made a lot of money fast. He advertised with a sign painted on the side of his boat: 'My #1 business is your #2.'"

Steve laughed. "Now that is creative."

"Yes, but he didn't last long. He out smarted himself. He went from boat to boat on a daily basis and charged less than the marinas to do the pump out. As the state and county offices became more powerful, they patrolled the waters in and out of the harbor. One day the Monroe County Marine Patrol caught him dumping his load out in Hawk Channel. That was the end of his #1 and #2 business."

"So that's why I had to empty my holding tank at the marina this morning."

"Yes, we're real serious about that stuff down here. That guy paid a stiff fine and actually served some jail time. Now only the marinas are authorized to do the pump outs. The county and the state monitor the water in the harbor closely and do on board checks to be sure visiting cruisers are using their holding tanks. Experience has shown us that the entrepreneurs will cut corners to maximize their profits, so we had to have some teeth in the laws to make them stick. We have that now."

"I'm glad I took care of that this morning. I wouldn't chance the penalties. All your work has paid off nicely. This harbor is one of the most beautiful I've ever seen. I can't get over how clean and clear the water is. I can actually see the sand on the bottom and the rocks and crabs crawling over them."

"If you're lucky, you'll see a nurse shark snoozing in the afternoon sun or the eyes of a stingray poking up through the sand. They like to burrow down into the sand and hide along the mangroves in the shallows. Sometimes we even see sea turtles in the harbor."

"I've seen a shark take off when I passed over what I thought was a pile of sand."

"We're lucky. We still have a lot of wildlife here and they're protected by tough state laws with hefty fines now."

"Yes, I'm aware of that from the literature I've picked up in the marinas on my way down the Intercoastal. You can't miss being informed about the regs for boating in the Keys."

"Yes, we're serious about protecting what we have. The Keys are a national treasure, but the economics are tough. You may not have thought much about it, but the Keys are a low-income area. The majority of the people here rely on the tourist trades for jobs in restaurants, motels and on the charter fishing boats. We have a few attractions like the bird sanctuary in Islamorada, the dolphin research center, the turtle hospital and the theater of the sea, and the parks all along the waterfront. After a few hours hiking, kayaking, or maybe a snorkeling trip, there's really not much to do but fish or sit in the sun."

"You're right, I'd be bored here if I weren't sailing my boat down the Intercoastal. The Keys are islands and suffer the same characteristics of other islands."

"We have a lot of social problems tourists rarely see. We aren't immune to the same problems you see on the mainland. Drinking problems are common. For the guys, hanging out in the bars is a popular past time. We do see some family violence and there is a shelter here in Marathon for women who need help."

"Where is that? I recently had a friend die from abuse from her husband. It was totally unexpected. Funny, I didn't expect that here. The Keys seem like paradise." Steve held back his emotions remembering the abuse Maria had suffered from Carlos.

"Don't forget, we're human beings, too. You'll find all the human foibles and frailties on the Keys. Alcohol can be the center of a lot of problems, including the ring of abuse. Even some of the snowbirds bring their problems along and can show up occasionally at the shelter. They're welcome to attend the 12 Step AA meetings. When the tourist trade drops, the drinking increases. My theory is that the men get frustrated standing around waiting for the tourists to show up. Right now the tourist trade is down as a result of Katrina and Wilma. The Keys made a concerted effort to minimize publicity about the damage from those hurricanes and everyone worked hard to complete all the repairs, but even the slow down in the economy has affected us. With gasoline prices up, people don't want to spend the extra money to drive all the way down here when there are more, better beaches farther north on the mainland."

"I see what you mean. I've hit some bad times now. That's why I'm running my boat down to Key West. That's where I found my buyer. I've had trouble connecting with him, so maybe he's lost his job."

"We've even lost jobs at campgrounds and trailer parks to developers who want to replace them with condos. They lost their funding when the hurricanes hit so even more people have lost their jobs. It's going to take some time for the economy to turn around again."

"Well, I stopped in to see if your technician could take a look at my VHF radio."

"Sure, as I said, that's Charlie, my husband. He should be back soon."

"I have to make a phone call and catch my friend while he's still in the office. I'll take care of that while I wait for Charlie to return."

"Great. I'll be right here tending the dock. There are a couple of pay phones up near the boat shed where the office is located. Do you see it?"

Steve looked up toward the buildings next to the parking lot. He didn't see any blue cars, or specifically a blue Toyota Corolla. "Thanks, can't miss them. I'll be right back."

Steve hustled to the pay phone and dialed Eric's number.

"Geez, Steve. Where are you? Are you still in Marathon?"

"Yes, I'm at the Boot Key Marina, waiting for Charlie to check out my radio."

"You've got to get out of there, fast." Eric's voice was tense and emphatic. He made no attempt to hide the anxiety in his voice.

"Yeah, yeah, I know the drill. I looked around for Carlos when I tied up at the dock. I might buy some more sardines while I'm waiting for Charlie."

"Stop. Listen to me, Steve. Forget the radio. Forget the sardines. Forget waiting for Charlie. You've got to get out of there."

"What? Why? What's the sudden panic? I need the radio. I don't know what's wrong with it."

"Don't you understand? It's Carlos. He's right there, in Marathon."

"Carlos? He's been tracking me all along. I checked this place out. He wouldn't know to look here for me. There's no one here but me, the woman at the dock and the cashier in the marina shop."

"You don't understand. He escaped."

"Escaped? Last night you said they were going to arrest him at a motel. I thought they had picked him up by now and I was free to enjoy the rest of my trip."

"Sorry to have misled you. I didn't have all the facts until this morning. Bellows called. They raided the Anchor Motel around 1:00 AM this morning, he was gone."

"Good God, the Anchor Motel is across the street. I can see the sign from here."

"That's what I'm saying Steve. You have to get out of there. He was at that motel. They don't know where he is."

"He's gone? Where would he go in the middle of the night?"

"They don't know, Steve. The lights in the room and the television were all left on, but no Carlos and no guns."

"When they knocked on the front door, he probably slipped out the bathroom window." Steve made light of the situation.

"Agent Bellow says they had the back covered from 9:00 PM on last night. He thinks their saturation plan backfired and Carlos out smarted them."

"What saturation plan? You're not making any sense. What's this all about?"

"They were worried about your safety. They thought if they spattered all the newspapers and television shows with Carlos' name and pictures, they would drive him into hiding and he'd leave you alone. Now Agent Bellows thinks Carlos saw his picture on the news in his room and left the motel long before they staked it out. He figures Carlos left the lights and TV on to throw them off."

"Maybe he's in hiding right now," Steve offered optimistically.

"Agent Bellows doesn't think so. Of course, there's an upside to this."

"Okay, I'm game. What's the theory?"

"They found the stolen car in back of the motel."

"The blue Toyota?"

"Yup."

"That's smart. He knew he'd be easy to track in a stolen car. Now you're scaring me. He could be around anywhere and I wouldn't be tipped off by the yellow Hummer or the blue Toyota."

"Sorry. I didn't tell you last night because I didn't know. I thought they had the situation under control and they would have him in custody by this morning. Sorry to upset you."

"Hmm. I see. He had to leave the motel in a hurry. He can't get far on foot. Did he borrow another car?"

"We don't know yet, but if the Anchor Motel is across the street from where you are now on Boot Key, he could walk over to where you're standing. He registered there yesterday afternoon around 4:00. That means he's had up to eight hours lead time to escape before they made the raid. He may even have taken the room to fake out the authorities. I figure he's had about sixteen hours to find you. That's why you have to get out of there, immediately. Even though Bellows promised to have you covered by now, he's not comfortable. Remember, Carlos is a master of disguise and blends in wherever he goes. He told me to remind you of the Grant case."

"I remember that one from the meeting in your conference room."

"He said while they were looking for Carlos, he registered at another motel across the street from their office and he was hanging out at a diner around the corner. He was watching them in the diner where the local officers routinely stop for coffee and donuts in the morning."

"That's close. I bet I can see the diner from here. There are a lot of cars parked out in front of the one near the motel right now." Steve started to get an ominous feeling in the pit of his stomach as he surveyed the cars across the street. "Do you know what kind of car he's driving now?"

"No, but guess who bought the officers coffee all afternoon?"

"Carlos."

"Right. That's why Agent Bellows wants you back out on the water in your boat, now, where you're safe."

"Okay. I got the message. I'm leaving right now, against my better judgment. I wanted to get my radio fixed. For my sake, you'd better be right about this one."

"I am. Please, go quickly. This may be your last chance to get away from Carlos. You're in dangerous territory now."

"Ok, I'll head for Big Spanish Channel over by No Name Key. I'll keep a safe distance as I cross Moser Channel and the Seven Mile Bridge."

"Please, do stay well off the bridges."

"Sure. The tides and wind are fine. I should have a nice sail across Knight's Channel."

"How long do you think it will take you to get to No Name Key?"

"It's just shy of twelve miles. I'd say about three hours. Tell Bellows I'll be sailing on the inside. I'll have to be careful of the shallows off Knight's Key Channel. I'll try to find somewhere to call in when I get to No Name Key. What about my buyer?"

"I haven't tried yet this morning, so there's no news. Just get out of there, now. I'm hanging up so you can go."

"Catch you later. Thanks, Eric."

"Good luck. I wish you had your radio working."

"So do I. This time I'm going to need all the luck I can get."

Chapter Eleven

A Place Called No Name

As he pulled up to the dock, the pelicans perched on the top of the pilings scattered like feathers in the wind. Shoestring followed them, flying low to the surface of the water in true cormorant fashion. Steve watched the birds disappear into the mangroves on the other side of the channel. Wrapping the bow and stern lines around the dock cleats, he sighed in relief at finding an out of the way stop conveniently at the edge of the channel a few hundred feet from the bridge between No Name Key and Big Pine Key. The docks were well weathered and the pilings were thickly crusted with barnacles. A building covered with white siding was set back a few hundred feet inland.

Steve headed for the building which turned out to be a small bar and restaurant. He entered through the back door. Half a dozen people were seated at tables scattered throughout the restaurant and two men were chatting at the bar. Checking the occupants carefully, he noted none resembled Carlos. As he stood by the payphone positioned between the bar and the restrooms, he could hear the chatter between the two men at the bar.

"You should have seen it. I couldn't believe the makeshift contraption they actually put together to get here. I would never have called it a boat. They had taken what looked like steel panels and riveted them together with screws. The whole thing was surrounded with foam about five feet thick to be sure it stayed afloat. They tied the Styrofoam to the steel panels with cheap orange line."

"Did they make it to shore? They're in trouble if they don't."

"Yes. There were about 9-10 men aboard. They were really haggard. Hadn't bathed or shaved in days."

"Where was this? Did you really see them come in? I've never witnessed a landing."

"Sure did. I was watching the dogs play ball over at Plum Beach in Marathon. They're fixing the beach up real nice now. Somehow their boat slid under the Coast Guard radar. I don't know how they did it with all that metal. Sure was an unsightly contraption. The Coast Guard was on their tail so you should have seen them dive over the side and make a bee line for the beach."

"So they made it."

"Yup. Their feet hit the beach."

"Well, there goes more of my tax dollars. They get a hefty sum when their feet hit the beach, plus medical coverage for a few years. I can see why so many of them make a break for the US of A."

"Yup, they're safe as long as their feet hit US soil."

"Life must be really tough over there for them to leave their friends and relatives to take a chance like that at sea."

"That's the problem. We used to have more trouble with drug runners and square grouper, now it's the constant run of illegal aliens coming in. You hear about new arrivals weekly."

"Sometimes a couple attempts each week."

"Take a run over to Marathon to see the boat they came in on. It's still sitting on the beach. The Coast Guard hasn't taken it away yet."

"I guess we can't stop 'em. They must be a bunch of desperate souls to take such risks. Last week they caught a boat full hanging off one of the moorings at Looe Key. They sent them back. They didn't make it to land."

"That's the risk. If they don't hit land, they send them back."

Steve turned away from the bar and dialed Eric's number.

"Eric."

"Hello, Steve?"

"I'm here, Eric," Steve was grinning.

"Where the hell is that?"

"No Name. I'm at a place called No Name."

"Talk to me. I've been worried sick about you. I've got the chart in front of me. Since you didn't fix your radio back in Marathon, I haven't a clue where you are. Is there a marina at the end of No Name Key?"

"No. There's nothing there, just me, the boat, the fish, the bugs and the birds. Lots of birds. I sailed around the north end of the island and back down between No Name Key and Big Pine Key. There's nothing there, just pelicans and cormorants. Maybe some Key deer, but no people, no cars, no trouble."

"Okay. That sounds good to me."

"I found a little joint. It's called Jimmy's No Name Bar and Grill."

"On No Name Key?"

"No, on Big Pine Key, about a half mile west of the bridge to No Name Key on your chart. If it wasn't high tide, I wouldn't have been able to get ashore here. I'm calling from the bar."

"Inside? What about your boat? Are you keeping an eye on the boat?"

"Don't worry. Carlos will never find me here. I've already asked. Everyone here is local. No one has seen anyone outside of the normal crowd, except me, and no one has driven across the bridge all day. Even if Carlos drove over the bridge, he wouldn't find anything out here. Believe me, there's nothing here. Oh, there used to be a ferry dock and a big hotel at the end of the road on No Name Key years ago, but there isn't a trace left of them now, just a pile of big rocks to make sure no one runs into the water."

"Steve, if I were Carlos and I had a map and was watching what you were doing, I'd check out every road, bridge or inlet on No Name Key. It looks intriguing and is a logical stop after leaving Marathon and the Seven Mile Bridge."

"Believe me Eric, it's a road to no where. Only pine trees and palmettos and birds are here. Back in the old days when there were no bridges from Marathon to Big Pine Key, the ferry came ashore at the end of the road on No Name. When they converted the railroad bridge to a highway that ended the ferry. No one wanted to ride the ferry anymore. It was easier to drive here. Anyway, what Carlos does now depends on what he has for transportation. He wouldn't drive a stolen car out here. He'd stand out and I don't think he wants to do that. Personally, I think he's already gone on to Key West where he can disappear into the crowd."

"You're probably right. He must have figured out when you left Marathon that the deal was in Key West. There isn't much between. He's on to your plan."

"Sure. My plan never included any stops between Marathon and Key West. I had planned to fix my radio in Marathon. I didn't want to be so vulnerable without a working radio. Today I was supposed to be off shore somewhere near here, but you made me leave Marathon in a hurry. Anyway, I'm here and I'm A-okay."

"It was for the best. I'm checking the chart. You marked No Name with a radio contact, not for a landing. I wouldn't be surprised if Carlos checked out No Name anyway. Be careful."

"Don't worry. I've got everyone in the restaurant on my side. They've all seen the pictures of him on the news. I told them he was dangerous and looking for me, and the boat. No one recognized his picture. This place is way off the beaten path. These Keys are larger, stretching north of Federal Highway. Besides, you'd have to be looking for this spot to find it. An outsider wouldn't have any business here. Not only is it No Name but it's No Where."

"Well, keep your eyes peeled. No one has a clue where Carlos is. He's vanished."

"I bet he's either in Key West or on his way there."

"Did it ever occur to you that he might have given up the chase? He's under a lot of pressure now. The Keys are not the place to have the law on your tail. There's no place to hide. Remember? And you told me, no place to go."

"Hey, you told me how steadfast Carlos is. You said once he locks in, he's got a mission and won't give up. If he's guessed my plan, he'll head for Key West. He can figure out where I'll dock and estimate when I'll be there."

"You may be right. In any case, Agent Bellows made reservations for you at The Harbor Inn. He wants to meet with you, the buyer, and the sheriff. He's asked the sheriff to cooperate with the search for Carlos in Key West."

"Any word from Owens?"

"Nothing. He hasn't shown up for work yet."

"I'll bet Carlos will try to intercept me when I come ashore in Key West. I'll anchor somewhere near Big Spanish Channel tonight. In the morning, I'll head for the backcountry around the lower Keys. Tell Agent Bellows I'll call him as soon as I'm on shore."

"Ok, I'll tell him. This chart makes me wonder, Steve."

"Why? What's the problem?"

"I'm concerned about that profile on Carlos."

"So far Carlos has been predictable, including slipping out from under their grasp the other night. I give him credit. He's clever enough to stay a step ahead of everyone."

"That's not what I'm getting at. The charts. Aren't they easy to get?"

"Sure, every marine and bait and tackle shop carries them. Why?"

"Carlos isn't dumb, couldn't he pick up a set of charts?

"Sure. What if he did?"

"He'd know you have to go through Northwest Channel to get into Key West. It's obvious looking at the chart. The Northwest Channel is the only way into Key West Harbor from the Gulf side. I'm not trying to scare you, but it makes more sense for Carlos to go after you on the water. That channel looks like the ideal place for him to make his move. It's away from the city crowds and all the authorities he knows are on his trail."

"But water isn't his turf. He'll be more comfortable making his move on land. Resorts and public places are his territory."

"I still think he may consider other alternatives. Profiles aren't a fixed science; they're only someone's best guess. Besides, anyone can change their mind."

"Okay. I'll keep that in mind, but tell Bellows I want help in Key West. I'm sure Carlos has a good idea of when that will be. That's what I'm worried about."

"Sure. Be careful. You're heading into the most dangerous leg of your trip."

"Don't worry. I have my crew watching out for me."

"You don't mean that bird, do you? Is that bird still with you?"

"You bet. He's back on duty, standing watch on the bow. He's been aboard with me for most of the trip. Why would he abandon me now?"

"He'll stop pooping on your deck if you stop feeding him."

"Captains don't starve loyal crew."

"You and that bird. Maybe he'll stay with the boat when you sell it. Then you'll be free. Don't get too attached, he's just a seabird. I doubt he'll follow you home." Eric paused to change the subject, "I'd better cut out for now. You need to get off shore even if that place doesn't have a name. Remember, Agent Bellows warned never to underestimate the enemy, and Carlos is the enemy."

"I'll be okay. I'll call you when I reach The Harbor Inn in Key West."

"Do you have a gun on board?"

"Hell, no. All I have is fire extinguishers and a flare gun."

"Don't discount what you have. Your safety equipment may be a weapon of last resort."

"I never thought of it that way. I'll keep them handy."

"A flare gun or a fire extinguisher may repel an unwanted boarder at close range."

"Thanks, that's a good idea. I never would have thought of it."

"Anytime. Be careful, Steve."

"Sure, Eric. Later."

"Goodnight, Steve."

"Goodnight."

Chapter Twelve

The Husband

From the edge of Federal Highway at the Jewfish Creek Bridge, Carlos watched Steve Andrews tie his boat to the marina dock. Steve's behavior convinced him of two things. First, Steve Andrews was following the sail plan he had left with the yacht club in Coconut Grove. Secondly, Carlos knew the sedan behind him was tailing him. The men in the sedan were conspicuous, even though they lagged behind and pretended to be bird watching. Carlos intended to follow Steve on his way to Key West to sell his sailboat with over half a million dollars in gold coins stashed on board.

If Steve stuck to his plan, Carlos would know his every move. With the knowledge of Steve's itinerary, Carlos could choose when and where to intercept him so he could recapture his gold. However, knowing he was being followed forced him to abandon his original plan to seize the gold at Jewfish Creek. His new objective became to evade the men in the sedan by abandoning his all too conspicuous Hummer, and replacing the bright yellow Hummer with a more inconspicuous vehicle.

From Steve's behavior, Carlos guessed Steve was unaware the gold was hidden on his sailboat since he continued to follow the sail plan. Carlos was concerned that if Steve discovered the gold onboard he would alter his itinerary. So, he planned to watch Steve's movements very closely. Steve had left the sail plan with the yacht club before Maria emptied the trust funds and stashed the gold on board. Clearly, Maria had selected an excellent hiding place for the gold. Since the sailboat was small, he would have fewer places to search to find where she had hidden the stash. Carlos anticipated that Steve would find the gold during his run down the Keys. If Steve found the gold before arriving in Key West, he might remove it from the boat as soon as he found it. The only likely place to do so was in Marathon. Since the banks and private dealers in Marathon were inconvenient to Steve's planned stops, removing the gold from the boat in Marathon was less likely. On the other hand, when Carlos checked the hotels, motels and resorts in Key West, he found Steve had a reservation for two nights at The Harbor Inn, a resort located within blocks of two major banks. If he found the gold, Steve would remove the gold prior to delivering the boat to the buyer. If Steve elected to sell the gold in Key West, two days would provide adequate time to complete the transaction.

Carlos guessed Steve would store the gold with one of the banks in Key West on a short-term basis due to the amount of gold involved and the limited market there. He was confident Steve would elect to take the gold back to Miami's international market where he would get a better price for the coins. Once Steve sold his boat, Carlos guessed Steve would rent a car to drive back to Miami. Carlos shuddered at the thought of attempting to intercept Steve in a car. He began to feel confronting Steve on the boat offered fewer challenges, so he began to devise a plan to intercept Steve on the water before he arrived in Key West.

After the incident at Jewfish Creek, his primary priority included shaking the agents trailing him in the sedan. From their behavior, Carlos guessed the agents were instructed to follow cautiously and keep their chain of command informed so they could react quickly if instructions changed. Carlos knew American law enforcement was slow to react but sure when they did. If he was sharp, he could stay ahead of the agents in the short term, but ultimately he knew he could make a mistake making his long-term prospects grim. He planned to escape to Brazil where the US had no extradition agreements and the gold would provide generously for the rest of his life. However, his greatest challenge required evading the authorities and recovering the gold from Steve's boat.

Watching for the sedan in his rear view mirror, he made a sharp turn onto a side road on Key Largo, quickly disappearing into a residential neighborhood. The sedan missed his turn, continuing down Federal Highway. Parked on a quiet residential road at a distance from Federal Highway, he waited for about an hour to be sure the sedan was well ahead of his position. When he returned to the main road, he searched for a busy strip mall set back from the highway. He selected a medium sized mall with a large parking lot filled with cars. He parked his Hummer at the back of the lot behind a row of red mangroves. Before locking the doors, he removed his duffle bags with his clothes and guns. As he crossed the parking lot, a woman rushed out of her car, leaving the car running in front of the drug store. As soon as she disappeared through the glass doors, he quickly slid into the driver's seat and sped back onto Federal Highway.

Putting several miles between him and the mall, he turned onto the parallel street along the side of Federal Highway looking for a public boat ramp. He found one where several cars were parked with empty boat trailers attached. Empty trailers meant that the owners would be out for the day on the water cruising or fishing, maybe for longer than a day if he picked lucky. Using a screw driver from his duffle bag, Carlos removed the license plate from one of the out of state cars and traded the plate for the plate on his stolen car. If the boat owners came in after dark or late in the day, Carlos anticipated they would not notice the switched license plates right away. Attending to the boat and trailer might even distract the owner from noticing the changed license plate.

Carlos checked Steve's next stop on the sail plan in Tavernier. He eliminated Tavernier for his confrontation, as it was too close to his recent activities. By waiting a little longer, he wanted to formulate a better plan. Experienced at hot wiring cars, he started the car and continued down the highway to inspect Steve's third stop at a location on Long Key scheduled for arrival the following evening. After checking the area, Carlos eliminated Long Key as his interception point. There were no houses, shops, restaurants, motels or even an isolated marina or resort nearby.

Again, he continued to drive down Long Key Viaduct, passing a section of the Keys as desolate as the American Southwest. The long open areas with no visible traces of civilization caused Carlos to become uneasy. He felt comfortable when he could "hide" in plain sight disguised in a large crowd. His modus operandi dictated avoiding open areas where he would stand out. As accurately described in the psychological profile, water was outside Carlos' comfort zone and crowds in public places were in.

Studying the information on Steve's sail plan, Carlos concluded, no matter what happened, Steve would take the gold all the way to Key West. Since the two stops scheduled in Marathon were at the extreme ends of Vaca Key and neither one was close to a bank, removing the gold and taking a long cab ride didn't make sense. Carlos gambled that Steve would be uncomfortable leaving the gold in Marathon and would opt to deal with the gold after selling the boat in Key West. Even if Steve didn't know about the gold stash, once he found it, Steve would want to keep the gold close by. To Carlos, Marathon seemed to be the best place to intercept Steve. He could take his time to recoup his gold when Steve came ashore. By having the sail plan, he could skip two days and two stops ahead of Steve to check out each scheduled stop.

In Islamorada, Carlos planned to abandon his latest stolen car in the parking lot behind his motel. He had made reservations there for the night when he first entered the Keys. Since it was winter, the tourist pressure on motels and resorts would increase the closer he was to Key West. The next motel he selected was near Boot Key Marina in Marathon where he planned to switch cars again, taking advantage of another owner enjoying his boat. If he picked well, the theft would go unnoticed for several days and give him ample time to recapture the gold from Steve. After inspecting both of Steve's scheduled stops on Vaca Key during the day, he found they were only a few miles apart by land, but at a much greater distance by water. Carlos had observed Steve's habit of coming ashore in the early evening, making a phone call before dusk, and returning to the boat to anchor off shore, out of his reach, before sundown. He would have to make his move while Steve was ashore.

Investigating the first stop on Vaca Key, Carlos found a gated resort with a manned guardhouse. Carlos ruled this stop out as a poor location to intercept Steve due to the presence of the security guards. Security guards manned the entrance around the clock and would have a direct alarm into the local police station. Steve would stop there today. The second stop was located at the base of the Seven Mile Bridge. Due to the distance on the water, Steve could make that distance before dark. Carlos checked out the second destination on Vaca Key, the one planned for the following day. Steve could buy fuel and ice and other provisions at the marina in the morning before heading on to Key West. Logically, Carlos surmised, at this stop, Steve would spend a significant amount of time at the dock and in the store provisioning. The marina and shop would be busy with enough people for Carlos to blend in. While Steve was occupied, he could slip on board undetected, hide in the cabin, affording him the opportunity to commandeer the boat at gunpoint once away from the dock. Forcing Steve to sail the boat to the public ramp where he had parked the car, he planned to leave Steve bound and gagged on the boat while he loaded the gold into the car to return to Miami.

With good weather, his plan should go well. After showering and shaving, he turned on the television to double check the weather report. As he watched the latest southern Florida news flash, his plans were shattered. The station blared his name and flashed a recent picture of him across the screen, warning people in the Keys to be alert for him. He shuddered as the newscaster warned the listening audience to call the local police if they saw anyone matching his description. The newscaster went on to say Carlos was wanted for questioning related to the recent death of Maria Santiago of Coconut Grove. He knew he was being followed, but he didn't think they had anything on him. After all, Maria had withdrawn the money from Steve's trust accounts and had hidden the gold on Steve's boat.

He was stunned to hear that Maria had died from the injuries in her fall down the stairs. He had called 911 two blocks away from the apartment knowing she was injured but had not believed her injuries were critical, besides she deserved it for moving the gold. He wondered, had the old lady seen him push Maria down the stairs? He did not think he had reacted that violently to cause such serious harm, but he had to admit to himself he lost control when she told him she had changed her mind and returned the gold to Andrews. He could not understand what happened. She had never gone back on him before. She insisted that she had changed her mind, but he believed she had convinced Steve to conspire against him.

Chills ran down his spine as he visualized the desk clerk still watching television in the lobby while waiting to check in motel guests. If she was watching and listening at that exact moment, she would recognize him as the last guest she had checked in. Carlos pictured her already dialing the local police to report him as a registered guest at the motel. He pressed the remote buttons to change the channel and increase the volume. He opened the front window and turned all the lamps on. Quickly repacking his duffle bag, he wrapped the guns in one of the motel towels, dressed and climbed out the back window. Once outside, he removed and emptied two plastic trash bags from the dumpster behind the motel and used them to rewrap the guns.

Cautiously moving along the back alley, he made his way down the marina dock where he picked the lock on a large fishing boat tied up at the end of the outer dock. Carlos slept on board the fishing boat that night. Waking before dawn, he wiped away all places where he had left fingerprints. As the sun began to send rays of light across the water, he crossed Federal Highway and slipped behind a small sporting goods shop in the strip mall. Detecting the lack of a security alarm system, he jimmied open the lock on the back door of the sports shop. Moving quickly, he changed into a pair of bright plaid Bermuda shorts, a flashy two-tone blue sports shirt and a new pair of sandals. He grabbed a pair of dark sunglasses from a display rack, a wide brimmed straw hat, and placed the guns and his old clothes in a large fishing rod case. To help authenticate his disguise, he grabbed a tackle box.

On the way out of the shop, he noticed the rack of marine charts. Instinctively, he grabbed one of the rolls containing a chart for the lower Keys. As he passed the dumpster in the back, he stopped and removed his old clothes from the fishing rod case, throwing them into the dumpster. Satisfied with his new look, he boldly started hitch hiking along Federal Highway southbound. Without much ado, a driver stopped and picked him up. He stayed with the driver until he saw the first motel after crossing the bridge into Key West from Stock Island. Thanking the driver, he hopped out of the car and began walking down Roosevelt Boulevard for about a mile until he found a large strip mall.

He crossed the street and slipped behind the buildings into an open field of tall grass. At the edge of the tall grasses, a narrow, but deep canal lined the edge of the mangroves. The water ebbed and flowed toward the harbor. Scattered between the grasses and the mangroves stood a row of temporary shelters made of large cardboard boxes and particleboard shored up with wire and miscellaneous pieces of lumber scavenged by the homeless occupants. The roofs were covered with thatches of palm and palmetto fronds like Native American Indian chickees. As he checked each shanty, he found only one occupied. When Carlos peered through the makeshift doorway, the occupant, a groggy, unshaven man, rolled over in his dirty, unkempt clothing and stared back through blood shot eyes. The old man clutched a small brown paper bag in his right hand.

"Hey old timer, is that your bicycle over there in the grass?" Carlos pressed the homeless man.

"It's for sale if you're interested."

"How's twenty bucks cash?" Carlos waved a crisp twenty-dollar bill towards the old man.

As the old man grabbed at the bill, he slurred, "You got yourself a deal. Only one hitch, no warranties and if you take it, you forget where you got it."

"Fair enough," Carlos responded as he dropped the bill into the old man's outstretched hand. "I'll be back a little later. I may need a place to stay, you got room here for one more?"

"Make yourself at home. Can't beat the rent anywhere else. Rooming here is first come first served."

"Good. I'll be back before dark. Here's another ten bucks to hold me a spot."

Carlos anticipated the authorities would make a sweep of the island looking for him. Most likely, the old man would be picked up along with all the homeless and other petty criminals they could find to review pictures of Carlos in hopes of finding someone who could say they saw him. This man could help spread some misinformation.

"Don't forget. I'll be back," he said as he wheeled the bicycle across the field to the back of the mall. The bike was rusty, but the tires looked good and held air. He smiled to himself as he climbed onto the seat and started pedaling. His smile broadened as he reviewed his good fortune so far.

In a discount store in the mall, he purchased a baseball cap, long tan pants, a blue and tan striped T-shirt, new sunglasses, two cans of purple metallic spray paint and a pair of tennis shoes, a package of shock cords and a roll of masking tape. Back outside, behind the mall, he used old newspapers and the tape to mask the seat and handle bars and the small baggage rack mounted behind the seat. Then he carefully spray painted the bicycle with the deep purple paint. After waiting an hour for it to dry, he used the shock cord to bind his tackle box onto the rack and changed into his new clothes. During the time he waited for the paint to dry, he had studied the marine charts for the entry into Key West harbor. He began to formulate a new plan.

An hour later, Carlos walked along the docks of downtown Key West wearing his new baseball cap. Inquiring about the shrimp boats, he learned they now docked on Stock Island, no longer operating out of Key West. Only a few small commercial boats hung on in the inner harbor and they were located on the north dock not far from the myriad of large, multi-million dollar yachts lining the docks and inner basin. On the north dock, he found exactly what he was looking for, an old wooden lobster boat with a weather worn For Sale sign taped on the windshield. He memorized the phone number and dialed the number at a phone booth at the town dock.

A woman speaking with a heavy Spanish accent answered the phone. Conveying his interest in the lobster boat, she told him the asking price was $2,500.00 and her husband would be back in the morning from Marathon if he had any interest in purchasing the boat.

"Tell him he has a deal," Carlos responded. "What time can he meet me at the boat?"

"Not before 9:00 AM" she told Carlos. "No sooner. He has to have his coffee."

"I'll be there, sharp." Carlos hung up the phone. He returned to the boat later, near dusk, wheeling the bicycle along the dock. He lifted the bicycle and placed it on the cabin floor when he reached the boat.

"Who the hell are you? And what are you doing on that boat?" a man hollered at him from a nearby boat as Carlos clambered aboard.

"The new owner," Carlos hollered back, securing the bicycle on board. The other man watched him curiously, then disappeared down the companionway. Exhausted from the day's activities, Carlos crawled into the V-berth, pulled a ratty old blanket over his body and slept soundly for the first time in over a week, maybe even sounder than the day he and Maria had exchanged Steve's trust fund money for gold coins.

Chapter Thirteen

The Backcountry

In the protection of the mangrove key, *Seaseeker* floated motionlessly in the center of rippleless water. With the rising sun, the changing thermals brought the first stirrings of a morning breeze. The puffs, increasing in frequency, blew gently into the windscoop mounted in the hatch over the V-berth. Hearing the rattling of the sailcloth and feeling the sensation of the wind ruffling the hair on his chest, Steve slowly opened his eyes to see the first rays of dawn spread through the cabin. Lazily he sat up and rolled forward out of the V-birth. With his first thoughts of food, he selected a can of sardines and peeled the lid open. Prying each soft body out of the can with his boat knife, Steve carefully selected four slimy fish, sliding their silvery bodies onto a plate. He poured a cup of cold, left over coffee into his cup, grabbed a slice of bread and climbed out into the dew-covered cockpit. Crouching down on the deck, he slid the plate of sardines toward the porthole window.

Hearing the sound of the dish slide across the fiberglass deck, Shoestring turned and waddled back from the bow to the porthole window. A long piece of green seaweed dangled from his beak. Steve watched Shoestring complete his mealtime ritual of peering at the sardines, dropping the seaweed onto the deck, and plucking the sardines from the plate one by one, swallowing them head first. Steve reveled in the companionship the cormorant afforded him on his journey.

Although Shoestring never responded to whatever he told him, Steve was grateful for the presence of another being to talk to. Somehow Shoestring had enhanced his enjoyment of the journey, taking his mind off the loss of Maria and the anxiety of knowing Carlos was out there somewhere, waiting for an opportune moment to accost him.

Gulping down two swallows of cold coffee, Steve smoothed a thin layer of peanut butter over the top of the slice of fresh baked oat bread he had purchased at the Last Chance Marina. Today he would be traveling deep into the backcountry of the lower Keys, following the unmarked inner channel of the Intercoastal. Shortly, he would enter the sanctuary of the Great White Heron National Wildlife Refuge, leaving all vestiges of human habitation back towards Federal Highway. Steve looked forward to sharing the next few days with Mother Nature and her multitude of creatures. They were far more pleasing to observe than the humans he had had to deal with recently.

Setting sail, he watched an osprey off in the distance soar into the sky after dive-bombing suddenly, feet first into the water. Successfully clutching a struggling fish in its talons, the osprey headed back to his nest above the mangroves.

Too soon, Steve thought, too soon, as he had crossed Big Spanish Channel at the west end of the Seven Mile Bridge. Carefully following the marks, he crossed into the edge of the open Gulf of Mexico. He relished this last opportunity to change his mind and cross back to the Atlantic to run into Key West through Hawk Channel. He held his course. When he reached the mark at Harbor Key Bank, he turned west, setting a course running along the outer edge of the Keys and heading in the direction of the mark for the entrance to Northwest Channel, the entry passage into Key West harbor. The course ran slightly off the shoreline along the lower Keys, at the edge of The Great White Heron National Wildlife Refuge. The nearest human habitation was at least five miles south along Federal Highway and 30 miles to Key West. By early afternoon he passed Johnston Key Channel.

Eric was right. The assumption that Carlos would stay on dry land and try to intercept him in downtown Key West did not make sense. Too many tourists in Key West this time of year could witness his actions. Also, Carlos knew by now, too many federal and local county agents were waiting for him to make his move. As Eric pointed out,

Carlos' desire to recapture the gold would motivate him to overcome his fear of the water. Most likely, Carlos would find a boat to track him away from observant eyes and ears.

Looking at the chart, Steve concluded the most logical point for Carlos to intercept him rested at the outer end of the jetty of the Northwest Channel. The mark was positioned at a considerable distance from land and afforded the deepest water leading into Key West harbor. With any map at all, Carlos could see that Steve had to pass through that channel to gain entrance to Key West. Steve's only advantage was that Carlos had no idea when Steve would make his entry. Clearly, the best time for Steve to pass through was early morning, before dawn.

Now was not the time to be anywhere near the entrance to the harbor. In fact, Steve wanted to find an out of the way channel or cove where he could rest for the evening. Logically, the best time to pass through the channel was 2 to 3 AM or later when Carlos would most likely be sleeping. Since Carlos was uncomfortable on the water, Steve guessed that he would patrol the entrance to the harbor during daylight hours, even Carlos had to rest.

What he wanted now was to find a small bay or tidal stream to hang out for a few hours to time his to passage into Key West before sunrise. He felt naked and exposed running along the outer Keys in the remaining afternoon light. Unfortunately, he had never sailed in this area and his chart warned that local conditions prevailed. With a light wind blowing out of the southeast, sailing conditions next to the mangrove islands turned fluky. The light and unreliable winds led Steve to furl his sails and motor slowly along the shoreline, watching the mangrove domes slide by.

Remembering Eric's suggestion, he removed the loaded flare gun from its orange polyurethane case in the lazarette and placed it on the cushion beside him. The flare gun might provide a weapon of last resort to repel Carlos if he attempted to board the boat. A feeling of confidence and security flowed through his thoughts as he grasped the handle of the small flare gun. For the moment, there was no imminent threat. The horizon was clear as far as he could see with no other boats ahead or behind. Although the passage entrance was miles away, he adjusted the throttle to the point where the boat was barely making headway so he could observe the birds along the shore and the fish in the shallow water.

Overhead a large bird circled the edge of the mangroves, with a wingspan that spread across the sky. Steve watched as the bird dove into the water ahead of him, bringing up a medium sized silver fish. As the bird streaked toward the upper branches of the larger trees deeper in the island, the freshly caught fish struggled to be free of the bird's tenacious grasp. "A bald eagle!" Steve exclaimed as he watched the bird glide into an enormous nest, high in the branches. A second eagle soared upward as soon as the first one settled into the nest. A handful of frigate birds followed after the eagle, but were not quick enough to steal the fish from his grasp. The frigate birds soared up into the sky, floating on the thermals, waiting for another bird with a fresh catch to capture for their next meal.

He continued to motor slowly as dusk settled in around him. Without warning, Shoestring dropped down into his position on the bow and, as usual, stared into the wind. As he watched the bird in his station on the bow, Steve alternated his focus between the bird and the horizon ahead. Suddenly, through the frame of the bow pulpit, Steve spotted a bright, white light shining close to the surface of the water. He was headed straight towards it. Up until this time, he had not seen any boats. Where had this boat come from so suddenly, seeming to appear out of nowhere? Could it be Carlos preparing to make his move?

The light remained constant, directly ahead. If he maintained his course, he would intercept the boat within minutes. Ignoring his rising fears about Carlos, Steve did not alter his course. Knowing that a sailboat could not outrun anything except a rowboat, he placed the flare gun in his pocket, moving his hand back into the pocket and running his fingers across the handle every few seconds. Although momentary thoughts of turning and running in the opposite direction ran through his mind, he continued to maintain his course. As he watched closely, the form of a small boat rocking on the waves, perhaps drift fishing in the low swells, emerged in the dusk. Peering through his binoculars, he could see a small flat-bottomed skiff with an outboard motor mounted on the stern. The light originated from a lantern mounted at the bow. A single occupant sat in the middle of the boat, fishing off the far side, with his back toward Steve. He continued to approach slowly with his running lights off, knowing the occupant must be aware of his approach.

His fears returned as he caressed the flare gun in his pocket. Could this be Carlos in disguise? Steve knew Carlos was a master at disguise and considered it a challenge to devise new personas to change his appearance. Remembering some of the pictures the FBI had shown him at the meeting in Eric's office, he closed his fingers tighter around the handle of the flare gun. Logic told him this was not Carlos. Carlos would not go so far as to actually fish. Unable to decipher how or where the boat had appeared, he knew the passage way could not be too far away. To have appeared so suddenly, the occupant had to be knowledgeable of the ins and outs of the ragged shoreline. Carlos would not have such knowledge. Insecurity prevailed as he kept his right hand on the flare gun and his left hand on the tiller. Gliding slowly nearer to the small skiff, the occupant stood and turned toward him.

"Evenin', sailor. You otta have your runnin' lights on. I barely saw you coming."

"I could see you. Your lantern was like a bright beacon. What brings you out here in such a small boat? I thought you might be in trouble."

"Me? Trouble? Hell, no. No trouble. I'm out here 'most all the time. If not fishin', I'm showin' folks birds and wildlife or saving some out-a-stater run aground or outa gas. Tonight, I'm trying to hook me a tarpon or a bonefish before dark. They won't bite after dark. Looks like you mighta spooked 'em. How come you're out here in the backcountry?"

"Sorry. I didn't mean to disturb your fishing. I'm looking for a small inlet or hole to tie in for a few hours before I head on to Key West. I'm ahead of schedule. I wanted to go in just before dawn so I need to kill some time."

"Well, you're in luck. You've just met the right guy, at the right time and in the right place." Mike scratched the back of his head and replaced his khaki colored cap backwards over his head of wiry red hair.

"It's getting on to dinner time and my stomach's beginning to grumble."

"Care for some chowder and a spot coffee?" Mike grinned through a full set of tobacco stained teeth.

"Where? I don't see any docks or restaurants. Steve surveyed the area and saw no trace of human habitation.

"'Been fishing here 'most all my life. I got me a few grunts for dinner. There's enough for two. You won't find any place on the charts. Follow me. I have a camp back among the mangroves that no one but me and my friends know about."

"Great. I'd appreciate a shelter for a few hours. My charts don't show a thing 'til the Northwest Channel into Key West."

"M' name's Mike, Mike Templeton. Most folks 'round here call me Mud Key Mike and probably some other not so favorable names behind my back. But you can call me Mike."

Steve put *Seaseeker* into neutral. When the momentum of the boat threatened to take him past his new acquaintance, he slid the gearshift into reverse to hold his position. "My name's Steve Andrews, Mike. I'm from Miami, on my way to Key West."

"That's a challenge to single hand all the way down from Miami. No crew aboard?"

"None, and yes, not just a challenge but a necessity. I'm delivering my boat to the new owner in Key West. I didn't have time to find crew."

"Look, afore you drift on by, follow me. You can hang out at my camp off Mud Key for the night. What's your draft?"

"I draw just under two feet."

"What kind of boat is that? I don't think I've seen one of those before."

"It's an Essex, designed for shallow water, like the Keys."

"Well, I might a heard of it, but I'm no sailor. Follow me. The camp's up in the mangroves where the tidal stream splits near Mud Key Channel. You won't know the opening from all the others without local knowledge. Go slow so you don't drift past me. Don't worry about where the channel is, it's plenty deep and wide. Stay in the middle 'til we get to the beach. Then you can anchor inside the basin. Follow me."

"I didn't see Mud Key Channel on the charts."

"It's there, and more. Ever hear of local knowledge? There's lots of things out here never gets recorded officially. Keeps the tourists at bay and saves the best spots for us locals. Most things out here can't be charted 'cause the weather and tides change the channels and shoals too frequently to keep the charts accurate," Mike instructed Steve as he reeled in his line and started up his outboard motor. He turned his boat toward the shore of a nearby Key.

Steve pushed his gearshift into forward, following Mike's lead. He felt at a disadvantage as he shadowed his leader under the branches of the overhanging mangroves. He followed the skiff, watching the digital readout on his Fathometer, hoping the depth would remain navigable. As they closed into what he expected to be a shoal, the depth reading surprisingly held steady between six and eight feet. An opening off to the side allowed them to pass easily through a narrow channel winding deeper into the thick growth of mangroves with a maze of exposed roots on both sides. The channel was wide enough for the boats to pass through easily, but allowed no room for Steve to turn around. He mentally acknowledged that he had to rely on Mike's knowledge that there would be ample room somewhere ahead for him to turn around for the return trip. He was thankful the mangroves were not thick or tall enough to tangle with his rigging. He relaxed as he followed Mike, knowing, for now, he was safe from Carlos.

Shortly, they entered a wide basin where the channel split, heading off in opposite directions between the mangroves. Mike slowed down along the perimeter, following a narrow spit of land densely filled with mangroves. As they approached a sandy bank, Mike cut off his engine as he glided toward the landing. Steve followed suit. He was thankful for his guide as he looked around. All of the domed dots of mangroves looked alike and the channels ran in all directions between them. He never would have found this basin without his guide.

"C'mon straight up to the edge. It's deep as hell in here back off the beach. Right now, you're about five hours from Key West so you might as well rest up a bit. Welcome to Mud Key."

Steve watched the depth reading on his Fathometer up until his bow crunched onto the beach. The reading had remained steady at eight feet right next to the mangroves, until they were about six feet from the beach where the shallows came up quickly. Mike stood, leaning toward *Seaseeker*, as the bow grated across the sand. He grabbed hold of the bow pulpit and collected the anchor and anchor line, securing them deep into the sand fifteen feet in front of the bow.

"This is amazing. I never would have found this place on my own."

"The Mud Keys are full of channels above and below land level. Tidal currents carved the channels out of the limestone eons ago. Then the mangroves filled in the shallow flats over time, making all these scattered keys we call 'the backcountry.' These little basins are great shelters if you know where they are. We have a lot of nice sandy beaches out here at low tide, like the big one over at Marvin Key. They're so far out, only us locals know where they are and how to get here."

Steve couldn't believe his good fortune. No one could possibly see his boat from the Gulf, the mainland or the Intercoastal. He breathed easy knowing he was safe from Carlos for a few hours. By now, Carlos must have commandeered a boat. Steve pictured Carlos on the jetty, waiting for him to cruise into Key West. He firmly believed that Carlos would not approach him in the crowds of tourists in Key West. On the water made more sense, as opposed to Agent Bellows who predicted Carlos would stay on land.

Steve pondered what Carlos would do when he found that Steve did not have the gold on board *Seaseeker*. This encounter with a local fisherman was a good sign. He would have a place to hide out for a few hours. He dismissed his thoughts about Carlos.

"Get yourself on down here, sailor. I'll make you some coffee. An' don't worry, there's no bugs out here this time of year. If there's a storm in the Gulf or Hawk Channel, this is the only place to hide from the wind and weather. Of course, you don't want to come here in the summer time."

"Why not?" asked Steve, finally deciding to replace the flare gun in the lazarette. He grabbed a flashlight and a light jacket as he slid over the side of *Seaseeker* onto the sandy landing.

"The gnats and skeeters'll eat you alive in the summer. Here's my painter. We'll tie the boats together on your anchor. We have a saying around here: Never tie your boat to a mangrove."

"You're sure full of good advice." Steve replied as he followed Mike along the sandy path through the mangroves.

"Watch your step. There's still water in here so the path is mostly mucky sand. Walk carefully. Your shoes can get stuck fast and you'll step right out of them if you're not careful."

Steve followed Mike through the scattered mangrove shoots sticking up like nails in a board. "I know this place like the back of my hand. That's why they call me Mud Key Mike. Anyway, sailor, welcome to my camp in the backcountry."

"Thanks. You can't imagine how glad I am to be here."

"Was that your pet bird that followed us in?"

Steve turned around and sure enough there was Shoestring perched on the bow of *Seaseeker*.

"Oh, no. That's Shoestring. He's not a pet." Steve laughed. "That bird is wild but seems to have grown attached to me. He's been following me down the Keys, all the way from Jewfish Creek Bridge."

"I'll bet you feed it."

"Yes, but he…"

"That'll do it, every time. Here we are. Wait here for a minute. I'll show you something really special." Steve joined Mike who was standing at the edge of an opening in the mangroves. "Watch carefully." At the edge of a dome shaped mangrove island in the distance, occasional cormorants flew into and out of the mangroves deeper inland. The full moon had risen above the eastern horizon and it's long beams of light reflected across the flats, shimmering across the water in the basin behind the two boats.

"Just stand quiet for a bit. If we're lucky we'll see a few Key deer. They'll be out soon. This is the time of day they come out to feed." Mike spoke softly, just above a whisper, leaning his bulky body sideways and speaking directly into Steve's ear.

"Key deer? There are deer here on Mud Key?" Steve whispered back.

"Yup. Everyone thinks they're only on Big Pine Key, but I've found several medium sized keys out here with small colonies of deer. Some swim out from the mainland, others live here. They survive because the islands below Bahia Honda have a limestone base that holds fresh water. The lower keys are different than up by Islamorada and north of

Marathon. The deer need the fresh water to survive and the limestone holds the rain in blue water holes."

Just as Mike finished speaking, half a dozen small deer, about the size of a Doberman pincher, entered the path and passed by them.

"Amazing. They weren't afraid of us. Look, they have a full rack of antlers, too."

"Well, now you've seen them."

"They're so small. I've never seen such small deer. They don't grow any larger?"

"No, they don't. Don't know why. They're a special species related to the Virginia white tailed deer. Most of them are accustomed to being around humans because we can't hunt them and we aren't allowed to feed them due to federal regulations. They have to feed on their own. They're on the endangered list. You won't find them anywhere else in the world. Not like your bird there. I think that one of yours has imprinted on you. My guess is that bird is standing fast to the bow of your boat 'cause it thinks you're his parent. He doesn't even recognize his own kind. He ignores birds of his own kind when they fly by."

"I've had the same feeling."

"We'll take another hike later, after we get to camp. I'll show you the rookery."

"Rookery?"

"Yes, there are thousands of mated pairs of your bird on a nearby key tending their young as dutiful parents. Does your bird have a name?"

"Shoestring. I call him Shoestring."

"Shoestring, huh. Seems like he's all screwed up. That's what happens to birds when they get too close to humans. They get too dependent and forget they're birds, eating human food and all. I bet most birds that happens to couldn't live in the wild anymore. They've learned to feed off human food and garbage."

"I think you're right. He's so confused he's followed me over a hundred miles down the Keys. I haven't seen him even look at other birds, especially other cormorants."

"Man does it all the time. Steps in the middle of a bird's life and they're never the same again. Your bird's gone a different direction."

"According to the story I heard up at Jewfish Creek, he would have perished if Birdie Svenson hadn't saved him."

"Perhaps, perhaps not. Man stepped into the middle and intervened. There's a guy I ran into a few years back that raised storks. He dressed up like them and invented a low flying machine to train them to be birds and migrate like their kind should. He flew the machine down the coast so they'd learn to migrate. That's the only way. Got to train 'em to be birds or they think they're human."

"That was a noble thing to do, train the birds to be birds."

"But there's a problem. Even though we're a part of the natural world, we really don't live in the natural world. We've created our own artificial world in our schools, office buildings and homes. Most humans haven't a clue about how to live in nature like the birds do. It's almost immoral to raise them in our way of life. Our way of life doesn't really exist in the natural world."

"Technology. That's what's different. Our life style is obscene in contrast with nature's creatures and their environment."

"Well, that's how complicated we've become. As much as I don't like it, we're still a part of this world, even with our technology. What we do and what we think is all part of this world, too, for better or worse. Probably worse. These birds here are doomed not because we can't talk about saving them, but really protecting them and their environment is the problem. When they do something we don't like, we get rid of them. Like the motel over on federal highway. The birds used to gather there just before sun down. Hundreds, no thousands of them collected on the electric wires about an hour before sunset, all watching the sun go down, like we do on Mallory Square. After the sunset, they flocked into the trees for the night. Well, some human took umbrage and they cut down all the trees so the birds lost their evening resting spots. Criminal, that's criminal."

"What? Why'd they do that?"

"Who knows? Someone probably didn't like to hear the birds chattering, or maybe some pooped on their cars. That's the way we are. Cut down over a dozen perfectly healthy trees to discourage the birds. And mankind wonders why the world is heating up and nature is lashing back. Can't keep cuttin' down those trees without something happening. Our unbridled population explosion smashes into their environment and damages any efforts to protect the other creatures we should be sharing the planet with. I believe it will happen. What goes around, comes around. One day, she'll win. Mother Nature will come back with a vengeance."

Mike stood and Steve followed him in the direction the deer had disappeared along the sand covered limestone path through the thick mangroves. When Steve looked down at the path, he could see the sharp impressions of the deer hooves in the loose sand. About five hundred feet into the maze, the mangroves thinned and they entered a clearing. A small, ramshackled shanty stood precariously off to the side of the clearing. Steve grinned at the crude construction, wondering how the old weathered boards and driftwood remained standing.

"Welcome to my hideaway, sailor. Have a seat and make yourself at home."

Steve sat down on one of the makeshift wood seats outside the shanty beside a large, crude wood table constructed out of weatherworn lumber. A foot thick section of a 50 gallon steel oil drum sunk into the sand beside the table served as a campfire ring. Flaked gray ashes from previous fires filled the blackened edges of the rim halfway to the top.

"Don't tell anyone about this place. The government doesn't allow camping or fires out here in the Refuge, so I'm real careful. I keep a water bucket full next to it when it's lit. And I don't cook long. Make yourself comfortable while I heat some coffee and clean my catch. I'll have a fish chowder in no time." Mike collected a sufficient number of logs and kindling and set an old blackened coffee pot on the fire as he cleaned the fish on the table in front of Steve.

"You come here often."

"Sure do. I spend most weekends here; sleep in the shanty if it rains. You can't beat the view of the stars here. There's no artificial light from human contraptions, so the moon and the stars provide the main light at night. The stars seem like they're right on top of you. I like coming here. It clears my head from all the interference caused by civilization."

Steve looked up into the darkening sky as the stars began to appear in the crisp, clear sky. "Wow. You're right. I feel like I could just reach up and grab a couple stars. They seem closer here."

"That's cause we're close to the equator. This part of the planet is closer than anywhere else on earth. Did you notice that the whole area around here is surrounded by a mud flat? That's the best protection Mother Nature ever came up with to keep out the human invasion."

"I get the feeling you think nature and the birds are doomed."

"You just don't know. I been here all my life. I don't see the number and variety of birds here that were around when I was a kid. I spent my youth poling around this part of the backcountry in a small skiff. That's how I know my way around."

"But I saw lots of birds along the mangroves, pelicans, egrets, seagulls."

"Cormorants, pelicans, seagulls. When you visit the state parks, you see lots of birds, grackles, pigeons, doves. We used to have more shore birds, egrets, and herons. The saddest one is the Roseate Spoonbill. I see one now and then, but the backcountry and the Everglades used to be teeming with birds, insects, fish and lizards. For me, they're a dead zone now."

"Wow. I really didn't notice."

"You're an office man. You live inside all the time. In the short term, I've been doing my share to protect what's still left. I spend my time out here chasing off offenders and teenagers joy riding in small watercraft and shooting off their guns at the wildlife. A few years back we had a big fight. Big Al, bless his soul, led the charge. They used to allow those small craft I call water mosquitoes in here. They were tearing up the sea grass and natural vegetation and scaring the birds off their nests. We fought them in the courts and won. They don't allow them in the Refuge now. They're illegal."

"That's good. I'm glad you won that battle. Those contraptions are noisy, too."

"You bet. But what are you going to do when you go back up to Miami? Go back to work in your fancy offices up there? You'll go back to Brickell Avenue and forget all about us and the birds down here. That happens with everyone. They come down here, enjoy the place for a few days or weeks. The snowbirds from up north drive down for a few months in the winter, then they all leave. Out of sight, out of mind. We few have a tough battle on our hands. You got to promise me one thing, sailor."

"Okay. What's that?"

"Promise me you'll look out for that bird of yours. He's all messed up and can't survive on his own now. He doesn't even recognize his own kind. Take care of him because he's dependent on people, you in particular."

"But I'm going back to Miami as soon as I sell my boat. I can't stay here. I don't have anywhere to stay."

"That's what I'm saying. That's what everybody does. That's why your bird is doomed. It's imprinted on you and you're going to desert it."

"But what can I do? I can't catch him. Whenever I get close, he moves away."

"Talk to the seabird station. They'll help."

"The seabird station?"

"There's one on Stock Island and one in the upper Keys, on Key Largo. I think you can get the phone number at any of the parks or the Chamber of Commerce. You have to do something to help that bird. It's half human now and nearly zero bird. They'll help retrain it and turn it back to nature and if not, he'll be part of their breeding program."

"But how do I do that if I can't catch it?"

"Call them. They'll know what to do. Let them intervene."

"I bet it's expensive."

"Nope, won't cost a dime. They're all volunteers, local citizens and retirees like me."

"Volunteers? That's unusual. No pay?"

"Yup, only love and appreciation. You lawyers don't recognize those traits, do you?" Mike paused and looked closely at Steve, then continued, "You guys already know life on this planet isn't fair. Love and appreciation are man's way of attempting to level the playing field, so to speak, to make things fair. But that doesn't work in the natural world. There isn't any love and appreciation in the natural world."

"There's no love for birds?"

"Not really, not in the natural world. The problem is, birds don't vote."

"Birds, vote? Now you're being ridiculous."

"Not really. That would solve the problem. One bird, one vote. Things would be different if the birds could vote, but that will never happen. Humans are all about politics and money. There's a place back in the upper keys where there was a pelican rookery. Some developers came along and cleared out the land to make time-share condos. They walled out the birds even though they called it Pelican Bay. They put pelican impressions in concrete, pelican logos on their stationary, and pelican statues all over the grounds and all but left no room for the real birds. The real pelicans couldn't survive there. They even put pointed ends on the pilings so the pelicans couldn't land near the docks. They're all gone up there. They didn't leave a thing for the birds."

"That's what man does. The birds and animals have no say."

"What I'm worried about is how they've designated the area out here as a wildlife sanctuary, all written out on paper. Then the politicians wave the paper around in meetings and fancy places to show off what they did. It's all a symbol. They don't know what the real thing actually is."

"You must be frustrated by anti-nature attitudes."

"There's only so much one person can do. You know what I mean. All I can do is spread the word and come out here to watch over the birds as often as I can. I try to do my share, but I'm only one little squeak in the darkness."

"Well, you've made an impression on me this evening. I appreciate seeing your camp and the deer. I'm glad to have met you and see what you are doing and hear how you feel about it. We need more people like you."

"Well sailor, you seem to be sensitive to nature. That makes you special, and maybe unusual. Unless I'm wrong, you're the type who could care. Do you know what the bigger problem is?"

"No, but I'm all ears."

"Indifference. If I can just reach one person in my lifetime, find someone to replace me out here, I'd settle for that. If I could reach two or three then maybe I'd have started something. It's a big job to tell six billion people we have enough of our own kind. Let's reduce our kind and make room for more of them. Maybe we can bring back more of God's creatures, closer to the way it used to be.

"If there is a God, I'm not sure myself. If so, then this world is his Garden of Eden, his gift to us. Those who run around and kill all these birds and fish and then go to church on Sunday bother me. Maybe that's why we don't hear from Him. I bet he's mad as hell about the slaughter of his creatures and ruination of his gardens. I better stop, I might be offending you. I don't know your views, but the way I see it, unless we control ourselves, it's too late to talk about limits. This world is doomed." Mike stopped speaking and looked tentatively at Steve.

"Oh, don't worry. I agree with you. Mankind hasn't figured out how to deal with his numbers and reproductive system to control population growth. Man likes sex too much to turn it off and we all feel we deserve our own babies. By the time we mature enough to think about it, it's too late, we've already made a bunch of babies."

"Well, everyone has a legal right to reproduce and the Bible directed mankind to be fruitful and multiply, so he did. And that's why these birds are doomed, sailor. What you see here is a miracle."

"A miracle?"

"Sure. At least what's left of one. In a generation or two, they'll all be gone."

"You really think so?"

"Sure. Look what happened to the Indians. It's the same thing. The Indians believe the land belongs to everyone, no one can own land. The land belongs to the Great Spirit so it was free for everyone. Then the white man came along and changed all that. How many Indians do you see living on prime land now? And the white man did it all legally, deliberately manipulating good, trusting people. The Florida Seminoles are the only tribe that stood up against the white man. They never signed a treaty with the US government."

"Hmm, an interesting parallel, the Indians and the birds."

"Sure. In the pioneer days, the victims were the Indians. Today it's the birds. No difference, same principal. Don't pay any attention to the rhetoric the politicians spin about themselves. They tell you what they want you to hear, then they go do what they want to do. You bet it will sound all nice and proper, but don't listen to what they say, watch what they do. Step back and look at history. There are lots of lessons there. Remember how the white man scammed the Indians out of all the valuable land. The Indians ended up holding worthless reservations on worthless land. Take a hard look at things."

"Legalized theft."

"They aren't the only ones, look at the whole world, especially China. They say China is the quietest place on earth."

"How's that?

"No birds."

"No birds? What happened to the birds?"

"They ate them, long ago."

"They ate them!"

"Sure, along with the dogs and cats and other small animals. With the population explosion there, food became a problem so they ate all the wildlife. It's happening everywhere."

"I never thought about that."

"You been too long running around chasing the almighty dollar, riding in fancy cars going to Dolphin games, or just chasing women to notice. You got a fancy education, Phi Beta Kappa from Yale, but no one taught you how to think."

"Hmm. Think about what?"

"Do you know what the real problem in Florida is today?"

"You said it, over population."

"Yes, but do you know why?"

"What do you mean? I'm curious about your opinions."

"No one could come here to live until two things happened, the first was cooling, like refrigeration, ice and air conditioning. Without those inventions, human habitation in Florida would be intolerable."

"Okay, so what's the second thing?"

"Mosquito spray. Mosquitoes used to flourish everywhere in Florida, particularly in the Everglades. But when man started migrating here, he couldn't live with the mosquito and all the other bugs. Now the problem has become the mosquito spray, the insecticide."

"How's that? I don't understand."

"The mosquito spray kills more than the mosquito; it kills the birds and other wildlife too. Birds, fish and reptiles, all depend on insects for food. Did you know that some species of birds fly all the way down to South America and up to Alaska to have their chicks?"

"Why?"

"Food. The chicks need the protein in the insects and larvae to grow and thrive."

"I never thought about all that. The birds migrate to find the food sources to survive?"

"Yup. That's what the food chain is all about. When we destroy the base, we destroy ourselves as well. The mosquitoes and other insects form the base of the food chain for everything."

"I never studied biology."

"That's the problem with mankind. He's blind sighted and only thinks about himself. But it's not just the birds and land animals. The minnows and most fish we call game fish for our food sources also depend on insects for food, too. Without that base, the whole system collapses, like what's going on today. Commercial ventures are fishing out more and more species of fish and starving the minnows by eliminating the insects and their larvae. Man won't tolerate the mosquito and other insects, they're nuisances for him. It's simple. You want to know something else?"

"Sure, I'm listening. You make sense, seems to me."

"Well every time they spray for mosquitoes, they kill millions of birds too. How many flies and other insects have you seen around Miami lately? They save a few human lives from diseases transmitted by insects, but kill millions of birds. How many bird obituaries have you read in your Miami newspapers? If I were you, I'd put my money on insect sprays, cause that's where it's going to come out in the end."

"You make a good point. Man won't tolerate insects, particularly mosquitoes. I read somewhere that mosquitoes carry the most diseases that are killers of people, worldwide. Look at the billion-dollar industry in pest control. They specialize in ant control, termite control, roach control. Now whenever you have a pest, you need the right specialist to treat the problem. I used to call the exterminator, now it's split into departments depending on the pest. You gotta get the right guy or the termites will get your house."

"I can't dispute that. That's the problem, the trade off. They spray the hell out of the mosquitoes in southern Florida so you don't hear of any deaths due to mosquito borne diseases. But you don't hear about the birds they killed, or the fish. They don't count them. And, you don't see any insects in Miami-Dade County."

"That's not news people want to hear. Like you said, birds don't vote."

"Sometimes I think you're getting smarter by the minute. You're catching on."

"So, is there any hope?"

"Look, sailor. You got to ask yourself something. What you gonna do with what's left of the rest of your life? If you ask me, you're a tragic figure, just like your friend the bird over there on your boat. You're both outcastes."

"How's that?"

"You're both orphans of this world. Hell, you may be good for each other. I'll tell you the story about old man Dawkins."

"Dawkins? Who was he?"

"Big Al. He used to run the seabird station over on Stock Island. He did it for free when he retired, all up 'til the day he died. I used to take him lots of injured seabirds, ones with broken wings, wings snarled with fish line, hooks hanging out of their mouths, those plastic rings from soda and beer can six packs stuck around their legs or necks. Society don't care. People just throw their trash in the water, along the highways. How many fires are started by smokers flinging lit cigarette butts out their car windows? They don't care. Walk along the shore and bridges down here. You'll find lots of discarded cans, plastic bottles and discarded fish line. They'd kill off all the birds anyway. That's how he got them, all injured or sick. In time, folks knew Big Al was there and brought him the injured birds. He told me he saved the birds and the birds saved him."

"How's that?"

"The birds were sick and he helped them. Helping the birds gave him a purpose to life in his old age, something meaningful since his wife and kids were all gone. He didn't much like watching TV, never played golf or cards, and didn't like sittin' around with a bunch of other old folks in rockin' chairs on the front porch. He figured the birds gave him another ten or fifteen years. He may have been right, too. He lived to be eighty-eight, as I recall. Think good and hard about what's important in life, sailor. You can't run around chasing fancy hood ornaments on your car and wild women forever. If you ever need to appreciate real value, come down here for a while 'n' sit in this shanty and watch the birds and the deer."

"I'll give it some thought. I won't forget this place."

"Big Al used to work for the government and did a study on the Spanish mackerel before he retired. Everyone said they were endangered so he took it upon himself to find out. He studied their migration and decided there were plenty of them around. They weren't endangered so he published his report."

"So what happened? Why do you mention this?"

"How many mackerel you seen lately? The commercial fishing people got a hold of the report and learned when and where the fish migrated. In the end, they fished them all out the next season as they passed through. I told him to redo his report, but he said they already spent the money and he stood by the report. Anyway, you do some research on your own. Go out there and ask them when the last time someone caught a Spanish mackerel.

"This may be the Great White Heron National Wildlife Refuge, but it's just a name on the map. You want to know the reality, you got to come out here and see it. I'll show you reality. The birds haven't got any friends, sailor." Mike stopped and sipped his coffee. "Look, I been jabberin' long enough. Let's drink our coffee and have some chowder."

Steve peered into the bubbling pot as the steam escaped out of each round spot of hot air. The aroma of fresh cooked fish and potatoes made his mouth water. Mike handed Steve a cup and poured the warm coffee into a cup for himself. Ladeling two scoops of chowder into each metal bowl, Steve's mouth watered for his first spoonful of Mike's fish chowder.

Chapter Fourteen

The Rookery

Mike poled the flat johnboat around the last bend in a narrow channel until the water was too deep for his pole. Looking back across the flats behind them Steve could see a continuous chain of dome shaped islands stretching south towards Federal Highway and civilization, east towards the upper Keys, and north and west towards the Gulf of Mexico. The backcountry, he thought to himself, goes on forever, miles and miles of forever.

Laying the pole down inside the boat, Mike pulled the starter on the outboard motor and guided the boat deeper into the mangrove islands of the Mud Keys. As they drew closer to a small island, Steve could see the dense clusters of mangroves at the edge of a sandy beach inside a short basin. A raccoon at the edge of the beach stopped, looked up at the approaching boat, and scurried back into the thick mangroves. Turning the outboard off and tilting it onto the transom, Mike allowed the boat to drift in toward the sandy beach on its own momentum. As they drew closer, Mike picked up the pole and pressed it vertically down into the soft, grassy bottom and held the pole firmly, stabilizing the boat in place.

"Did you see the raccoon?"

"Yes. I didn't realize there were raccoons in the Keys."

"Yes, we have a lot of small animals here. Raccoons, rats, rabbits, lizards, snakes. You just don't see a lot of them. The raccoon population is thin here, but they've become a nuisance in Key West. They raid the garbage so food is not a controlling factor there. In Key West, they have plenty of food and lots of shelter."

"I never thought about the small animals. I expect to see lots of insects and spiders living here. I've seen lots of little lizards and an occasional large iguana sunning in the mangrove branches."

"Watch over the tops of the mangroves. You'll see the birds now, coming and going into the rookery." Steve looked up as Mike began to pole the boat across the flats. As they drew closer to the beach, Mike grabbed one of the overhanging branches and pulled the boat up onto the sand. Once the bottom ground over the sand and crunched to a stop, Mike jumped over the side, dragged the bow onto the beach and secured the anchor in the sand. "Here we are. What do you think?"

As clouds raced across the sky above them, the moon slid out from behind the billowing clouds sending scattered light beams over the tops of the dense vegetation. A steady flutter of wings passed over their heads, heading into the inner core of the island in a steady rate. In the fading daylight, the black bodies of the cormorants cast a striking but eerie contrast against the glowing golden red, pink and yellow colors of the fading sunset. The dome shape of the islands appeared like apparitions silhouetted against the horizon.

"Amazing," Steve muttered as he watched the steady stream of black ducks flying in and out of the rookery. Each one flew in a characteristic straight line, low over the smooth glassy surface of the water until they disappeared into the mangroves.

"The rookery is just ahead. Hundreds of birds nest in there, lots of birds like your friend sitting on the bow of your boat and anhingas come here to nest and rear their young. That's how I found this place. The cormorants led me here."

More birds continued to cross over the top of their heads. Steve felt like he was sitting under a major airport with jet liners soaring in to land and take off every 20-30 seconds, only many more than one bird passed overhead at a time.

"I brought you here, like I promised. There's a few things you might miss," Mike whispered. "Cormorants usually don't fly at night.

They settle in and wait for the sun to come back up. You might see some in a full moon, but they need light to fish. When they dive down to nab a fish, they need a sandy bottom to see their prey. Personally, I think the ones you see flying in and out now are the parents who need a break from their young 'uns. I think when the young 'uns go to sleep; the last one to return gets the night off. Anyway, the wildlife officer that was out here last week told me he thought there were about 1300 breeding pairs in here this season, so this place is even busier in the daylight."

"I can imagine. I'm glad you brought me here. I sense a serene beauty here."

"You got it. These birds are God's gift to mankind. They don't help us in any way. They're no good to eat so they have no value, but they don't harm us neither. They're just here for us to appreciate them. So there you are. That's my job out here."

"What is?"

"To protect them."

"How do you do that? You're not armed."

"No, I never carry a gun and my role isn't official. I took this job on my own. I just tell folks about the birds and why we need to let them be as they are. I figure there's three types of people that are a threat to the birds. When I meet up with one of them, I try to educate them to give the birds some peace."

"What kinds of people are they?"

"The first and worst are the teenagers with BB guns and some with 22's. They come out to target shoot and use the birds to see how many they can kill. Then, second, there's the macho ones driving those personal jet powered contraptions, water mosquitoes I call them." Mike snarled angrily. "They're a danger not only to the birds from the noise, but the sea grass gets ripped up when they zip over inches of water, tearing up the bottom. That destroys some of the food sources and protection for the water creatures and the noise spooks the nesting birds. If the nestling's parents don't come back, we lose a whole generation due to abandonment. I see less of them now that they're illegal in the refuge."

"What's the third category? I understand the first two."

"Fishermen. Oh, the only ones that are a threat to these birds are the ones with nets tied to sinkers that drop to the bottom. The net disturbs the bottom fish, the crabs and other food for the birds. People need to stay away from the rookery and the backcountry if we really want to save the birds and their nesting grounds."

"But that's not realistic. People want to explore and play in areas like this. For many, a place like this represents their escape from civilization."

"You bet. That's the conflict. When I was young, I saw a lot more birds, fish, insects and other wildlife out here. When the fish and insects go, so do the birds. The officials and government people call this a wildlife sanctuary, but it's only a label compared to what it used to be. Did you notice all the trees down?"

"Yes. I wondered about that. I did see a lot of dead trees knocked over all along the lower Keys as soon as I passed Bahia Honda. I didn't think about it, but now that you mention it, what happens to the birds in a storm? Where do they go when the wind builds up?"

"That's the other problem. They're creatures of nature. They hunker down in the trees so when the hurricanes and tropical storms do their damage, they wipe out large portions of the bird population, too. We're just starting to recover from Wilma. We didn't get a direct hit, but the winds and storm surges took their toll. We lost a lot of what made this area special...birds, mangroves, even the deer. There are only a few Great Blue Herons now and the ospreys are slowly beginning to come back."

"Oh, I saw a bald eagle nest earlier today and an osprey the other morning."

"Yes, some of the lucky ones are coming back, but it will take years and generations before the survivors can make a difference. We're like the Everglades. Katrina hit them bad, too. I don't think they'll open back up like they were. They closed the campgrounds and the lodge. About the only thing left are tour boats and mosquitoes."

"But isn't that a good thing? Then the environment can go back to nature, with less pressure from man."

"Well, I guess that's so. Nature will win in the long run, just as long as she keeps bein' nasty."

They remained silent for some time, watching the birds flying in and out of the rookery. As the sky darkened, the number of birds diminished.

"After a bit, they'll all settle down for the night. We might as well head back. I wanted you to see the largest rookery in the Lower Keys since you're traveling with one of them. Who knows, sailor, maybe your bird was actually born down here and is hitching a ride home."

"Oh, I don't think so. I believe the story I heard back up in Jewfish Creek. I think my bird hatched up near Card Sound and by some fluke it's imprinted on me. Anyway, I appreciate your bringing me here. Thanks."

"My pleasure." Mike paused, then turned facing Steve directly, "By the way, why are you so set to go into Key West in the dark? Boaters don't usually plan to make nighttime entries into an unfamiliar harbor unless it's an emergency. What's your emergency, sailor?"

Steve was startled by the question and taken off guard. He sputtered, "It's her husband. He's waiting for me at the entrance to the Northwest Channel."

"Say no more. I'll bet she was your secretary. Foolin' around don't lead to good endings."

"That's true, but..." Steve stopped. He didn't know how to explain himself or the situation.

"I see the whole story. I bet she was much younger and a real looker, too. Hell, that's why you hired her. Nothin' like a pretty face to decorate your office, huh? He didn't catch you in the act, did he?"

"Well no, not exactly." Steve hesitated to tell the whole story. He felt silly and betrayed at the same time. He realized that for someone like Mike, the details really didn't matter and he didn't want to go through the pain and agony he had experienced in Eric's office again. Better to let Mike have his fantasy version of the truth. Out here, the truth didn't matter. He responded slowly, "Yes, she was a looker and she did a good job, too."

"Say no more. I know the story. Now her old man wants to get his hands on you. Spare me the details. He must be mad as hell."

"I think he's going to jump me at the Northwest Channel."

"Can't say I sympathize with you, you brought this on yourself. But you seem like a good sort, so I think I can help a bit. Knowing men folk and their ways, I doubt he'd chase you all the way down here to Key West, rent a boat and nab you at Northwest jetty just to beat you up. Sounds far fetched to me, unless there's more to the story than you're telling me. Your imaginations may be getting the best of you. But, if you figure that's what he's gonna do, that's your opinion. Since I've takin' a liking to you, I can help you a bit with some local knowledge."

"Thanks. Are you telling me there's something else I can do?"

"Yup. I know another way into Key West Harbor so you don't have to go through the main channel or even pass by the jetty."

"There's another way into the harbor?"

"Sure is. Like I said, local knowledge. All the old salts 'round here know about it. I'll show you when we get back to camp."

"Thanks again. I'd be forever in your debt."

"Think nothing of it."

The two men returned to the skiff and Mike shoved the boat back into the water. Once in deeper water, he started the outboard and quickly guided the skiff back to the basin by his camp. They followed the same path into the center of the mangroves where Mike struck a match and lit the mantle of his lantern, placing it in the center of the crude table.

"Here, let me show you." Mike bent over and pulled out a roll of plastic encased, but well-worn charts from his duffle bag. "I don't need these charts, but I keep them with me in case I meet a stranger, like you. Then they come in handy." Mike spread one of the charts out on top of the driftwood table and placed the lantern on the edge to keep the end from rolling back up. He turned the light up so Steve could see the whole chart. Steve recognized the chart for Key West Harbor.

"I can't see where we are. There are marks all over the chart. You sure you really can help me?"

"Sure, don't let my marks confuse you. When I notice something changes, I make a mark on the chart. That way I don't forget. There, over there, Calda Channel. That's the alternate route the locals use to go into Key West." Mike pointed to Calda Channel on the chart.

Steve peered at the spot Mike was pointing to. "Calda Channel?"

"Yup, located well inside the jetty. You don't have to go all the way around to come in. See? Turn into the harbor when you see the first flashing green marker after you leave here."

"When I looked at my charts, I didn't think there was enough water there."

"Things change out here with the wind, water, and storms. Calda opened up a few years ago, like this basin, where we are now. None of the charts show this basin or what the water depth is now. You'd never find this place following the charts. Y'er lucky you run into me. Local knowledge makes all the difference. Your charts are useless for finding your way through the mangroves in the Mud Keys and most of the islands in the backcountry. Once they get out here, most tourists get confused since they all look alike. I kin tell the difference, know 'em like the backs of my hands. I spend a lot of time rescuing stranded boats on the flats when they run aground or outa gas."

"So it seems."

Mike and Steve continued to pour over the chart until Steve was sure he understood where the channel marks were and what he should watch for.

"The world don't always conform to what you want it to be, particularly in the backcountry. You gotta be smart and learn to read Mother Nature's cues to get by here. The water depth varies according to the weather conditions, wind, storms, and the phase of the moon."

"Local knowledge. That's what I need to know. I'm not familiar with this area."

"Of course not. You know Biscayne Bay like the palm of your hand. I know the backcountry down here."

"Yes, that comes with time and boating in the area frequently."

"Have to. Conditions change. Down here, sand bars and channels change with the wind and waves, everywhere, so it's always different. After a while, you learn to read nature's cues. They become second nature. If you learn to sense changes in barometric pressure, you know when a storm is coming. Then, when the wind dies suddenly, you know to pull into shelter or take the sails down fast so you don't get blown down."

"Exactly. I've done that many times when I sense a front coming in."

"Well, we've just had a few days of front weather blowin' in from the north."

"That wind blew me down the Keys."

"Sure, but down here it blows the water up into the mangroves where they shelter the channels. Then the water drains back into the channels slowly. The bigger the blow the more water makin' the channels a little deeper when the water all drains back."

"What does that mean? What are you saying?"

"Once you leave here, the mangrove keys thin out before Key West. The backcountry fades out and becomes mostly flats, big sandy flats before the Northwest Channel. If the wind has been coming in from the northwest, it'll blow the water up onto the banks. That'll throw off the tide tables as long as the water drains back out of the mangroves slowly against the wind. That means the water will be deeper later, so if you go through Calda Channel after 3:00 AM the tide will still be running out and won't stop until dawn. The other part is that no matter when you go through Calda, you'll run into the tide change. If you go in with the tide, by the time you get half way through, the tide will change against you."

"Then how do I time going in?"

"Listen carefully. In Calda, the tide won't make much difference for the draft of your boat. You got a shallow draft. That's why you can do this. Any deeper draft and you'd be dead meat and have to go in by the jetty. So listen up, you'll be going in an unknown channel in the dark so you need to concentrate."

"Ok, I'm with you."

"Good, when you go in, you want the current running against you so that if you run aground, you can back off with the current. In addition, if you go in with the current against you, your buddy Carlos won't be expecting your arrival then and may not even be out there. Once you get far enough in, it won't matter because the closer you get to Man 'O War Harbor, the channel gets wider and deeper so the current won't matter."

"That's a good point. I never would have thought of that."

"Second, the moon may be going in and out of clouds so you won't be able to count on steady light."

"Without light, I won't be visible to Carlos, and he won't expect me to be running in against the current."

"You got it. If you go in Calda Channel, you'll be goin' in way behind the jetty. If he plans to wait for you there, he'll be looking in the opposite direction, out at the Gulf. You'll be far enough away if your sails are down he won't see you. Your engine is real quiet. I didn't hear you until you snuck right on top of me and I was a lot closer than Carlos will be if he's waiting at the jetty."

"Wow, am I glad I met you Mike. That sounds like a plan I can use to get into Key West safely."

"Sure, he won't see your mast with the sails down and you keep your running lights off. He'll be too far away. Your hull will be below the mangroves."

"How about the channel marks?"

"The mark's there on the chart, the quick flashing green. Watch for it carefully because the moonlight won't be dependable. Going in against the tide means the water will be draining, so watch the banks for the ripples where the water runs into the channel. The bigger the wavelets, the deeper the water. That's how you can gauge where the channel is. Don't hug the shore too close, either. Even in a breeze, the surface will be flat calm, almost like glass since it's protected. The water will reflect the moonlight like a mirror. That's why I call the channel the 'black mirror' because it's so smooth. Just follow the channel carefully because it snakes in. When the moonlight comes out, memorize all the little details along the mud banks and follow the dark ribbon in the middle."

"You make it sound easy."

"It is, but don't be complacent. You gotta to be sharp as a tack to pull this one off. If you turn on a flashlight or running lights, that'll give you away. The trick is to feel your way in with the current against the boat. Keep a sensitive touch with your boat. It's a good thing you've got a shallow draft. I doubt your buddy Carlos will be smart enough to find a shallow draft boat for himself."

"What if Carlos finds out about Calda, too?"

"That's the risk. What do you know about him?"

"He doesn't like water and has no boating experience."

"That's your advantage. He'll follow convention and expect you to come in the main channel. Novices follow the main channel. The biggest risk is if he finds someone local who knows about Calda."

"He's a loner, I don't think he'd bring anyone along with him."

"Then my guess is you'll be safe. Only the locals go in Calda."

"What about the marine patrol or the Coast Guard? Will they be out there?"

"Forget about them. They'll be off looking for drug runners or more likely people smugglers, the illegal immigrants attempting to reach shore. Maybe you'll be lucky and they'll be out in the channel, but they won't stop you."

"Why not?"

"They don't usually profile sailboats, especially ones coming in from the north. You'll be coming in by Fleming Key. Once you're in the harbor there's plenty of water. No need to worry there. Then you can find a slip. If you're in early in the morning as you plan, you'll have no trouble."

"You're sure this isn't too risky."

"Hell sailor, you just sailed all the way down here from Miami. You already covered the hard part. You got a good boating head. That's obvious or you wouldn't have made it this far. Trust your instincts and you'll be safe while your buddy is hanging out on the main jetty."

"What about Bluefish Channel?"

"Forget it. The last big storm after Wilma filled that in permanently. They took out all the markers because the channel ends in the mud banks."

"You're sure about this…"

"You bet. I'm not just someone with local knowledge; I'm an old conch what grew up in the backcountry. Stick with Calda and you'll be fine."

"Thanks Mike. You may have saved my life."

"Unless I miss my guess, you're dead meat unless you outsmart him. So, go in by Calda Channel before dawn, with no lights, no sails, and motor right up that channel. If I'm right, Carlos will be over here on his own, holding an empty bag. If he won't ask for help or pay for a local guide, he won't find out about that way in. He may have the same charts, but no local knowledge."

"That sounds smart."

"Yup. I use it all the time. Calda goes through. Not for big boats, but small ones like yours can make it easily. Just be careful and follow the surface of the water. The full moon will help."

"I have my fathometer."

"Forget the fathometer. The meter shows the depth of water you're in. That's too late. You need to anticipate the depth where you're going fifty yards ahead. By the time you see the reading on the meter, it's too late. You have to run in blind. Watch the ripples on the surface. You may bump bottom occasionally, but go slowly and carefully. Slow up if you hear the bottom grind so you can back off right away. Go slow so you don't run hard aground. If that happens, you're stuck."

"Okay. I've got the picture."

"The whole area around Calda is a sandy mud bank, which means the surface of the water will be still and flat like glass. Remember, the bigger the ripples, the deeper the water. That's how to gauge the depth in the channel. Stick to the plan." Mike pointed to the chart again. "Once you're in, the harbors are plenty deep."

"Will I see the channel marks in the dark?"

"No problem. Look at the chart. You can't miss. After the flasher at the edge of Calda Bank, all the marks running from the beginning down to Man 'O War Harbor have reflectors on them. I don't know where you're headed then. If you go left of Fleming Key, you can tie up at the town docks or find a marina in Garrison Bight. If you go west of Fleming Key, you'll run in to Key West Bight. That's where all the hotels and restaurants are."

"I have a reservation at The Harbor Inn. It's a resort. I think it's in Key West Bight. So you're sure I'll be alright?"

"Sure, just be careful going through Calda, just like you did with all the other channels in the upper Keys. If you made it through Big Spanish Channel, you'll have no problem with Calda. Hell, you came all this way, why are you worried about Calda? Calda is wide and it's marked. You'll do fine. Hell, sailor, this is the easy part. Take it from an old conch, you'll do fine in Calda Channel. Trust your instincts and watch the channel markers. You'll be safe in the harbor and your buddy Carlos will be hanging on the jetty in the main shipping channel, waiting for you to come in."

Chapter Fifteen

Key West

At 8:30 PM on Wednesday evening, the District Office of the Florida Marine Patrol dispatched the evening patrol boat out to the Northwest Channel from the Key West station. Following his orders, the captain turned east at the channel marker at the end of the jetty rocks. He ran eastward along the outer shore of the Great White Heron National Wildlife Refuge, all the way to the marker at Harbor Key Bank for Big Spanish Channel past Big Pine Key where the Keys meet the Gulf of Mexico. At the marker, the captain reversed his course. On the way back to Key West, he recorded the description and registration numbers for the three small fishing boats near the outer entrance to the channel. He radioed the report in, stating no boat matching the description of Steve's sailboat was located anywhere along the entire length of his course, nor was there any unusual or suspicious activity along the Northwest Channel.

The office dispatcher typed up a brief report and faxed it to the local office of the DEA. The desk clerk at the DEA checked the file records for the fishing boats the patrol boat had identified. All three had been boarded and checked for contraband and illegal aliens over the past two weeks. On the basis of the report, the desk clerk cancelled a repeat run for the patrol boat scheduled for midnight that evening. Instead, he sent the patrol boat to the Marquises Islands. The navy blimp,

"Fat Albert" had detected a suspicious vessel about a mile southeast of the islands, which potentially had illegal aliens aboard attempting a landing on US soil.

The clerk sent the Marine Patrol report to the Coast Guard. In response to the report of a small boat of refugees headed toward Key West, the Coast Guard dispatched a second small patrol boat in the opposite direction to cover the waters between the Main Shipping Channel and the Southeast Channel towards Sand Key Light at the edge of the Gulf Stream. The commanding officer cancelled the scheduled run to the Northwest Channel to investigate the alleged refugee boat.

The clerk also faxed the Marine Patrol report to the FBI office in North Miami, where Agent Bellows reviewed it. Bellows concluded that Steve had altered his plans delaying his entry into Key West since there was no observation of his sailboat along the backcountry Keys. He anticipated Steve would leave Big Pine Key later, if not the next day. He was unaware that the other patrol boats for the Northwest Channel were cancelled for that evening. Assuming Steve was safe for the night, he called to confirm his flight to Key West mid-morning on Thursday.

******

When Steve paused to look at his watch, the LED read 4:30 AM. He stood, swaying like a drunken sailor on the dock at The Harbor Inn in Key West as he double-checked his dock lines. Steve was thankful that the pier was well lit as he admired the pseudo antique gaslights on poles spaced about forty feet apart. Checking the dock lines again, Steve adjusted the length of the lines for the three bumpers hanging between the dock and side of his boat, keeping the boat from bumping the dock. The hull rocked in response to the gentle waves in the harbor as the dock also rose and fell with the waves rolling in from outside the harbor. Each gentle swell raised the dock slightly; then the dock slid back into the trough with the rhythm of the waves. He watched how the boat and the bumpers responded to the wind and water for a few minutes. The boat was riding well against the bumpers with the adjustments he had made to the dock lines. Confident *Seaseeker* was secure, he dropped the keys for the cabin lock and ignition into his pants pocket before heading up the gangway. Lodging his feet securely on the wedges on the ramp, he paused to survey the area for Carlos. No one was visible on the water, on a boat, and the docks were clear. He had been tense and anxious during the entire trip down Calda Channel into Key West Harbor, expecting Carlos to confront him at any moment. Exhaling his pent up anxiety, he continued up the ramp to the hotel.

As he acclimated to land, Steve surveyed each portion of his body noting the exhaustion from the trip. His legs wobbled as he placed one foot in front of the other and his body swayed as if he were still on board *Seaseeker*. Slowly he regained his land legs. Halfway up the ramp, he glanced around again, expecting to see Carlos lurking somewhere nearby. Remembering the profile for Carlos, he tensed at the thoughts of a confrontation. The risk of the anticipated meeting had escalated exponentially now that he was in Key West.

When he had confirmed his reservation, the clerk had informed him the registration desk was open 24 hours a day. Due to the early hour, Steve was sure he would have to wake the desk clerk to check in. He was also concerned that Carlos may be sitting in a chair in the lobby, waiting for his arrival. His greatest fear was that there would be no witnesses for the anticipated confrontation. On the other hand, Steve believed that Carlos could be waiting for him at the entrance to the Northwest Channel. Fortunately, Steve had motored quietly down Calda Channel, following Mud Key Mike's directions. So, if Carlos had obtained a boat, he could still be waiting for him to arrive at the jetty. At the top of the ramp, he glanced toward the main channel out of the harbor toward the Gulf. The solitary channel marker flashed beacons of light across the surface of the water at regular intervals. He detected no boats motoring in the harbor and no sign of Carlos on the water or on land.

Nearing the entrance to the Inn, he realized Shoestring was missing from his post at the bow of *Seaseeker*. He wondered if Mud Key Mike had been wrong. Perhaps the bird had finally joined the other cormorants at the rookery and had found a mate. The last time Steve had seen Shoestring was when he reboarded *Seaseeker* at Mike's camp in the Mud Keys. He had not unfurled the Genoa during the entire trip from the Mud Keys to Key West. Shoestring had not reappeared even though the foredeck was clear. Steve was disappointed and missed his companion.

Contrary to his fears, Steve found the front desk and lobby busy in spite of the early hour. The desk clerk checked him into his room after he requested a room change so he could observe the docks. The clerk complied. When he entered his room, he dropped his duffle bag and clothes on the floor and took a long, hot shower to rinse the salt and exhaustion of the trip from his nerves and muscles. Feeling refreshed from his days at sea, he collapsed onto the bed, failing to check the boat as his eyelids closed and the tension ran out of his body. His last thoughts as he crashed into a deep sleep included a sense of freedom from the tension of Carlos tracking his moves. Soon he would be able to concentrate on rebuilding his failing law practice and rebuild his income and savings. With Carlos and the boat out of his life, his first task would be to replace Maria in the office.

Steve woke to the shrill sound of the telephone ringing. Before picking up the receiver, he checked the time on his watch. The room darkened by the closed drapes belied the hour. The LED reflected a reading of nearly twelve noon. He picked up the phone.

"Welcome to Key West," a deep voice greeted him.

Steve recognized the voice of Agent Bellows.

"Morning," Steve mumbled through his stupor.

"Good morning, or should I say afternoon? We've got a room just down the hall from you."

Gently parting the drapes, Steve could see the water in Key West harbor glistening in the mid-day sun. The boats anchored and docked in the harbor rocked in response to the white caps lapping through the fleet.

"Don't worry about your sailboat. Our room is also an observation post. We can keep an eye on your boat from here. In fact, we've been directed to do so by the FBI."

"Great. Thanks."

"How was your trip last night? The desk clerk told me you checked in a little bit before 5:00 AM."

"Thankfully, uneventful."

"That's a relief. Did you see anything unusual? Did you see Carlos out on the water?"

"No. I didn't see any boats on my trip in."

"Both the Coast Guard and the DEA made a run out to the Northwest Channel last night. Apparently they went out and back before you came in. Neither one reported seeing your boat or any other activity."

"I didn't see them either."

"The only boats they saw were locals that checked out. You must have come in so late they missed you. I was surprised to see your boat tied up at the dock this morning. We suspected that you postponed your arrival for tonight."

"I planned that deliberately. No one saw me because I came in through Calda Channel."

"Calda Channel? Where's that? I didn't know there was another way in."

"That's the point. Calda is a smaller channel running parallel with the Passage. It's shorter, but more importantly, it kept me out of the main channel and shielded my exposure in the Northwest Channel."

"I'm impressed. That was good thinking. Frankly, we were beginning to think Carlos had overcome his fear of water, hijacked a boat, and intercepted you where we couldn't help."

"That's why I used Calda Channel. I thought he might be so desperate that he forgot his anxiety in his passion to recapture his phantom gold. If he was out on the jetty, he wouldn't catch me slip through the smaller channel. There weren't any phone booths out there, so I couldn't let you know my plans."

"You did the right thing. It looks like our profile was valid and he'll make his move here in Key West. So far our analysis has been right on."

"Thanks for watching out for me. I appreciate your efforts."

"That's our job. I've set up a meeting at La Concha Grille & Café at 4:00 PM today with the sheriff, your buyer and the owner of the café."

"You found Paul Owens, my buyer? Where was he?"

"No, actually we didn't find him. Chuck Everson, the owner of the café, rents a house trailer on Stock Island to Owens. Since he knows him both as employer and landlord, he's assured us he can bring him to the meeting."

"I'm relieved. After making this trip, I'll be glad to turn the boat over to him."

"We'll see you then. In the mean time, if you're hungry, the restaurant downstairs serves some fine food. I don't recommend that you wander around town until we have Carlos in custody. If you decide to go to the restaurant, return to your room immediately after you've eaten. No tourist stops for you until we have Carlos. Understand?"

"How about I call room service?"

"Even better. Be careful when you head to La Concha. We'll meet you there. No deviations, don't take any side trips."

"Got it. Thanks for the help."

"Enjoy your snack. Remember, Carlos is probably close by."

"See you later."

"Oh, Steve, one more thing."

"What's that?"

"They buried Maria today."

Steve was silent.

"Steve, are you there?"

"Yes. I'm listening."

"There were no relatives and Carlos never showed up to claim her body, so they buried her in a pauper's grave in South Dade."

"No, that's not acceptable. I'll pay for her to have a proper burial."

"Steve. That's not possible. You can't. You're not related by blood or marriage. You don't have any legal papers."

Steve was silent.

"Steve? I'll see that she has some flowers on her grave, in your name. Okay?"

"Roses. Red roses."

"Steve."

"Jesus. I don't know what to say. My hands are tied by Florida laws, and I'm a freakin' lawyer."

"I'm sorry. Rodriguez from Metro-Dade made the determination."

"Okay, okay. I don't have any say. What can I do? She set me up, stole all my money and dragged me into a phony marriage. Yet I still have feelings for her. I still love her. In a strange way, I can't give her up."

"Steve, my advice is, the sooner you let go the better. You're screwed and you need to go forward. I can't say anything more. Just be sure you make that meeting this afternoon at La Concha at 4. Do you know where it is?"

"I'm looking. I'm looking." Steve thumbed through the yellow pages in the phone book on his night table. "Here it is. Jesus, it's almost next door. It's across the street, less than a block away. I'll be fine getting there and I have plenty of time to get something to eat."

"Don't worry then. We're watching your every move now. The Monroe County Sheriff and the FBI are all here."

"Maybe they'll arrest me. Has the Sheriff eased up on me yet?"

"Just make that meeting. As long as you're there to meet with the buyer, he'll be cool."

"No problem. I'll be there."

After he hung up, Steve slid the drapes open. From his room, he could see the entire harbor as well as *Seaseeker* tied at the dock below his window. Several people were tending to their boats at the dock while other boats ran in and out of the harbor. Smiling, Steve saw Shoestring had returned to his station at the bow of his boat. He would have to go against Agent Bellow's instructions. Shoestring needed to have his plate of sardines. He had no idea how long Shoestring had been back at his post. He was late for breakfast. Before he did anything else, he had to feed his loyal crew.

Chapter Sixteen

The Man Who Wasn't There

On his way to the meeting with Bellows and the Monroe County Sheriff, Steve passed one of the many tobacco shops scattered throughout Key West. He made a mental note to stop in later, after the meeting, to pick up some Cuban cigars for Eric. He remembered seeing the partners smoking them occasionally. He found La Concha Grille & Café on Duval Street, two blocks down and across the street from the hotel. The ambiance in the café represented the typical tropical decor found in Key West. The scent of grilled meat and fish greeted him as he approached the open entrance to the dining area. The large open windows filled the outer walls of the building allowing the gentle sea breeze to blow into the restaurant and carry the aroma of the grilled fish and beef out to the sidewalk to tantalize the passersby. He found Agent Bellows seated at a table near the windows with two other gentlemen. A large, heavyset man dressed in khaki pants and shirt topped with an official looking hat stood and shook Steve's hand as Bellows introduced him.

"Steve, meet Agent Scott Turner with the DEA in Miami and Monroe County Sheriff Arnold Woodson from Key West."

"Pleased to meet you." Looking at Agent Turner, Steve frowned and asked, "Is there a drug issue affiliated with my case? I wasn't aware that the DEA was involved."

"Oh, don't worry. Mr. Owens, the gentleman buying your sailboat is a material witness in another case. We've been trying to locate him to corroborate someone else's story."

"We're looking for your buddy Carlos. He's been on the lam for a few years. We consider him armed and dangerous and are aware he's stalking you," Woodson spoke boldly.

"Carlos." Steve repeated, automatically.

"Yes, Carlos Santiago. We have his file," Sheriff Woodson responded tapping the manila folder on the table. "What I'm trying to understand is why he's here tracking you in the Florida Keys. Las Vegas or Reno make more sense to us. Bellows explained the case to me, but I'd like to hear your assessment of this guy. You've met him so you may be able to give us some insight into his personality and motives."

"Yes, I've met him. My wife, err former wife, Maria told me he was her brother."

A waitress greeted the men at the table handing them menus. "Chuck says your first drink is on the house."

"Chuck? Who is Chuck?" asked Sheriff Woodson looking at Bellows.

"Chuck Everson, he owns this café. He'll be joining us soon. He knows Paul Owens."

"Okay." Sheriff Woodson turned to the waitress, "Iced tea for me. Do you have lime?"

"Yes, lemon and lime."

"A wedge of lime, please, with the iced tea." He passed the menu back to the waitress.

"Coffee, black," said Agent Bellows.

"I'll have iced tea," Steve ordered.

"Thank you. Chuck should be back within the hour. He asked me to convey his apology for running late. He wanted to check a couple of places he knew Paul frequented."

"Fine, thank you." Agent Bellows began to peruse the menu.

"Who is Paul Owens?" asked Sheriff Woodson.

"Paul Owens agreed to buy my sailboat. And Carlos is the one stalking me. He thinks I'm 'Midas Man' with a pile of gold coins stashed on board, gold he and Maria converted from my escrow funds."

"We're looking for Carlos on charges of grand theft auto. We have reports of two cars he's stolen since he arrived on the Keys a few days ago, one in Marathon and one on Long Key. We found one of the cars parked behind the motel where the manager recognized him after he had checked in. We were able to confirm his ID from fingerprints lifted from the car and the motel room. He can't be far if he's on foot. We suspect he's here somewhere in Key West."

"Thanks for the warning. I need to find Paul Owens to transfer ownership of my sailboat and get Carlos off my back."

"Carlos is clever. Somehow he's consistently given us the slip since we started tracking him at Jewfish Creek. Unfortunately, we still need you to be the bait to catch him. We're aware he thinks you have his stash of gold on your boat."

"I understand. I didn't know about the gold until a few days ago. I've been cooperating with all the agencies. I'd like to see this guy apprehended, too. The sooner the better."

"We're trying to goad Carlos into making his move. He's closer to the gold now so he's more likely to make mistakes. You and your boat are on 24/7 surveillance. Fortunately, we have Maria's statement before she died. Unfortunately for Carlos, she told us he pushed her down the stairs when she told him she'd stashed the gold on your boat. In addition to the criminal theft charges, we have filed charges of premeditated murder. He's not a nice guy."

"I didn't know anything about the gold until Agent Bellows told my friend Eric. He wanted me to know so I would understand how desperate Carlos is."

"Are you sure the gold isn't on your boat?"

"Absolutely. I think Maria made up the story to get him off her case. I haven't found any gold on board and I've been looking everywhere since Eric told me."

"Why would he believe Maria?"

"Why not? She was his wife and partner in crime."

"Yes, of course, but she was living with you, as your wife. How would he know she hadn't changed her mind about you? Maybe you do know where the gold is and you and Maria were planning to double cross Carlos. I think that's why he's so desperate. Maybe he's not after the gold, maybe he's after you."

"I've been worried about that. That's why I'm cooperating with you. I want to get this boat off my hands so I can go back to my law practice."

"How do I know you're telling the truth?" Woodson countered.

"He's cooperated fully with us." Bellows interrupted Woodson in support of Steve. "Besides, a guy who's covered the missing escrow funds with his own assets wouldn't do that if he were going to bolt. His clients are happy and haven't registered any complaints with the bar. We don't have any evidence for a case against Andrews."

"Yes, but if Mr. Andrews has both the insurance to cover the loss and the gold, he's in for double recovery. What do you know about Essex sailboats?" Woodson asked.

"The Essex? Nothing. Is there something I should know?"

"I checked with the manufacturer. Despite being a shallow draft boat, the Essex sails well in blue water. How do I know Andrews won't take off on us? I've researched a couple of articles where the authorities recommend the Essex for sailing the east coast of Mexico and South America."

"I trust Mr. Andrews. He's been honest with us, plus he's here right now. He showed us his contract to sell the boat to Mr. Owens and we have a copy of it. Let's not lose focus."

"Okay, but if the gold isn't on board your boat, Andrews, where is it? Obviously Carlos doesn't have it."

"Maria claimed she stashed the gold on Andrew's boat. She was angry with Carlos for pushing her down the stairs so she ratted on him. I think she was tired of their life of crime and living with Andrews gave her a taste of a life she preferred. The doctors only let us have a little time with her before she slipped back into a coma. She's the only one who knew where the gold is and now she's gone."

"Maria could have hidden the gold anywhere," Steve offered.

"So could you," snapped Sheriff Woodson. "I'd like to meet this buyer to validate your story. Until he shows up, I have to consider all options in this case. I've been fooled before, as you know. We had a similar case a few years ago where the guy ran off with both the money and the insurance claim. He came down here in style, set up his law practice and skinned us alive. Everyone important in town was his friend, everyone trusted him, including me. Now I trust no one."

"Well, I haven't done that. I'm not moving my law office down here. I just want to sell my boat and go home. You've seen the contract."

"Agent Bellows said Owens was going to be here for this meeting. Didn't you want to see him for something else?"

"Yes, he's a witness for another case we're investigating."

"I find it strange that you continued down here without making contact with Owens."

"I've been trying to reach him. My friend Eric has been calling for me while I've been making good on the delivery."

"Chuck is looking for Mr. Owens and promised to take us out to the trailer park if he can't find him in Key West this morning."

"How do I know Andrews won't take off with the boat? As I see it, he could have made a deal with Maria to take the gold and leave the States."

"Maria is dead. I can't go anywhere with her now."

"So, you adjust. You can still take off with the gold. There are more single, beautiful young women in the world to begin a new life."

Steve remained silent. He was angry that Woodson put him on the hot seat. He understood Woodson's sensitivity considering the previous case, but he refused to accept false accusations. He looked to Agent Bellows to help defend him.

"Steve has cooperated with all of our efforts. Let's not keep this pseudo-trial going. As I said, no one has filed any complaints against Mr. Andrews. Let's focus on finding Paul Owens." Bellows spoke fiercely, beginning to show his annoyance at Woodson's insecurity.

A tall, muscular blond haired man wearing a brightly colored tropical shirt and khaki shorts and sandals approached the table. "Gentlemen, welcome to La Concha. I hope you have enjoyed your drinks. I've asked the chef to put together a sandwich platter and some conch chowder for all of us. He'll be serving us shortly so you can pass on the menu."

"Everson?" Agent Bellows asked.

"Yes, Chuck Everson. Nice to meet all of you."

Each of the men stood and introduced themselves. "I have bad news. I can't find Paul. No one has seen him for days."

"He agreed to buy my sailboat. He put a deposit on it a few weeks ago."

"Yes, I remember how excited he was about the boat. He showed me the pictures you sent him." Chuck offered.

"So he really did plan to go through with the deal?" Sheriff Woodson asked.

"I've been concerned all week since Eric wasn't able to contact him," Steve commented.

"Sure, Paul planned to buy the boat. He thought he had a good deal and was anxious for Mr. Andrews to deliver the boat."

"Well, I've done my part. The boat is here. I haven't heard from him since he wired the deposit and signed the contract."

"I haven't heard from him either. He hasn't shown up for work for the last three nights."

"So how does a body keep his job if he skips out a few nights without calling in?" asked Agent Turner.

"You have to understand how Key West works since we've become an 'in place' for tourists. Real estate values have soared so I can't keep good help."

"Why is that?" Steve asked.

"To own or rent in town is too expensive for service workers. Their jobs don't pay enough to afford nearby housing, so they live as far away as Big Pine Key and Sugar Loaf and then commute to work. The cost of living has soared as real estate values escalated in Key West."

"And Stock Island, like Paul Owens?" asked Steve.

"Yes, Paul rents an old trailer from me over on Stock Island. He's been my tenant for over six months, plus he tends bar here three to four nights a week. He asked for flex hours, so he works when he wants. He always does a good job and has been helpful on and off the job."

"Has he paid his rent on time?" Agent Turner asked.

"Oh, he paid the rent six months in advance."

"Isn't that unusual? Why would someone do that?"

"Well, down here people frequently come with strings."

"Strings?"

"Attachments up North. They're really not as free as they'd like us to believe. They hang around for a few months, then the strings from up North pull them back home. I've found tenants unreliable, so I ask for three months rent in advance and sometimes six. I've been burned too many times when a tenant leaves me high and dry."

"He can't be too far, his phone is still connected," Steve said. "We've been leaving messages for several days now."

"Up until yesterday I was leaving messages, too. Today the answering machine doesn't click on any more," Everson informed them.

"That's odd. Maybe the tape is full if he hasn't erased the old messages."

"I'd like to go out there and check his trailer. It's been too many days. Maybe something happened. He normally calls in when he can't make it. His answering machine has never been full when I've called. I have a key to the trailer. Do any of you want to go with me?"

"Sure, sounds like a plan."

"I want to know if I still have a buyer for my boat."

"We're all of the same mind. Andrews needs his money and we need to ask him some questions. Mr. Owens' whereabouts are important to all of us. Let's go."

"My car is parked behind the café."

"We have a patrol car. Let's take two cars. We'll follow you, Chuck."

After lunch, Steve rode with Chuck Everson and Agent Bellows while Deputy Turner rode with the Sheriff. Stock Island was only minutes from downtown Key West. As they crossed the bridge onto Stock Island, Steve could see the power plant, the destination for the fuel barge that nearly crushed him and *Seaseeker* at Black Bank. A steady stream of smoke drifted up from the tall stack filling the sky with billowing clouds of gray smoke. The poles from the rigging of the shrimp boats in the harbor filled in the space between the tops of the palmettos and the height of the power plant stack. Passing the local residences, Steve compared the marked differences in the plain architecture on Stock Island to the quaint gingerbread Victorian homes and shops in Key West.

As they turned off Federal Highway, the number of houses decreased and the frequency of trailer courts increased. When they turned into the Stock Island Trailer Camp, the coarse grass disappeared. Coral gravel and cactus interspersed with rows of palmettos filled the space between the trailer sites. The two cars bumped clumsily over the ruts in the coral roads between the trailer sites. Frequently, an old boat in various stages of disrepair was stored upside down next to the trailers, laying like dark dreams long lost and forgotten. Chuck Everson pulled into one of the trailer sites. Steve noted that the trailer appeared to be in better condition than most of the other units in the park. Although appearing clean and neat, Steve sensed an air of abandonment. Paul Owens did not answer when they knocked on the door and there was no car parked near the trailer.

"This is one of two trailers I own here. This doesn't look good. Paul's bike isn't here."

"I was looking for a car. He rides a motorcycle?"

"Yes, a big Harley. I'm not sure what year or model; I'm not into the biking scene. I just know it's a big one. So, he's not here. At least I can leave him a note to get in touch with me. Let's go in and have a look around."

"You're the landlord."

When Chuck checked the mailbox, he removed mostly junk mail fliers and two bills, the electric company and the phone bill. Chuck knocked on the door. When no one answered, he opened the trailer door with his master key. They entered the living room just as the other officers arrived and parked behind Chuck's car.

Everything inside the trailer was orderly and neatly arranged. Chuck checked the answering machine. The red message light was flashing, indicating the message center was full.

"Here's a note for you," Agent Bellows picked up a page torn from a three-ring notebook with writing on it and handed it to Chuck.

Chuck paused to read the note silently, then when he finished, he read the note aloud:

Dear Chuck,

I'm sorry to leave without talking to you personally. I hope you find this message soon. I tried to call a few times, but your line was busy. My mother called from Ann Arbor to tell me my father had a stroke, so I've gone back to Michigan to help take care of both of them. The prognosis is poor. If my dad survives, he'll be wheelchair-bound for the remainder of his life. The doctors recommend keeping him a week or two for observation before he goes home. My mother said he asked for me, so I left after checking the weather forecast. They predicted excellent weather for the time I need to go north, so, I'm off.

Since I prepaid the rent, keep the balance for what I owe you and to pay any outstanding bills. I don't know if I'll be back. Feel free to re-rent the trailer and fill my job at the café. I'll send a forwarding address for you to send my paycheck for what I'm due from working at the bar.

I'll call when I arrive. My free and footloose days in Key West are over. I have to take care of my mother; she's a nervous wreck without my father and needs me to drive her to the hospital to visit him.

Please contact Mr. Andrews about the boat. I have to back out of that deal also. I am very disappointed. I hope he can refund part or all of my deposit, but I leave that for you to settle for me. I'll accept whatever he decides to do. I apologize for causing everyone so much trouble.

Best,

Paul

"That's it?" asked Bellows.

"That's it," Chuck responded. "There's nothing more. He's gone. I'm sorry. Looks like you've gone to a lot of trouble for no deal."

"I'll have to put the boat on the market here. I don't have time to take it back to Miami."

"If you make a sign, I'll post it at the bar. We get a lot of male customers. Who knows, one of them may be in the market for a sailboat."

"Without Owens, we'll have to find another witness to our case. I have a tough task ahead. Thanks for your time Andrews, Chuck. We've done enough chasing windmills here. Andrews, you're clear."

"My sailing days are done. I can't sail the boat back to Miami. I'll have to find a broker to sell the boat here. I was counting on having the money from the sale."

"The boat should sell; the Essex is popular here on the Keys," Chuck offered.

"Your reservation at the hotel is good for tonight," Bellows reminded Steve.

"We'll keep looking for Carlos. Finding him is our top priority now." Sheriff Woodson and Agent Turner abruptly excused themselves.

"We'll cover the bill for two nights at the hotel, but we can't continue with that expense beyond tonight." Bellows was apologetic. "Budgets," he muttered softly to himself.

"That's okay. I can stay on the boat. I'll anchor off Wisteria Island and sleep on board until I find a marina to store the boat and handle the sale."

"Where is Wisteria Island?"

"Just off Mallory Dock, the little island to the northeast. The locals call it Christmas Tree Island. I'll be fine there and save some money."

"You forgot one thing."

"What's that?"

"Carlos. We can't protect you out on the water. That's impossible."

"I'll have to count on his fear of the water. Your profile has been accurate so far. You can use binoculars to watch me."

"I don't like your plan. Our profile is only a theory. It's not infallible. Carlos should be growing more desperate. He has to make his move soon if he's going to get his hands on the gold."

"That's what I'm worried about, but I have to be mindful of expenses now. On the boat I'll only have to buy food."

"Maybe we can round him up before tomorrow night."

"I hope so. Carlos scares me. I won't sleep well until you have him in custody."

"You're not the only one."

"I'm sure he's on the island."

"Me, too."

"Maybe we can change that."

"I hope so."

"One other thing I forgot to mention. I have a plan to flush Carlos out."

"What's that?"

"Can you meet me for breakfast tomorrow? I'll treat."

"Sure, what time?"

"Eight sharp, before the banks open."

"Sure, I'm curious."

"Ill explain at breakfast tomorrow."

"Okay, tomorrow is Friday so I'll see you in the restaurant."

Chapter Seventeen

A Simple Deception

The next morning, Steve met Agent Bellows for breakfast in the restaurant next to the hotel lobby. "Deputy Turner was right. We've been taking advantage of you."

"How so?"

"You're the bait in a dangerous game to snare Carlos."

"Perhaps. He hasn't made anyone's life easy, including Maria. I don't mind helping. I had to come to Key West anyway. Knowing he's stalking me hasn't made my trip easier or soothed my nerves." Steve sipped his coffee.

"Frankly, I thought we'd have him in custody by now. Since he doesn't like the water, we're running out of land for him to hide. There's only one road in and the same one out."

"That's true, Key West is the end of the road."

"Let's hope it becomes the end of the road for Carlos."

"Yes, but no one has seen Carlos, right?"

"Sheriff Woodson dragged every known petty criminal, wino and homeless person they could find and questioned them about Carlos. They showed them pictures and engaged them to watch out for Carlos. Hopefully that will help find him."

"Any luck?"

"Actually, yes. They found one wino down by the canal who claimed to have sold Carlos a bicycle."

"A bicycle? That's strange."

"Apparently the bicycle was stolen so he made a few bucks off Carlos to buy another bottle. The story is thin since the guy is rarely sober. He may have made it up to get attention or he was hallucinating."

"That's not much to go on. Key West is loaded with bicycles."

"There's actually more to the story. The wino described him as a tourist dressed like he was going fishing, tackle box and pole in hand."

"Fishing? That doesn't sound like someone who dislikes the water. Why would he go fishing?"

"At first we discounted the story until Sheriff Woodson received the report of a break in from the owner of a small fishing and sporting goods store near the Anchor Motel. The shop is across the street from the motel where Carlos escaped our raid the other night. The owner reported only a few items stolen, including a tackle box and sports clothing. We think his objective was to pick up a new disguise to use here in Key West. No money was taken and the register was untouched."

"Interesting. With a disguise like that, he'd look like everyone else visiting Key West. So Carlos is dressed up like a tourist going fishing, somewhere here in Key West."

"Yup, but that's all we've got. It's not much. We know he has to show up sooner or later. Someone will spot him. The problem is he's brazen and has no fear of the authorities. Instead of running, he charges into the situation head on. He could even be sitting somewhere in this hotel right now."

Steve glanced around the restaurant looking for anyone resembling Carlos. Knowing Carlos could be nearby increased his anxiety.

"Carlos is an interesting character. He's confident that he can stay one step ahead of us and up to now he's been successful. We're sure he's working on his opportunity to recapture that gold he thinks is on your boat."

"Yes, but there isn't any gold on my boat. What will he do when he finds out I don't have any gold on board?"

"We'll nab him before he boards your boat. He knows he has to get the gold before you sell the boat, so he has to make his move soon."

"Do you have a plan? You sound like you do."

"We want to divert his attention away from you and shift it onto the gold. If we succeed, we think he'll leave you alone."

"That sounds good. What do you have in mind?"

"I've placed an empty brief case next to your chair. Take it with you when we finish breakfast and go back to your boat."

"I see. You want me to pretend to move the gold off the boat. Where do you want me to take it? I'll need a bank or office in on the plan."

"Absolutely. Wait about twenty minutes on the boat to feign enough time to load the gold into the briefcase. Then take it to the Key West Bank and Trust two blocks down Duval Street. Actually, the bank is across the street from La Concha where we had lunch yesterday. The manager there will be expecting you. Ask for Sam Pritchard. He'll help you open a safe deposit box."

"If I'm supposed to have the gold, won't I have to make more than one trip?"

"Make three trips. We'll have you covered every step of the way. We have five agents working on this case and Sheriff Woodson assigned three undercover officers from his force this morning."

"What about guns? Is Carlos armed? What do I do if he pulls a gun on me?"

"We'll be watching and ready for whatever he does. Don't try to be a hero. Do whatever he says. Once he makes his move, we'll move in. When this is over, you'll be a free man. We'll have Carlos and you can go on with your life."

"Okay. I'll do it. I have to check out of the hotel by noon today. I'll anchor off Wisteria Island until I find a broker for the boat. Then I can go back to Miami."

"As I see it Steve, there are two possibilities here. Either we nab Carlos this morning during this caper or he's realized his chances are futile and he'll give up on the gold. Either way, you should be out of this situation by noon today."

"As long as you and your men are there to back me up, the plan sounds workable."

"Good. Once we're done this morning and you've checked out of the motel, keep in touch with me when you come ashore."

"I'll anchor off Wisteria later this afternoon. First I need to find someone to fix my radio."

"Let's hope Carlos takes the bait this morning. If he sees you off load the gold that will take the heat away from you. Maybe he'll give up when he sees there's no chance to get possession of the gold. Maybe he'll realize Key West is too hot for him and he'll move on."

"I should be so fortunate. I can't think of a better plan."

"Don't worry. We'll be right here. We'll get this bad guy off the streets today."

"Ok, I'm off." Steve took a deep breath and picked up the briefcase. "Thanks for the breakfast."

"My pleasure."

Chapter Eighteen

One Small Shoe

Steve woke the next morning to the familiar sound of tapping on his porthole window. He smiled. Bright sunlight streamed into the cabin and Shoestring was telling him it was time for breakfast. He opened a fresh can of sardines, placed two of the lifeless bodies on the small plastic plate that had become Shoestring's meal plate, and carried the plate out to the cockpit. Several other boats were anchored off the south end of Wisteria Island. As the last arrival the night before, *Seaseeker* was the most exposed to the rolling waves. The closest boat anchored near Steve was a large, black wooden schooner he couldn't help admire. The stern identified the boat as *Black Draggon* with Boston as the port of registry. The finely polished brass fittings on the deck reflected the rays of the morning sun giving the schooner an aura of sparkling majesty. Many hands had worked long hours to produce such a fine, polished finish. Steve thanked himself for having a fiberglass boat with minimal metal and teak fittings not requiring such intense labor.

Remembering his millstone, Steve surveyed the anchorage for any sign of Carlos. Yesterday, the ruse of moving the gold to the bank in Agent Bellows' briefcase had proceeded uneventfully. Either Carlos had observed him and knew he was protected by dozens of agents or had missed the activity entirely and was still planning to intercept him elsewhere. Steve assumed that Bellows had not apprehended Carlos yet or he would have informed him. Steve and Bellows had met at the restaurant in the hotel last night and discussed a new strategy while Steve remained in Key West. Steve planned to row to shore in his dingy and Bellows and his agents would continue to monitor his movements on land. On the water, they would do the best they could by observing his movements through binoculars. Chuck Everson had posted his sign for the sale of his boat at the restaurant and Steve had successfully found someone to repair his radio in the afternoon.

All of the boats in the anchorage were headed bow to shore in spite of the steady breeze blowing out of the northwest. Steve relaxed at the rhymic lap of the small waves against the hull. The outgoing tide was stronger than the force of the wind, holding the boats perpendicular to the wind. The contrary forces of the wind and current caused *Seaseeker* to rest over the top of the anchor rode, a curious condition seasoned boaters experience in such conditions. He could see the rode run straight back under the hull in a taught, straight line for only a few feet before it disappeared from view. The anchor was holding firm.

As Steve leaned forward to place Shoestring's plate on the deck, he noticed Shoestring had delivered an unexpected object instead of his customary piece of seaweed.

"Hold on there, Shoestring. What did you bring this morning?"

When Steve moved closer to the object, Shoestring waddled back toward the bow, keeping his usual safe distance from Steve.

"Hey, this is a shoe, a baby's shoe. Where did you get this, Shoestring? Someone surely will miss this."

Steve picked up the small shoe. The shoe appeared new, clean and dry and had not been in the water.

"Whoa, Shoestring, where did you get this?"

Steve examined the shoe more closely. He noted that it fit the right foot of a small child he guessed to be three to four years old. Since the shoe was pink, the owner must be a little girl. The shoe was amazingly light and crafted of baby soft leather. Steve doubted that Shoestring had brought the shoe across the harbor from Key West, so he scanned the other boats in the anchorage. He noticed a dingy beached on the shore of the island, about 100 yards directly in front of *Seaseeker*. Two figures stood near the craft, a woman and a little girl. As he watched, they appeared to be looking for something in the exposed coral rocks along the shore. Through his binoculars, he could see that the little girl was barefoot, carrying one pink shoe in her right hand. After some time, the two stepped into the dinghy and set a course back towards the anchored boats. They headed directly towards *Seaseeker* until they reached half way, where they turned and headed for the schooner.

Attempting to attract their attention, Steve stood on the lazarette, waving his arms and hands over his head. Convinced the little girl in the dinghy was the owner of the shoe, he cupped his hands and shouted in their direction. In response, the woman changed the direction of the dinghy and headed straight for *Seaseeker*. As she neared *Seaseeker*, she cut off the outboard, turned the bow slightly, gliding perfectly parallel with *Seaseeker's* hull. Her long black hair fluttered gently below her canvas sailing hat and settled slowly down her back as the motion of the dinghy subsided. She stood and grabbed the gunnels of Steve's boat with both hands to steady the motion of the dinghy.

"You in some trouble, skipper?" she asked, smiling.

Steve was immediately captivated by her friendly manner and the glowing bronze color of her skin from days at sea.

"I flagged you down, but not for help."

"Then what's up? Need a ride to shore?"

"I saw you looking for something on the beach. Perhaps this is what you were looking for?" Steve held up the tiny shoe.

"Mommy, my shoe." The little girl's eyes brightened with excitement.

"Yes, Mandy. He has your shoe." Looking up at Steve, her brow furrowed, she asked, "How did you get that shoe out here?"

"Here, she better put her shoes on." Steve handed the shoe to the woman who passed the shoe to her daughter.

"Tell the man thank you, Mandy."

The little girl looked up at Steve, "Thank you Mr. Man."

"You're very welcome. My name's Steve."

"Pleased to meet you. My name is Talia and this is Mandy."

Mandy struggled to put on her shoe.

"Pleased to meet you, too." Steve turned toward the little girl, "Next time you go wading, young lady, wear some old shoes so if you lose one you won't worry so much. It's not good to walk around on the sand in bare feet."

"Okay, Mr. Steve."

"So, Steve, are you some kind of magician or wizard? How did you get Mandy's shoe all the way over here? I watched her take her shoes off on shore. How did her shoe get from there to here without a boat?"

"I promise to tell you, but I'm not sure you'll believe me. It's a long story."

"Have you had breakfast yet?"

"No, I was just feeding my bird."

"You have a pet bird?"

"Sort of, he's a cormorant. See the one on the bow?" Steve turned and pointed to Shoestring, standing at his post on the bow.

"He doesn't look like a pet. I've seen hundreds of them. They're wild birds. They're all over here in the Keys and plenty of them here in the harbor."

"That may be true, but he keeps coming back so I feed him sardines. He's been with me all week."

"Why don't you join us for breakfast? That's the least I can do to thank you for finding Mandy's shoe. I just bought them for her yesterday and they were really expensive. She loved them so I couldn't say no."

"Are you sure your husband won't mind?"

"There's no husband to mind. It's just the two of us. That's our boat, over there." She pointed to the schooner Steve had admired earlier. Steve's eyes widened in surprise. How could such a small woman with a small child handle that schooner on her own? "Okay, I'll join you on one condition."

"What's that?"

"That you tell me how you handle that boat with such a little girl for crew."

Grinning, Talia responded, "Okay, I'll tell you how we do it if you tell me how you found Mandy's shoe."

Steve grinned back, "Deal. Wait a second while I grab a few things." Steve dropped below and grabbed his jacket, half a dozen eggs, the rest of his loaf of oat bread and three oranges. He stuffed them into his backpack and rejoined her on deck.

"I invited you for breakfast. I didn't expect you to bring it."

"I always bring something when I'm a guest." He handed her the backpack. After closing the companionway cover, he slid under the lifelines into the dinghy.

Pulling the starter cord, she adjusted the choke as the outboard sprang to life. "Welcome to *Serpent*."

"*Serpent*?"

"The dinghy for *Black Draggon*."

Chapter Ninteen

A Widow's Tale

Talia cleared the table as soon as they finished breakfast. "Don't you want to take the rest of these eggs back with you? I didn't use them all."

"Keep them. I have to start cleaning out my boat. I plan to sell it. I'll be heading back to Miami as soon as I find a broker to handle the sale. Why don't you boil them? I find it's easier to store hard-boiled eggs. You don't have to worry about them cracking and making a mess in your cooler."

"Okay. I'll boil them and put them in the icebox. I just added two new bags of ice yesterday." Talia slid into the seat beside Mandy. Looking sternly at Steve she asked, "So now, tell me how you transported Mandy's shoe from the beach where we lost it to your boat in the anchorage?"

"Promise, but first tell me how you manage this big boat by yourself. How did you get to Key West from Boston?"

"I met Sal when we were kids. We were neighbors."

"Sal, who is Sal?"

"Oh, I'm sorry. Sal was my husband. We married because we were supposed to, everyone expected it. Our parents were close friends. He was, you know, the boy next door." She smiled sadly. "I guess I was like the other girls my age, marriage was expected."

"You don't sound happy about your marriage."

"What can I say? He wasn't my first choice, but he was always around so the guys I was interested in thought I was 'Sal's girl.'"

"Jealousy?"

"I don't think so. I think they assumed because we were together so much that we were going steady or getting married. No one else asked me out. I think that happens to a lot of girls."

"What happens?"

"The guys made assumptions about what they saw, rather than asking if I wanted to go out with them. They just decided from the looks of it I was dating Sal."

"Weren't you?

"He was there. My parents didn't have the money, so I didn't go to college. Then I couldn't get a really good job or meet any other prospects. That's what happens, the one who pops the question is the one who wins. No one else asked and he was there. What else was I going to do?"

"So you married Sal."

"My parents were happy about it. His parents were happy about it."

"Was Sal happy about it?"

"He seemed to be, so I worked hard to keep him happy. That was seven years ago. I didn't find out what that meant until I got pregnant. That's when he told me he was saving to buy a boat to sail to Belize and open a hotel there with one of his buddies. The problem was, Sal wasn't a businessman."

"I see. This was all a surprise to you?"

"Yes. He hadn't planned the hotel thing very well. I think the whole idea came out of a spontaneous conversation where his friend talked him into it. After we bought this boat, I found out he wasn't a sailor either."

"The boat is magnificent. How did you find it?"

"Well, I know it looks expensive, but older wooden boats are known for requiring a lot of hard work to keep them up. Sal was good with his hands and he was working for a shipyard in Connecticut at the time. The previous owner tried to sell it to a marine museum but there were too many modern improvements that destroyed the historical value. When the museum explored the possibility of purchasing the boat, they found it would have been too costly to retrofit the boat, so they lost interest. The owner was running up yard fees so he sold it to Sal for next to nothing rather than give it away or dismantle it." She paused to pour more orange juice for Mandy.

"More juice?"

"Sure. Go ahead, your story is interesting. The boat was in Connecticut, so how did you get it down here?"

"When Sal decided to move to Belize, I had to go along with the plan. I was pregnant so I couldn't leave him. We sold everything except some clothes, some tools and kitchen items we packed in the boat and gave notice on our apartment. What I didn't know was that Sal was lying to me."

"I thought he told you about his plans for Belize?"

"He did, but he also told me he had signed up for navigation and sailing courses, but he never finished them. He didn't have any experience on the water. All he knew was how to repair boats, not run them or sail them."

"None? I can't believe someone from New England who worked on boats had no boating experience."

"Well, he did take some sailing lessons on little boats in the bay, but he didn't finish those classes, either. He quit when he thought he knew everything."

"I know the type, very hard headed and difficult to get along with. They know everything about everything. What happened to Sal?"

"On our way down here, we were sailing in the Gulf Stream. A storm blew up on us one afternoon not too far from here so I took Mandy below. I was afraid she would blow or slip over board. Suddenly the boat started rolling out of control. Everything seemed to have gone awry. When I hollered up to Sal, he didn't answer so I put on my foul weather gear and secured Mandy in the V berth. When I got up to the cockpit, the boat was turned sideways to the waves and the wheel was spinning wildly. Sal was gone."

"Gone? Did you look overboard?"

"I couldn't see a thing. I was scared to death. I had to get the boat under control. I was afraid the waves were going to broadside the boat and we were going to capsize drowning both Mandy and me. I focused on getting control of the helm and heading the boat into the wind and the bow into the waves. I never saw Sal again. Frankly, I was scared to death and too seasick from the heavy waves to do anything more than stabilize the boat."

"That must have been horrible."

"It was horrible. The storm went on for hours. I hung onto the wheel until the wind and waves died down. I wasn't sure what I was doing. The wind blew us in close to shore. Thankfully, Chuck came along and rescued us. He saw we were in trouble and came along side to help just in time."

"Chuck?"

"Charlie Everson. He and one of his buddies were out fishing in the Gulf Stream when the storm hit. They were in a big fishing trawler so they fared better than we did. They threw me a line and towed me here. When we got to the anchorage at Wisteria Island, Chuck set the anchor. Since I didn't have any money to pay him, he hired me. He runs a couple of restaurants here in Key West, including the one I work in at The Harbor Inn Marina & Hotel. To help me get back and forth to work, he gave me the dingy. He told me he had another one he could use. This one was a spare. Now I commute by dinghy to work there as a waitress. Sometimes I fill in as receptionist at the front desk if they're short handed. He's special. I don't know what I would have done without him."

"He sounds like a really nice guy. I stayed two nights at The Harbor Inn. The hotel rooms are comfortable and well kept. I enjoyed my stay, including the food at the restaurant."

"One of my benefits is meals when I work. Chuck set up a playroom for Mandy in one of the storerooms so she has someplace to hang out while I work. He extends my meal perks to her, too."

"He sure has taken the two of you under his wing. At least you don't have to pay rent and utilities."

"That's true. Money is a big issue for me now. I have some cash that we had on board but Sal had transferred all of our savings to a bank in Belize before we left Connecticut. Chuck helped me find an attorney here in Key West to help with the legalities."

"Legalities? Don't you own the boat?"

"Yes, but I have to find our bank account in Belize. Sal didn't tell me where he moved the money and I'll have to have someone declare Sal missing at sea or something. Right now I don't have a death certificate until they determine if he really is missing. That's why I need an attorney. In addition, I have to change the title of the boat to my name and I don't know where that document is."

"What do you think happened to Sal? Do you think he jumped overboard?"

"Sal was a klutz on the boat. He was always standing up on the lazarette to steer. He said he could see better. I'm not sure he could steer better. I didn't see what happened but I think the boom must have suddenly swung across the cockpit in the wind and struck him, knocking him overboard. The boom was always hitting him. It's really low on this boat. He thought he was a sailor, but he never followed the rule to keep one hand for the boat."

"I'm sorry. He wouldn't be the first to make that mistake. It's good you got control of the boat. You and Mandy could have been lost, too."

"So, there you are. That's my widow's story," she smiled wanly.

"Now I understand why you're out here alone."

"You didn't tell me if you were married."

"That's another story," Steve began. He told her his story about Maria. Not wanting to frighten her, he left out the parts about Carlos tracking him for the gold. When he finished, he sighed. "You know, in spite of what she did, I still have feelings for her. That's hard to change suddenly. I've been doing a lot of thinking about what happened and what Carlos did to hurt her disturbs me. I've promised myself to support a domestic violence shelter when I get settled back in my practice. Women need to have a safe place to go and counseling to break the pattern of violence."

"That's frightening to think how some women find themselves in a violent relationship. I'm so sorry about Maria."

"Thank you." Steve hung his head.

"So we're both in the same boat, so to speak, missing spouses," Talia observed.

"We are?"

"Well, we both had bad marriages and we're both still legally married."

"Almost, but with one exception, Maria died."

"I'm sorry."

"It's okay. Apparently, I was not legally married because she's still married to Carlos."

"Well, I was legally married, but no one is sure what really happened to Sal. He's missing at sea." She paused, then continued. "Okay, I've fulfilled my part of the bargain. Now, can you answer my question about Mandy's shoe? You have to tell me. Are you a magician? I can't figure it out. I watched her take both shoes off and place them near a coral rock on the beach."

"Sure, look out your porthole window. I'll show you."

Steve's cheeks turned red as he felt the heat of the blood rush to color them. He pointed toward the bow of his boat, but Shoestring was gone.

Chapter Twenty

An American Atoll

Talia was too scared to ask, but when Steve approached Charlie Everson about taking Talia for a three-day trip to the Marquesas Islands, some thirty-five miles west of Key West, he enthusiastically supported the idea. He helped provision *Seaseeker* for the trip from the kitchen at the Inn. Talia had not taken any time off since she had started working for him. In spite of being anxious about spending so much time with a new male friend, she was looking forward to the mini-vacation.

Agent Bellows presented another matter. He reminded Steve that Carlos had not been apprehended yet and still posed a serious potential danger for Steve. Reminding him that there was little they could do to help on the water, Steve remained adamant that he have this last trip on *Seaseeker*. Having Talia and Mandy with him, Steve felt secure that Carlos would not bother them.

"You said if Carlos bought our deception with the phony movement of the gold and did nothing, he was most likely on his way back to Miami or had left the country."

"Yes, but we have no confirmation that he saw you or believed our deception," Agent Bellows countered.

"If he didn't, he'll hang around when he sees I'm not unloading the gold. That will give you more time. Besides, my radio is fixed and the

Coast Guard has my sail plan. If we run into any trouble, I can call the Coast Guard or the marine patrol on the radio."

Agent Bellows studied the chart Steve brought for him. "Three days?"

"One day to sail over, one day to walk the beach, picnic, go swimming, and the third day to come back," Steve explained. "It would be too much to cram the trip into two days."

"Okay, it's possible Carlos is still hanging around. He could easily rent a boat and follow you. Because it's remote, you must be prepared if he does show up."

"That's why I want to go. There's no human civilization on the Marquesas."

"I'll see if I can schedule some assistance to watch out for you in case Carlos follows you out there. If Carlos is around, your trip could buy us time. Spending time with your new lady friend may be dangerous, but we can't stop you if you want to go."

The trip west to the Marquesas would take close to eight hours. They left early in the morning as the sun rose in a cloudless sky. *Black Draggon* floated silently in the anchorage off Wisteria Island, bobbing up and down with the steady current flowing into the harbor. Steve, Talia and Mandy motored toward the Southwest Passage in *Seaseeker*. They waved, smiling as a Coast Guard patrol boat heading in the opposite direction sped past them. Steve wondered how far the patrol boat would go before it turned around to head back out of the harbor. Averaging a steady five knots in a stiff breeze, they sailed past Crawfish Key, Man Key, Woman Key, Ballast Key and Boca Grande Key into the open channel to the Marquesas. The view was spectacular with open water and blue skies stretching undisturbed to the Dry Tortugas beyond.

Reviewing his previous trip to the Marquesas four years earlier, Steve pictured the shallow lagoon in the center of the ring of islands. Knowing that the water surrounding the atoll and the center were shallow, he was thankful that Talia had agreed to take *Seaseeker* on this trip. Having a boat with a shallow draft hull would be an advantage exploring the small keys. His memory of the channel entrance into the islands helped to be prepared for the tricky trip in through the shallow flats.

From Boca Grande Key, the shallow flats had dropped away and deeper water prevailed across the Southwest Passage. Sailing through the open water, they had enjoyed a steady lift from the prevailing southeast wind. The strength of the wind had made the crossing smooth and swift in spite of a moderate chop that was not unpleasant. The vast expanse of the Gulf of Mexico and the Atlantic Ocean stretched out to Belize, Mexico, South America and the southern shores of the States to the north.

Once in the deep water, Talia suddenly exclaimed, pointing off to the side of the boat, "Look, dolphins!"

Steve turned in time to see half a dozen dolphins leaping out of the water in the direction she was pointing as Mandy exclaimed, "Wow, Mommy, dolphins. Look, Mommy. Look at all the birds." Talia looked in the direction Mandy had pointed and saw a large area where an enormous group of shearwaters had collected, floating on the surface of the water. The occasional call of the birds broke the quiet slice of the boat cutting through the waves.

Steve recognized the sea birds. "Those are greater shearwaters. I've never seen so many in one place."

As they watched the events unfold, the number of dolphins approaching the maze of birds in all directions increased exponentially, swarming in a huge circle. Suddenly, the shearwaters bolted into the sky above, swarming like bees after honey. The sky above the dolphins was filled with hundreds of birds circling above the agitated water. Snarling calls of "*eeyah*" filled the air as the birds dove repetitively into the churning water where the dolphins surfaced, leaped into the air, and disappeared back into the water.

"The pod must have driven a school of fish up to the surface. Both the dolphins and the shearwaters are having a feeding frenzy." As the three watched, they could see a mass of smaller fish jumping frantically out of the water. The number of dolphins leaping into the air also increased as the shearwaters madly dove into the water like Kamikaze fighters. The birds dove deep down into the depth of the water picking off the frantic fish the dolphins had driven to the surface. Steve, Talia and Mandy watched in awe as the swarming creatures continued their feeding frenzy. Once all the dolphins and shearwaters were satisfied, the maelstrom died down and the swirling surface of the water slowly calmed. The pod of dolphins stopped circling and headed towards the Gulf and the shearwaters dispersed in all directions.

Enjoying the warm, clear weather and the company of enthusiastic companions, Steve, Talia and Mandy found the trip to the small atoll slip by quickly. Approaching mid-afternoon, Steve rounded up along the shoals south of the ring of islands. They had arrived safely at their destination, the Marquesas Keys, leaving the distant Dry Tortugas another forty miles to the west.

Throughout the day, Shoestring appeared and disappeared until they passed Boca Grande Channel. Since the Genoa was unfurled for the entire trip, Shoestring stood forward of the cabin on the windward side leaving a respectable distance between the sail and the mast. When anyone approached him on the foredeck, he flew off and returned when the deck was clear. The closer they approached the islands, the more frequently Shoestring disappeared and returned to his post.

"Look Steve, the islands appear to be horseshoe shaped."

"The locals in Key West call them the American Atoll, but they really aren't an atoll at all. True atolls form from the erosion of volcanic eruptions in the water over time. Just like the Keys, the Marquesas formed from mangroves that grew up on shallow sand banks and limestone outcroppings when the primordial oceans retreated, exposing the coral reefs. The Keys aren't formed from volcanic action."

"How lovely. Look at the beautiful beach over there. Will we be able to walk the beach?"

"Sure. We'll walk the beach and have a cookout for dinner. I brought firewood to cook our hamburgers and hot dogs."

"Sounds yummy. I'm beginning to get hungry thinking about it."

"Outdoor activities always make me hungry. I'm starving. I don't know why. Must be the fresh air. We'll anchor out here for the night later, but we'll go into the center between the islands to go ashore. Even though the water looks fine inside the atoll, it's a shallow, mucky basin. See the channel over there? Between the mangroves? That one is deep enough to motor in. It's a little tricky, but I found the way in a couple years ago when I was here."

"Steve, this is beautiful, no cars, no houses, no people. Thank you for bringing us here."

"I like exploring out of the way places. This one is special since few people come here. Because of the shallows and the distance from Key West, the locals discourage people from attempting the trip."

After furling the Genoa and dropping the mainsail, Steve guided *Seaseeker* into the narrow channel, threading his way between the two sandy, mangrove islands. After Talia flaked the mainsail and secured the sail cover, she returned to the cockpit.

"Can you get a dock line out of the lazarette for me?"

"Sure," Talia opened the seat and pulled up a neatly coiled dock line. "Here."

Steve maneuvered the boat along the side of a mangrove out cropping and grabbed one of the larger overhanging branches. Tying one end of the dock line as close to the base of the mangrove as he could, he played the line out as he walked toward the bow. Shoestring had abandoned his post, flying into the center of the island, out of sight. He fed the other end of the dock line through the chock below the bow pulpit and secured the end to the bow cleat. *Seaseeker* drifted back from the mangrove in response to the slow moving current.

"There we are. Now we can take a walk ashore and set up our campfire for a nice cookout. Let's get the food and beach towels. We'll have plenty of daylight to make our dinner."

To reach the beach at Crescent Key, they would have to cross the center of the open lagoon. "I'm not sure we can all three ride safely in the inflatable with all our gear, so I want to make two trips."

"Sure, I'll go first and Mandy can go with you on the second trip. Maybe we should split the food and supplies."

"Sounds good to me."

They collected the things they needed for dinner and Steve handed them down to Talia after she slipped into the inflatable. "Mandy, you wait here while we take some of these things over to the beach."

"I'll be okay, Mommy."

"Good girl."

Steve slid into the inflatable and pulled the starter for the outboard. They quickly crossed over the lagoon and transferred the items to the beach. "I'll set things up while you go get Mandy."

Steve headed back to *Seaseeker* and Mandy passed the remaining items for their beach excursion over to him before slipping into the inflatable. Steve knew they would be fine while the sun was up and the steady wind blew the mosquitoes, no-see 'ums and other annoying insects out to sea. Later, he would move *Seaseeker* out to the edge of the sand bank to anchor for the night. There they would be out of reach of the local insect population. In the morning, they could return to picnic and walk the beach again. Steve was looking forward to getting to know Talia and Mandy better.

"Mommy, mommy, here we are." Mandy waved excitedly at her mother who was standing at the edge of the water, waiting for their arrival.

"Did you enjoy your ride here?" Talia hugged Mandy as she hopped easily out of the inflatable.

"Sure, it was fun. Can I take my shoes off and run on the beach and wade in the water?"

Steve scowled as he pulled the inflatable a safe distance from the water's edge. "I think we'd better keep our shoes on here. These islands are too far from civilization if one of us gets hurt. Things we can't see live here."

"Like what? This looks like the beach we went to yesterday. I want to take my shoes off."

"Listen to Mr. Andrews, honey. He knows more about the islands here."

"There may be broken shells or exposed limestone that can cut your foot. Horseshoe crabs may be buried in the sand. Sometimes sting ray barbs or even man o' war tentacles and jellyfish wash up on the beach. They can cause serious problems we don't want to experience out here. Be sure to shuffle your feet too when wading in the water. That will scare away any stingrays or sharks buried in the sand. Stingrays have poisonous barbs next to their tails so you don't want to step on one."

"Oh, that's scary. I don't want to get hurt."

"The things we can't see often are the ones that hurt us. So, wear your shoes, even when you go wading." Steve turned to Talia, "Have you two had tetanus shots recently?"

"Mandy has. Now that you ask, I'm not sure about me. I don't remember so it must be a while ago. You have a good point. I'm going to wear my shoes, you too Mandy."

"But I'll ruin them in the water."

"Better your shoes than your feet. We're too far from a doctor, young lady."

"Okay, Mommy, but I'd rather stick my bare feet in the sand." Mandy skipped off toward a group of sea gulls, disturbing their rest in the sun. The flock simultaneously fluttered into the air as Mandy approached them.

"She's well behaved. I'm impressed with your young lady."

"Thank you. Let's do a little exploring before we start dinner. I need to stretch my legs a little."

"Me, too."

Steve and Talia organized their supplies and covered the food with the beach towels. They headed in the same direction Mandy had darted, but walked along the edge of the water, exchanging light conversation when suddenly Talia stopped and pointed into the channel.

"Look, a baby shark. Do you see it? Mandy, come look." Talia pointed at the two-foot long, gray form swimming a few feet away from them.

Mandy skipped over to join them, peering into the water. "Wow, I don't want to go swimming here. He might bite me."

Talia chuckled softly. "He's only a baby and probably would be more frightened of you if he ran into you in the water." Turning toward Steve, she asked, "What kind of shark is it?"

"I don't know. I'm not that familiar with sharks. From the shape of its head, it's not a hammerhead." Steve bent over and picked up a broken piece of coral and threw it at the shark. The coral hit the water next to the tail. In response, the shark zipped out of sight, returned and circled the area where the coral had entered the water, then swam away.

"Wow. Sharks are fast."

Steve reached over and took Talia's hand, guiding her gently away from the edge of the water. They walked hand-in-hand toward a cluster of mangroves, while Mandy scampered over the sand.

"I agree with Mandy. I wouldn't want to meet that guy in the water. Even though I didn't see his teeth, I bet he has a mean bite."

"The bite isn't the problem, it's gangrene."

"Gangrene?"

"They don't brush their teeth," Steve said sternly.

Talia giggled. "How do you know?"

"I tried to find a shark dentist and couldn't."

They both chuckled at Steve's joke "I keep informed." Steve realized that he was still holding her hand as they continued along the beach.

"Did you love her?"

"Maria?" Steve hesitated. "I thought I did. I'm still hurt at her betrayal and angry at my failure to see through her deception."

"You made the decision, you asked her to marry you."

"Yes, you're right. How about you? He asked and you said 'Yes.'"

"I felt cornered, that I didn't have an alternative. He was the only one I knew. Both of our parents pushed us. It's a mistake to do what everyone else expects. I knew I wouldn't be happy."

"I bet a lot of young people go with the flow. They take the road of least resistance, particularly if they want to please their parents."

"Ugh, look, a dead fish. Quick, bury it so Mandy doesn't see it."

"I see it. It's not a fish, it's a turtle. It looks like it's been cut in half. That's what's left of the bottom shell."

"I don't want Mandy to see it. She still doesn't understand death and she likes turtles. This would upset her."

"Sure." Steve dug a shallow grave with the heel of his sneaker and shoved the smelly carcass into the depression and covered it with sand. "Let's head back to the dingy. Look over there. I think we're going to get wet. I see a squall heading towards us."

"Mandy, Mandy, come back here. We're going to start dinner." Talia shouted to her daughter who had found another field of sea gulls she proceeded to frighten into the air. She looked in the direction Steve was pointing. "Oh, no dinner. We're going to get wet. Did you bring a plastic tarp?"

"Yes, if we hurry we can put it up as a shelter." As soon as he had spoken, a strong gust blew from the northwest bringing the smell of rain as the first drops began to fall. Out on the Gulf, Steve watched as a lone trawler disappeared into the thick clouds of the rapidly approaching squall. The previously calm water had whipped up into a froth of white caps.

"We'll never make it. It's coming on too fast," Talia cried.

"Don't run. We're going to get wet so let's just enjoy the rain." Steve stopped, grinning, he said, "Let's sing and dance in the rain."

Talia started laughing as she realized there was no reason to run. She dropped Steve's hand and began spinning like a top with her arms outstretched. As the rain soaked her long dark hair, she turned her face to the sky letting the rain run over her face and down her body. Mandy followed her lead giggling at the childlike frolic her mother led for the three of them.

As the storm swept in, the thunder and lightening followed as the rain turned into a thick torrent reducing visibility to a few feet. By the time they reached the dingy, they were soaked to the skin, water dripping from their hair and clothing.

Talia shivered, "I don't like the lightening," she said as a bright flash crossed the sky above them. A deafening clap of thunder followed. Mandy snuggled under her mother's arms.

Steve pulled the blue tarp out of his duffle bag. "Okay. I see we're beginning to get chilled. I'll get this up to give us some shelter. I don't like lightening either but there's no place else to hide." Another flash of lightening streaked into the channel followed by a sharp clap of thunder.

"We're lucky."

"You call this lucky?"

"Sure, so far we haven't been hit and we're safe under the tarp."

"What about the boat? Won't the lightening hit the mast? The mast is metal. Doesn't metal attract lightening?"

"Yes, but there's a grounding wire that runs from the mast to the keel so the lightening grounds into the water. You don't have to worry about that. The boat is safe even if the mast gets hit."

"Are you sure it works?"

"Sure. I've heard of lightening blowing a hole in the hull at the water line and sometimes frying the electrical system, but the grounding wire will prevent that."

"I hope so. I sure don't want to get stranded out here. I can't believe I'm shivering and it's eighty degrees." Mandy whimpered and snuggled closer to her mother.

"Here, I've got some beach towels to wrap around you. Actually, I think the temperature has dropped to about seventy degrees." Steve handed them two brightly colored beach towels. The three huddled together as the warmth from their bodies spread through the towels.

"I've heard you can get hypothermia, even here in the tropics."

"Yes, but that's not going to happen to us. We're okay."

The lightening continued to streak through the sky above over and over again as the thunder rumbled behind it.

"This is not letting up. I think we should head back to *Seaseeker* if it doesn't stop soon. I want to get you two into the cabin where it's safe and cozy. We won't be able to light a fire here today."

"I could use some dry clothes and a warm cup of coffee."

"Dry clothes would be nice right now," he agreed, in spite of enjoying being so close to Talia.

Chapter Twenty-One

Missing At Sea

After huddling under the blue plastic tarp for about an hour, the blustery wind dropped down to mild puffs and the thunder and lightening receded into the distance toward Key West. They watched the repeated flashes of lightening pierce the sky spiking downward into the water. The rain continued and a deep mist hung heavily over the mangroves reducing visibility to no more than a few yards.

"Well, that settles it. Our dinner on the beach has been rained out."

"I'll take a rain check for tomorrow."

"Okay, but let's get back to the boat. We should be safe on the water now. If we wait much longer, we'll have to deal with the insect population when the rain stops. I want to move *Seaseeker* out from under the mangroves."

"We left the hatch open. I hope the cabin didn't get wet inside."

"Are you ready for a ride back in the rain? I think we'll all go together. I don't want to leave anyone behind in this weather."

"You sure we'll be okay?"

"The inflatable is rated for 450 pounds, we'll be on the edge. I'd rather we all go together."

"Ready, Mandy?"

They grabbed all the gear and stuffed it into the dingy. Steve pushed the craft into the water after Talia and Mandy climbed aboard. He hopped in and once they were in deeper water, he dropped the propeller shaft into the water and started the outboard. "Is everyone set? Keep the tarp over your heads."

Talia nodded in reply, leaning her head against her daughter's damp curls. They were safely on their way back to *Seaseeker*. Steve kept checking between his two charges and the course ahead. He was concerned about Talia and Mandy. He wanted to get them back aboard *Seaseeker* as quickly as possible. The water in the lagoon was relatively smooth due to the shallow depth. He headed directly across the center to find the channel where he had tied *Seaseeker* to the mangrove. Once he reached the channel, he hugged the shore of the mud bank where the current was not as strong and he could touch the mangroves hanging over the water. He proceeded slowly, moving away from the mud banks when he felt the propeller hit bottom and churned up white mud and sand behind them. He was not as afraid of going aground as he was of losing connection with the mangroves. He knew he could jump over the side into the muck if needed to push the dinghy off the mud.

Talia and Mandy were curled up together in a ball of arms and legs in the front of the inflatable. Talia was resting her feet on the wet bundles of wood Steve had brought from Key West to fuel their campfire. She appeared to be dozing. The mangroves thinned as he passed by the first mangrove key. A distant flash of lightening showed the way ahead about two hundred yards to the next mangrove key. After that, he knew he only had another hundred yards of the channel to the next key where he had left *Seaseeker*. He maneuvered the inflatable carefully along the mangroves, watching Talia intently. She appeared young and vulnerable and he began to chide himself for leading her into this nightmare, instead of the idyllic campfire he had planned.

"What's that?" Talia startled awake at the sudden sound.

"It's okay. It's only the mangroves scraping against the side of the inflatable."

"I hope you know where we are. I can't see a thing. How do you know how to get back to the boat when you can't see?"

"I remember the way. I've been here before. There's only one more open passage before we get to the boat. Trust me."

"Well, you act like you know what you're doing."

"I'll need your help later to navigate."

"Navigate, how can I do that when I can't see anything?"

"Just look out ahead for the boat. We're almost there. Only this channel and we're there."

For some time they continued in silence until the inflatable ground to a halt.

"Oops," Steve said as he reversed the propeller.

"Oops what? Where are we? I don't see any land only mangroves. How can we have run aground?"

"I missed the channel." He turned the boat to the west.

"What are you doing?" Talia protested. "Are you heading to South America?"

"See, you do have a good sense of direction. Just watch for the mangroves."

"I can see mangroves coming up on your left."

"Good. That means the island is coming up. See the dark shadow?"

"I see it, but I don't see the boat or the mast."

Steve turned again, but the inflatable ran hard aground.

"Okay captain, what do we do now?"

"Stay put, I'll push." Steve tilted the outboard motor exposing the mud-coated propeller. He slid over the side and sank into the mud up to his knees. Surprisingly, the mud was not as deep as he anticipated. He waded slowly through the sandy muck, pushing the dingy into deeper water. Once aboard, he rinsed the muck and sand from his legs and started the outboard. They continued to scrape along the mangroves. "We're almost there."

"Steve, I don't see the hull or the mast. Isn't this the channel where we left her? Where's the boat?"

Unsettled, Steve had to agree with her. This was where he had left *Seaseeker*, but there was no sign of her or the dock line he had used to tie her to the mangrove. Feeling queasy he searched along the branches of the mangroves. He didn't take long to discover what had happened. The thick limb he had tied the line to was missing. Instead, the base of the mangrove was seared with a long, creamy yellow scar where the wind had severed the limb from the trunk. *Seaseeker* had blown away in the storm.

"Talia, the wind broke the mangrove where I tied *Seaseeker* to the branch. She's gone. The wind and current must have carried her out into the Gulf." Steve's voice deepened and his hands began to shake.

Talia's face fell and turned ashen, "You mean we're lost at sea?" Her voice quivered with fear.

"Don't panic. There's little to no wind. *Seaseeker* can't be far."

Chapter Twenty-Two

A Change in Circumstances

"What are we going to do?"

Under the stress of the moment, Steve reacted immediately, "I'm going after *Seaseeker*. I'll drop you and Mandy off on the beach at the edge of the mangroves. I'll tie the tarp to the mangroves to make a shelter."

Pulling the inflatable onto the nearest sandy beach, he and Talia quickly stripped the inflatable of everything except the outboard and fuel tank to make it as light as possible. He helped Talia set up the shelter to protect Talia and Mandy and the gear from the rain and wind. Using the charcoal briquettes and lighter fluid, he coaxed a small flame in the center of the damp firewood. "That should dry the wood out. As the heat increases, move the logs closer, but don't burn them all at once. The fire will keep you warm and give me a beacon to return." He gave Talia a reassuring hug and quickly shoved off.

Steve settled into the wet dingy hoping that *Seaseeker* had drifted only a short distance and run aground before reaching open water. He steered the inflatable through the channel towards the Gulf looking through the waves of fog for *Seaseeker*. The mist cleared as the sun sank lower towards the horizon. He had only a few hours until dark. He had to find *Seaseeker* before dark. *Seaseeker* must still be tied to the branch adrift with the current.

As he passed a second set of channel markers, he realized that *Seaseeker* had drifted into the open waters of the Gulf of Mexico. He continued through the mist, following the channel to the west. He was disappointed and discouraged *Seaseeker* had not run aground before drifting out of the channel. He checked the LED on his watch; twenty minutes had elapsed since he had left Talia and Mandy on the sand bar. To find *Seaseeker*, he knew he had to stay cool and use his head. He began to calculate the current and distance his boat had possibly traveled during the time they were inside the atoll. The current must have carried *Seaseeker* about one to two knots giving *Seaseeker* a two-hour head start. That meant *Seaseeker* had drifted at least two to two and a half nautical miles ahead of him. He knew the tides in the Marquesas were running a steady two knots from South to North. Since he had already traveled twenty minutes, he would have to continue to head North with the current.

After twenty minutes, he throttled back to take a good look around. He anticipated that by now his boat must be nearby. Studying the surrounding water through the mist, he could see no sign of *Seaseeker* in any direction. He pushed the throttle forward to run full ahead when the outboard sputtered momentarily, started up, sputtered again and shut down, leaving Steve in a world of silence. All seamen know the risk of sudden changes on the water. Often, changes can create life-threatening events. By anticipating the risks, the prepared sailor avoids the dangers by being well equipped and mentally sharp. Often the difference between survival and loss is reduced to controlling emotions and making good decisions under stress.

Once again, Steve found himself at the mercy of poor planning. He had not made one, but three mistakes. Remembering Mud Key Mike's warning, he had to admit that tying *Seaseeker* to a mangrove was a serious mistake, particularly with the arrival of the unexpected squall. He should have taken the time to secure the anchor to the island, not tying the bowline to a mangrove. With the sputtering and sudden death of the outboard, he had to admit he had failed to check the fuel tank for the outboard before he left Key West. Without looking at the small red neoprene fuel tank, he knew it was empty.

"Damn, now what do I do," Steve cried aloud, throwing his hands into the air. "I've run out of gas." Looking up into the sky, he pleaded,

"God help me, I'm such a fool." To reinforce his agony, he reached for the fuel tank. As soon as he picked it up, he confirmed his fears. The tank was light, and empty. Dark panic and desperation fueled his embarrassment and shame. He had really blown his image with Talia.

Perhaps he should give up and return to the sandy bank where he had left Talia and Mandy. He could hang off the back of the inflatable and propel the dingy back to land by pushing with his hands and kicking. He knew he was a strong swimmer, but the current was running in the wrong direction. He doubted he could overcome the force of the current which was running north, away from the Marquesas into the Gulf. He contemplated visions of returning to the shallows and Talia and Mandy sheltered under the tarp. In the face of the current and his vanity, he discarded his plan to return. *Seaseeker* must be drifting to the north as well, moving with the current.

He began to formulate a new plan. He considered dropping the outboard into the water to lighten the inflatable, then propelling the boat by swimming behind it with the current, toward *Seaseeker*. Without a strong breeze, the current would carry him in the inflatable to the north like a balloon on the wind. He castigated himself for having removed the paddles with the other items he'd left with Talia and Mandy. He could not return to the Marquesas on his own power due to the contrary force of the current. His flippers would have helped, but they were stored in the lazarette aboard *Seaseeker*.

He was committed. His only option now was to go forward and find *Seaseeker*. Waves of blood rushed to his cheeks as he thought of how Talia had trusted him. He had to find his boat to save face with Talia. He had promised her he would return with the boat and he had seen how that promise had calmed the growing panic in her face. Talia had trusted his promise. He promised there was no danger and he would return shortly. *Seaseeker* had to be nearby.

He reviewed his predicament. He had no fuel, no flashlight, no oars or paddle, no life jacket and a useless outboard with an empty fuel tank. His thoughts returned to Talia and Mandy alone on the sand bank. He wondered if he had set their camp back far enough from the shoreline to be safe from the incoming tide when it turned. Picturing this new scenario, Steve feared for their plight if the returning tide washed into their camp and doused the fire. They would be wet and cold and he would lose his beacon to find them in the dark. With the setting sun, Talia and Mandy would be swarmed with mosquitoes and no see-ums without smoke from the fire to discourage their attack. He shivered in response to the new picture he had created.

The mist flowed in fluctuating streams of heavy and light waves across the inflatable. Changing his focus, he put his visions of Mandy and Talia and the sandy beach behind him and peered into the gloom. For a brief instant, he thought he saw the white hull of a boat roughly a few hundred yards north and west. Concentrating, he listened carefully for any sounds. He could not hear the sound of a running engine and he had not seen sails above the hull of the ephemeral vision he thought he had seen through the mist. Convinced the vision in the mist was his boat, he had second thoughts. Perhaps he was too far out to have found *Seaseeker,* but remembering the heavy gusts at the onset of the front, he felt the vision could be *Seaseeker*. He listened again and could not hear voices or sounds of human activity, which would be audible at this distance if it were a fishing boat. He paused, waiting for another break in the mist. Loss of the outboard now placed all three of them at risk. He was thankful he had filed his plans with the Coast Guard. In addition, Agent Bellows and Chuck Everson knew where they had gone and when to expect them to return. These thoughts reassured him that if they did not return on time, both Chuck and Agent Bellows would become concerned and notify the Coast Guard to look for them.

His thoughts turned to surviving the immediate dangers. Realizing the chances of being rescued within a few days was high, he relaxed and focused on the mist ahead. He knew he had to act as if the image he had seen was *Seaseeker*. To lighten the inflatable, he freed the fuel line fitting from the outboard and jettisoned the outboard overboard. Reducing the weight of the inflatable would increase the speed he could propel the boat by pushing it from behind. With only a fleeting reference ahead, Steve stripped off his pants, shoes and shirt. In a flash, he was over the side. A brief tug of doubt crossed his mind as he began to kick in a steady rhythm, pushing the inflatable towards *Seaseeker*. As he kicked he kept his eyes focused in the direction of the vision, hoping his vision was not a mirage, like a thirsting soul imagining an oasis in the desert. A second break in the mist showed that he had reduced the distance to his target enough to confirm his hopes. In the clearing, he could see several hundred yards ahead. *Seaseeker* was floating in the current with a large mangrove limb attached to the bow with the dock line. The break in the mist confirmed that he was propelling the inflatable faster than the *Seaseeker* was drifting away.

As the mist cleared again, Steve caught sight of *Seaseeker* for the third time. He was getting closer. Just as feelings of relief began to grow, the welcome vision of his boat faded from view and another vision of something moving in the water off to the right sent chills down his spine. The shapes of two, gray triangular fins pierced the surface of the water and were heading directly toward the inflatable.

Chapter Twenty-Three

Denizens Of The Deep

Human beings instinctively recognize danger in the face of potential predators. Steve knew the difference between the fins of dolphins and porpoises and that of a shark. The two fins approaching the inflatable were distinctly characteristic of sharks, and judging the size of the fins, the sharks were large. He did not know what kind of sharks they were, nor did it matter, as most species of sharks inhabited the open waters of the Marquesas. Steve maintained a respectful awe of sharks and the power they represented. He also remembered that in addition to being dangerous, they were curious, like cats. He feared that one puncture from the action of the jaws of a shark could make the inflatable, inflatable no more. He comforted himself that there were few documented shark attacks on small boats, but on second thought, maybe this was the case because the victim didn't survive.

Steve froze. Holding tightly to the transom, he ceased moving and drew his legs into a ball as close to the small craft as he could. Mesmerized by the approaching fins, he kept his eyes fixed on the two triangles cutting through the surface of the water. The only sound breaking the stillness of the air was the occasional drop of water out of the mist onto the surface of the inflatable. When the two fins came closer, their noses bumped the bow then veered back into the distance between the inflatable and *Seaseeker*. Steve could feel the vibration echo through his body.

Wet, cold, and fearful, Steve contemplated his dilemma. With two sharks lurking somewhere between the inflatable and his boat, he was rapidly losing hope and the opportunity to reach *Seaseeker*. Without thinking, he quietly eased up on the transom and grabbed the empty fuel tank. He flung it to the side of the inflatable, but away from the direction towards *Seaseeker* where he had last seen the two fins. Instantly, he recognized the stupidity of his action when the fins reappeared. The tank hit the water with a dull thud half way between the inflatable and where the fins had surfaced. Both sharks, startled at the sudden noise, turned and headed back toward Steve and the floating fuel tank. Steve monitored the rapid swish of their tails as they responded to the splash. Steve cursed his stupidity. Not only had he failed to frighten them, he had increased their curiosity. The two fins continued to disappear and resurface, circling the fuel tank floating about ten feet away. Perhaps, if he had not thrown the fuel tank, the two sharks would have continued on their way without incident. But now, due to his foolish action, the two sharks had returned to more thoroughly investigate the foreign objects floating in the water.

Steve remembered the incident earlier in the day when he had thrown the piece of coral at the baby shark swimming in the channel. Anticipating these two adults would behave in a similar manner, he watched them continue to circle the fuel tank. His heart beat heavily like a bass drum. He talked to himself, breathing deeply to stay calm and control his emotions. He remained motionless, curled up in a ball, hanging off the stern of the inflatable. As they neared the inflatable, Steve could see the eyes, jaws and dorsal fins of both sharks, the tail fins, and the full length of their streamlined bodies emerge out of the darkness of the water. Both sharks were about twelve to fifteen feet long, longer than the length of the inflatable. After circling the floating fuel tank, they approached the bow of the inflatable. Steve remained frozen in time, holding his breath, hoping to be interpreted as an inanimate attachment on the larger, strange object. One of the sharks bumped the bow of the inflatable. Steve felt the impact again as the vibration traveled from the bow to the stern. He remained motionless, holding his breath. As quickly as they had returned to investigate the fuel tank, the two fins turned away, circled and disappeared.

Hanging from the transom, Steve reviewed everything he knew about sharks. They were common inhabitants of his usual sailing territory, Biscayne Bay. Whenever he had entertained friends snorkeling, he had assigned one person to act as lookout. When the lookout spotted sharks in the area, they slapped the surface of the water with a wooden paddle to warn the swimmers to methodically return to the boat with minimal splashing. The sound of the paddle on the water did not necessarily frighten the sharks away, but served as a warning to the swimmers. He knew sharks best be avoided due to their unpredictability; however, statistically only the occasional rogue attacked a lone swimmer. More frequently, encounters took place without incident, especially when the human controlled his motions and did not panic. Acting like a regular inhabitant of the water resulted in favorable encounters. Minimizing splashing so that the predator did not interpret the human as a fish in trouble was critical, as well as avoiding entering the water with open wounds. Splashing and fresh blood send attack signals to hungry sharks nearby.

Steve waited a few moments, reminding himself of the baby shark's behavior when he startled it earlier in the day. The two adult sharks had mimicked the same behavior by returning and circling the fuel tank and the inflatable. Hopefully, the two sharks had satisfied their curiosity and had departed for more appetizing water. If he waited much longer, Steve felt he would lose his window of opportunity to reach *Seaseeker*. Building his courage and continuing to survey the surrounding water for triangular fins on the surface, he decided to make his move. Uncurling from his fetal position, he dog paddled to the front of the inflatable and grabbed hold of the line attached to the bow. If he swam using the frog kick, he would minimize his disturbance in the water. Pulling instead of pushing the inflatable freed his arms to add more power to his efforts. Stifling his instinctive reaction to panic and facing the potential that more sharks could be in the vicinity, Steve began swimming towards *Seaseeker*.

As he paddled toward *Seaseeker*, pulling the inflatable behind him, he maintained a slow, steady, powerful rhythm. Exhaustion now was his foe. Remembering his run across Biscayne Bay to Black Bank, he controlled his body to conserve his strength for the distance. To buoy his spirits, he pictured Talia's reaction when he returned with *Seaseeker* to retrieve her and Mandy from the sandy beach back at the Marquesas. Replacing the frightening images of the sharks and the potential of the damage they could inflict with thoughts of Talia and Mandy lifted his spirits and turned his focus to success. He created mental pictures of what he would do once he reclaimed *Seaseeker*. He reinforced his positive images with memories of winning awards in swimming competitions when he was younger. Swimming towards *Seaseeker* elicited memories of the competitions he had won for long distance underwater and breaststroke. Overcoming feelings of panic had contributed to his success in these competitions. He remembered pushing himself to take two more strokes when his body demanded air. His tenacious attitude had won over the competition. Successfully reaching *Seaseeker* demanded mental control, overcoming fatigue, and a strong sense of survival. Steve focused on cultivating all three. He had survived an encounter with the denizens of the deep and now *Seaseeker* was within reach.

Chapter Twenty-Four

A Bird In Time

Heading steadily towards *Seaseeker*, Steve continued to reinforce his confidence that he would reach his destination. He knew he was not the athlete of his youth, but he was comfortable in the water. Thoughts of past trips to the Keys reminded him of snorkeling trips while barracuda watched in the distance or an occasional shark passed nearby. He was confident he could make the distance but he wished he had his flippers. His flippers would have increased the power of each kick. He clutched tightly onto the end of the line attached to the inflatable. If he lost the dinghy, he would not be able to return to the mangrove key where he had left Talia and Mandy. Fortunately, the current was running in his favor.

After the front had passed, the air became calm. Suddenly, a gust blew out of the southeast, catching the inflatable and dragging him in a direction away from *Seaseeker*. He listened carefully for the familiar sound of the halyards striking the mast, helping him to calculate the direction he needed to go, and to adjust for the strength of the current. Steve applied his navigating skills to determine the angle of his approach. If he swam in a direction upwind of *Seaseeker*, the wind would blow him down toward the boat. If he misjudged the angle and was swept downwind of *Seaseeker*, he was doomed. He would never be able to overcome the forces of the wind and the current dragging him and the inflatable away from *Seaseeker*. He was sure that the gust had blown him off course.

Instinctively, Steve let go of the inflatable. The inflatable darted off like a helium balloon in the wind. Eliminating the drag of the inflatable on his ability to swim would make the difference between success and failure. If he reached *Seaseeker*, he knew he could retrieve the inflatable later. Now he needed every advantage to reach his boat. He felt alone, totally unsupported, and naked to the forces of nature. He felt the pressure of the current on his skin and the force of the wind on his face and hair. Looking through the mist, he prayed for another glimpse of *Seaseeker* and when that failed he listened for the sound of the halyards on the mast. He strengthened his resolve to reach his sailboat or drown.

On the borderline of panic, Steve stopped to rest, treading water. A break in the mist reinforced the sound of the halyards confirming his bearings to make his final sprint. If he made the wrong decision, he could be swept out into deeper water and drown or be consumed by sharks. As visibility improved slightly, Steve saw a black duck flying towards him through the gloom. The bird did not waver in its direction, characteristically maintaining a distance of a few feet above the surface of the water and flying in a straight line. He watched as the bird flew directly toward the inflatable, passing over his head. Astonished, Steve saw a piece of seaweed hanging from its beak. "Shoestring," he thought. The bird had to be Shoestring. He watched the bird circle the inflatable and head in the direction he had last seen *Seaseeker* and heard the clinking of the halyards.

"Shoestring," he called out. The bird ignored him and continued to fly in his intended direction. The bird had to be Shoestring, he thought, as the bird disappeared into the mist. He fixed the direction of its flight in his mind. Remembering Captain Bill's words as he had read from the Audubon field guide, cormorants feed by diving in three to fifteen feet of water. The water here was too deep for the bird to be interested in feeding. Cormorants were shore birds, spending most of their time resting on posts or trees or other objects a few feet above the water where they could dive to feed. This bird had flown by to inspect the inflatable and return to where it was resting. The seaweed was a telling clue. Was that a gift to exchange for sardines? Was this assumption any less accurate than the others he had made? He had seen his boat through the mist close by. If this bird was actually Shoestring, it had just shown him the straight-line direction to his boat. He had no other alternative but to trust the direction Shoestring had shown him. Relying on the bird's instinct, Steve took a deep breath and ducked under the surface of the water. His life depended on having made the right assumption. He reinforced his theory; no other bird would carry nesting materials so far from shore. As he blocked out thoughts of the consequences of a wrong decision, he thanked Shoestring for saving his life again.

Steve took another deep breath and slid below the surface. Falling back into a steady rhythm, Steve drew on the competitive training of his youth. He concentrated his full strength on taking a deep breath, three powerful breast strokes, resurfacing for air, three powerful strokes, air. Returning to the surface, he repeated the pattern focusing on forcing as much power as he could into each stroke to glide towards *Seaseeker*. If his estimations were correct, *Seaseeker* was a few hundred yards away. With the assistance of the current, he could be making progress at the rate of two knots and would reach *Seaseeker* in less than twenty minutes. Even at his age, he could easily make the distance before exhaustion set in. He worked the three-stroke pattern into a regular rhythm.

A vision of Talia returned to his thoughts. He barely knew her. He wondered if she spelled her name with an "i" or a "y" or if there was an "h" in her name. He tried to recapture the sensation of her hand in his as they had walked the beach earlier in the afternoon. The sound of her laughter echoed in his head and the imprint of her smile reflected a pleasant vision in his mind. He remembered how cute she had appeared when he first met her. Her sailing hat had not covered the long, glistening strands of her dark hair draping down to her shoulders. He realized that in spite of her petite stature, she was capable of handling a sailboat on her own. He admired the tenacity of her spirit.

Remembering the carcass of the turtle they had found on the beach, he knew it had not been severed by a propeller. Most likely, a shark had taken a bite and the turtle had succumbed to the jaws of nature. Here he was, mimicking the motion of a turtle, thinking he could camouflage his presence in the water. Obviously, being a turtle would not keep him safe. He missed his rhythm. Think about Talia, think rhythm. Focus on reaching *Seaseeker*. His rhythm returned. Surface, take a deep breath, head down, three strokes and glide. Feel the water as it flows past, new water, closer to *Seaseeker*.

His thoughts returned to his youth and swimming competitions. He remembered the girl he had wanted to impress. She had inspired him to win the competition when she caught his eye in the bleachers prior to the start of the race. He had instantly been attracted to her. Winning, he had thought, would gain her attention and maybe her affections. As he had applied his efforts toward winning, he envisioned her as his prize. He won the competition, breaking his prior record. His enthusiasm faded, however, as she left the competition holding hands with their football team's assistant coach. Remembering this vision for inspiring his motivation, Steve replaced her with saving Talia as his prize. The contest was similar, but the stakes were now much higher. Victory required maintaining his mental and physical focus.

Like riding a bicycle, swimming the breaststroke was not tiring and the motion of his legs became an automatic, even rhythm. As Steve sensed fatigue creeping into his arms and legs, his hands hit something hard in the water. Momentarily recoiling in fear, thoughts of the sharks resurfaced. Once overcoming his fear, he discovered he had hit the branch of the mangrove floating alongside *Seaseeker*. Feelings of relief and success spread through his body, renewing his sagging energy. He turned toward the stern knowing his marathon with the denizens of the deep was over. Maintaining his focus had succeeded.

Out of the corner of his eye, he detected a sharp movement on the surface of the water and a chill ran through his body. The unmistakable shape of shark fins were moving toward him. With a sharp spike in adrenalin, Steve used every ounce of strength to reach into the upper branches of the mangrove. The sharks had returned. Swinging quickly onto the top of the floating mass, Steve camouflaged his body among the branches, sliding out of the water as fast as he could. As the sharks veered away within feet of the floating mass of branches and leaves, Steve watched the ominous gray shapes dive deep toward the ocean's floor. Once they disappeared, Steve closed his eyes, holding his shaking arms and legs as close to his body as possible. Breathing deeply, he knew he was safe, protected by the mass of tangled branches and leaves, even though both he and the mangrove were now partially submerged. He waited, not moving until he gained confidence the sharks would not return. Circling around to the stern, Steve climbed aboard *Seaseeker* by placing one foot on the top edge of the rudder, the other on the tail of the exhaust pipe and grabbing the edge of the toe rail. Standing behind the transom and holding on to the backstay, he swung his right leg onto the edge of the deck and pulled his body under the lifeline. He was safe aboard his boat. When he looked toward the bow, Shoestring was standing at attention with his head cocked to one side and a strand of seaweed dangling from his beak, peering back at him.

Chapter Twenty-Five

Final Encounter

Steve anchored *Seaseeker* off the edge of the sandbar by setting his Danforth anchor securely in the sand at the edge of the channel. The mist had cleared as the sun dropped closer to the horizon. The late afternoon sky was turning a bright golden yellow. The flickering light from the bonfire Talia had built had guided him back to the mangrove key. This time he made no mistakes in securing his boat. He had dropped the anchor and backed down until the boat stopped short, setting the anchor securely. *Seaseeker* drifted sideways in the current when he turned the engine off. Taking the spare paddle out of the lazarette, he boarded the inflatable and paddled to shore. Talia and Mandy rushed to greet him, their faces reflecting relief at his return.

On the way back to the camp, all three collected more mangrove branches to add to the fire. Stoking the fire with a new supply of wood, they sat by the flames as they roasted their hamburgers and hot dogs. Wrapped in a dry blanket from *Seaseeker*, Steve enjoyed the heat radiating from the fire. The warmth of the flames melted the physical and nervous chill out of his body. As they ate their hamburgers and hot dogs, they watched the brilliant glow of the sunset as the colors in the sky ran through the spectrum of fading yellow and golden brilliance to muted pastels. They finished the evening with roasted marshmallows. Mandy cuddled up next to her mother and dozed off to sleep. Talia wrapped her arms around Mandy and tilted her head against her daughter's shoulder. Shoestring stood guard on the bow of *Seaseeker*.

A loud snap jarred them out of their sleepy reverie.

"What was that?" Talia asked, half asleep.

"It must be the breeze in the mangroves," Steve said as he poked the dying embers with a long stick.

Another loud snap of cracking branches came from the direction of the mangroves, followed by a loud splash.

"The wind is not that strong. That sounds like an animal moving through the mangroves," said Talia.

"Wait here, I'll look around," Steve said as he jumped up and headed toward the thick vegetation. He knew the sound was not the wind and there were no large animals resident on the Marquesas. Something large and heavy was moving through the mangroves, breaking the stems and branches. As he entered the thicket, Steve detected a large, dark shape in the direction of the cracking branches. Steve bristled, knowing instinctively that the shape was human and it was Carlos.

Having waded through the shallow tidal channels, Carlos had struggled toward their camp, also following the glow of the fire. Exhausted, his mind was caught between fear, hunger and greed, his body driven by rushes of adrenalin. Like a wild boar, Carlos was anxious for his final confrontation with Steve to regain possession of the sailboat loaded with gold. As Steve approached Carlos, he positioned himself between Carlos and the campfire where Talia and Mandy were near *Seaseeker*.

Struggling with sleeves that were too long, Carlos reached into the pocket of his yellow foul weather jacket and retrieved a small revolver. In the fading daylight, Steve did not see the gun barrel as he moved boldly toward Carlos. He fiercely held on to the goal of preventing Carlos from getting past him. He had to protect Talia, Mandy and his boat. He stopped short a few feet from Carlos as the glimmer of the campfire reflected off the barrel of the gun. Carlos raised his arm and pointed the barrel at Steve.

Suddenly, Carlos looked down at his feet, inadvertently loosing focus as the gun lowered. "What the…" he sputtered.

Steve followed the direction of Carlos' gaze. A large black form was struggling at his feet. Shoestring was tugging with all his strength at one of Carlos' shoelaces. The moment Carlos lowered the gun; Steve lunged forward wrapping his arms around Carlos in a bear hug. His sudden momentum caught Carlos off guard. Carlos lost his balance and tumbled backward with Steve wrapped tightly around his waist. Attempting to counter his fall, Carlos flailed both arms grasping at the mangrove branches. Distracted from his goal, he lost his grip on the gun as it slipped out of his hand, splashed into a pool of water and disappeared below the surface.

Unable to regain his balance, Carlos fell backwards into the water with a great splash and crack of mangrove branches. With the weight of Steve's body holding him down, Carlos' foul weather jacket filled with water. Carlos was trapped, barely able to keep his head above the surface to breathe. On top of the situation, Steve controlled Carlos who was now desperately trying to keep his head above water. The struggle was over almost before it had started. Like a medieval knight in a heavy suit of armour, Carlos had fallen and the weight of his waterlogged suit imprisoned him.

"Talia, get the gun. It's in the lazarette on board *Seaseeker*," Steve yelled back toward the camp.

Steve maintained control of Carlos as Talia rushed back to *Seaseeker*. Returning, she held the flare gun pointed at Carlos.

"Shoot it," Steve directed.

"Shoot him? With a flare gun?"

"No, not him. Shoot it up, in the air. Hopefully, a Coast Guard patrol boat will see it."

Steve had guessed correctly. Agent Bellows had alerted the Coast Guard to remain on watch for *Seaseeker*. The Coast Guard patrol was only a few miles away, investigating the abandoned lobster boat beached on the north side of the Marquesas. Within minutes the patrol boat arrived and the officers handcuffed Carlos. They assured Steve Carlos would spend his remaining days far from the Keys.

After hearing of Carlos' apprehension, Agent Bellows commented to Steve over the Coast Guard radio, "Congratulations, Steve. You did it. I knew Carlos would make big mistakes on the water. Thanks for your help."

"You're welcome. I'm exhausted," Steve didn't dare reveal who the real hero was. No one would believe him.

"You were the perfect bait. Have a good evening Steve. Your ordeal is over."

"Good night. I'm going back to my boat to get some sleep." Steve felt the energy drain from his body as his arms hung limply at his sides. He was physically exhausted and emotionally drained from a very long, trying day.

Chapter Twenty-Six

Sunset

When they returned to Key West two days later, Steve called Eric to explain that he needed another week to sell *Seaseeker* before he returned to Miami. What Steve really wanted was to spend more time with Talia and Mandy. At the end of the conversation, Steve looked down at his feet, "Stop it."

Eric responded cynically, "Shoestring?"

"No. A dog. He's acting like he thinks I'm a fire hydrant. Shoo. Go away. Beat it."

"You can't fool me. It's that crazy bird of yours."

"No. It really is a dog. I don't know where Shoestring is."

"Sure, Steve. See you next week."

"Really. I'm headed back to the boat. See you next week."

Every morning, Mandy served a generous plate of sardines on the deck and a second helping in the evening before sunset. For each meal, Shoestring arrived with a gift of seaweed, which he readily exchanged for the plate of smelly sardines. The ritual continued until Friday when Steve and Talia noticed by midmorning the plate of sardines had remained untouched. By mid-afternoon, the sardines had dried out in the sun. Steve dumped them overboard causing a feeding flurry from the nearby scavengers. The uneaten fish had attracted a myriad of green-headed flies that were annoying everyone. Seagulls and killies devoured the morsels in the water within minutes.

That evening, Mandy placed a fresh plate of sardines on the deck for Shoestring's evening meal. After two hours, they continued to check the plate and became concerned when Shoestring failed to make his appearance. Steve and Talia yielded to Mandy's request they go ashore to Wisteria Island because that was where Shoestring had found her shoe. "But Mommy, Shoestring is hurt and needs our help. I just know he's laying on the beach and he can't fly. Maybe he broke his wing. Please, we have to save him. I know he's there." Mandy convinced Talia and Steve to check the Island for any sign of the missing bird.

Piling into the inflatable, Steve, Talia and Mandy returned to the beach on Wisteria Island as the shadows began to lengthen and the sun had become a large, red ball hanging above the horizon. Once ashore, they combed the island looking for the missing bird. Dozens of cormorants rested on branches, alternating between stretching and closing their wings to dry in the fading sun, watching the rays of the setting sun fill the clouds with tints of gold, yellow and pink. The dormant cormorants ignored the three humans scouring the island.

None of the resident cormorants on the island appeared familiar to the three humans.

Once they rounded the far end of the island, returning to the inflatable, Mandy ran ahead of Steve and Talia, pointing to a cormorant swimming a short distance from shore.

"Shoestring, Shoestring," she called.

As she approached the edge of the beach, the startled bird flew in the opposite direction, across the channel toward Tank Island. By the time Steve and Talia caught up with Mandy, she was kneeling on the sand, crying. Laying among the rocks was the dried carcass of a cormorant, just above the tide line.

"Mommy, it's Shoestring. Shoestring is dead."

Steve knelt down to examine the remains. For a moment he frowned. After studying the dried body, he smiled. "Don't cry, Mandy. This isn't Shoestring."

"How do you know?" she asked through her tears. "It looks like Shoestring."

"This bird has been here for a long time. Shoestring has been missing for less than a day."

Steve's words lifted her spirits and she wiped away her tears.

"Are you sure?"

"Mandy, I'm sure."

Mandy smiled and skipped off in the direction of the inflatable. "Shoestring, here Shoestring," she continued her search.

When Talia caught up with her at the inflatable, she joined Mandy calling for Shoestring. Steve joined them.

"Shoestring. Shoestring," Steve, Talia and Mandy called for their lost friend. Their voices floated over the soft evening breeze. No bird responded to their calls.

Across the harbor in Key West, the tourist crowd gathered on Mallory Dock to celebrate the daily sunset ritual. As usual, the crowd was shoulder to shoulder with local vendors selling their wares. Bicyclists peddled into the square and clowns carrying helium balloons wove in and out among the tourists. A man with a dog act set up his props as the dogs waited obediently. A flame swallower, a juggler and a monocyclist hawked the tourists to stay for the show as other tourists sampled the vendor's booths. Artists painted children's faces with rainbows, stars, stripes and dots of red, white, blue, yellow and green face paint. As the sun dropped closer to the horizon, it grew into a huge reddish-orange orb resting precariously at the edge of the sky and water. The anxious crowd watched the burning orb slip into the ocean. When the sun had disappeared below the water, the crowd clapped, cheered and hooted in appreciation. The catcalls echoed across the harbor to Wisteria Island. The applause and voices dispersed on the evening breeze as sailboats returned to the harbor, their sails crossing the golden glow of the sun on the horizon. The crowd on Mallory Dock scattered back toward Duval Street, dispersing into nearby restaurants and shops. Spirits were high with the promise of a new day and another sunset celebration at the next day's end.

Some say, if the crowd had been silent, they would have heard the calls on Wisteria Island, but sunset in Key West is a time of jubilation. For Steve, Talia and Mandy on Wisteria Island, there was no celebration. They sat on the edge of the inflatable with tears in their eyes.

"He's gone," Mandy sobbed.

"He may still come back," Steve reassured her. "We just don't know when."

"This time he's not coming back," Mandy replied.

"Do you remember when we sailed out to the mangrove islands?" Steve asked.

"Yes."

"He flew off many times, but he always came back. When he disappeared, we never knew whether he would return. It was always his choice. He's a wild bird, Mandy. If he never comes back, we have to accept it."

"I never said goodbye."

"Sometimes you don't have to. He'll always be with you. He doesn't belong to anyone. Maybe he was homesick."

"Do you think so?"

"Maybe someone else needs him more than we do. We need to learn to share him with others. Can you do that?"

"I think so."

As the night settled around them, they climbed back into the inflatable and returned to *Seaseeker*. Steve picked up Shoestring's plastic dish and slipped the stale sardines into the water. As he steered the dingy back to *Black Draggon*, all three were silent. Each knew in their hearts the sun had set for Shoestring and would never rise again.

Chapter Twenty-Seven

The Story Teller

On a sunny winter day thirty-three years after Shoestring disappeared, a tourist boat motored along a shoal on the Gulf side of the backcountry in the Lower Keys. A green and white striped Bimini top covered the open pilot station at the back of the boat. A full capacity of tourists circled the glass bottom observation well and gazed intently at the underwater vista below. The pilot, sitting under the protection of the Bimini was an attractive young lady in her mid twenties with jet back hair protruding from the back of a tan baseball cap emblazoned with a US Department of the Interior logo. She wore the khaki Bermuda shorts and matching long sleeved shirt of the government uniform with her sleeves rolled up half way to her elbows like the other park service rangers. Her bare feet slipped loosely in and out of a pair of well-worn Docksiders. As she steered the boat, she peered through large, dark sunglasses looking for channel markers ahead and checking her position against the mud bank. After sipping water from a plastic bottle, she placed it in the cup holder mounted on the chart table. She cleared her throat to speak into the microphone in her left hand.

"Although Shoestring had become an integral part of their lives, Steve knew it was only a matter of time before the bird would leave and not return. The endurance of their relationship depended entirely on Shoestring's tenacity for his sardines.

"After Shoestring's disappearance, the days seemed uneventful and lonely. No one mentioned the missing bird. During the week after Steve and Talia returned from the Marquesas, they rafted their boats together, anchoring off the shore of Wisteria Island. Chuck suggested that Steve post a For Sale sign in the Café to advertise *Seaseeker*. His suggestion was a good one and an enthusiastic buyer contacted Steve within a few days. While Talia helped clean out the cabin before the sale, she found three canvas bank bags stashed in the forward anchor locker, under the chain and coiled anchor line. On opening the bags, Steve discovered the gold coins Maria claimed to have hidden on the boat before she died. The coins were valued to be over half a million dollars.

"Steve returned to Miami long enough to turn over what was left of his law practice to Eric. He used part of the money from the gold coins to buy the trailer on Stock Island from Chuck. Subsequently, Chuck promoted Talia to manager of the restaurant in The Harbor Inn, while Steve took a job teaching at the local community college. Within a few months they were married in an informal ceremony on the beach at Wisteria Island. Mandy was the flower girl.

"A year later, when Talia became pregnant, she sold *Black Draggon* and *Serpent*, intending to end their lives on the water. Not long afterwards, with Talia's blessing, Steve couldn't resist buying an old wooden houseboat they moored using an old engine block just ahead of us. Both Steve and Talia spent many hours after work and on the weekends out here protecting the rookery. They also spent time assisting the local shelter for women escaping abusive relationships. They were truly conscientious citizens concerned about the quality of life for both humans and the birds.

"Pamphlets with information on the birds nesting here in the rookery are circulating for each of you. If you would like extras to take home, there are more in the rack by the gangway amidships.

"Steve died a year ago from a heat attack. With the old houseboat empty most of the time, vandals set it on fire and it sank over there where you can still see the remains."

She paused to put the microphone down, take a sip of water, clear her throat and continue her speech.

"Please, excuse me. My throat gets dry occasionally from speaking so much. One of these days, I'm going to record my speech so I can just push a button to play the tape," She said with a smile. "If you can imagine, Steve was everything to Talia. She never recovered from his passing and her physical and mental health declined soon after. For some time, most people thought she would just pine away from missing him. Fortunately, her daughters prevailed and her spirits returned. She lives today in the Fisherman's Nursing and Convalescent Center in Marathon. If you visit her there, she sits silently in a wheel chair, clutching two framed pictures. One is a painting by a local artist of a cormorant drying its wings at sunset in Key West Harbor. The second holds a family picture of Talia, Steve, and their two daughters. Remarkably, she holds these two pictures all day. In the evening, her aide places them on her dresser where she gazes at them until she falls asleep. Each morning after bathing and breakfast, the aide returns the pictures to her arms and she hugs them for the remainder of the day."

The young woman put the microphone down on the chart table and cleared her throat again, momentarily using both hands to steady the boat.

"I don't know what you think," said an elderly woman to her husband, "but that is a beautiful story." Her husband grunted, mouthing an unintelligible response.

The young woman cleared her throat again and took a sip of water. Picking up the microphone, she said, "Thank you for your attention ladies and gentlemen. I hope you enjoyed your tour of our cormorant and anhinga bird sanctuary."

Chapter Twenty-Eight

The Curious

The glass-bottom tour boat rose and fell softly on the gentle swells as they rolled and broke along the mud bank. Numerous cormorants and anhingas flew in and out of the rookery bringing seaweed and small fish to the hatchlings nested among the mangroves. A slight smell of bird dung hung in the air and scattered droppings could be seen coloring the leaves with a snow-like dusting. Some of the tourists stood with their cameras catching birds in flight and other birds perched near the edge of the mangroves with their wings spread wide, drying in the sun.

Breaking the hush of human voices, the young woman began again, speaking over the intermittent calls of the birds and the sound of the waves washing over the mud bank.

"Most of you have noticed the small number of beaches in the Florida Keys, especially in Key West. In contrast to mainland Florida which is known for hundreds of miles of spectacular beaches, we celebrate beautiful clear water, abundance of fish, a fresh, clear sea breeze, multitudes of birds, and, of course, spectacular sunsets. People travel hundreds of miles to experience the unique tropical islands of the Florida Keys. We are not known for our beaches but for the mangrove islands, built from the extensive root systems of the mangroves, which retain mud, sand and silt to create the scattered keys. We call this area 'the backcountry,' which is typical of the keys with mud banks exposed at low tide, extensive open bays and shallow channels running through the mangroves. If you are looking for a tropical paradise with palm trees and sandy beaches, the Keys are an illusion. Sandy beaches are few and far between.

"Notice the dome shaped islands surrounding us, nearby and in the distance. The mangroves create this image on the mud flats. The island here on your right we call Bird Island. It's named after the famous island in the southern Caribbean off the coast of Venezuela. An American ornithologist is credited with naming the island due to the numerous sea birds living there, which are rare on the mainland.

"For all of you dedicated birdwatchers, our Bird Island supports the largest double breasted cormorant rookery in the Florida Keys. This rookery happens to be the same rookery I referred to in my story about Mr. Andrews and his wife Talia. Since the tide is high, we are able to idle closer to the rookery without disturbing the birds that are nesting.

"If you stop in the Audubon house in Key West, you will see many of his drawings and in the Hemingway house, the six fingered cats who are the current residents. Be sure to check out the cormorants featured in Audubon's drawings in all the major field guides for North American birds. For those of you who bought your tickets at the Starfish Gift Shop on Front Street, you can find most of the popular guides for sale there, as well as poster-sized reproductions of Audubon's cormorants.

"Authorities have estimated that cormorants have been nesting here for thousands of years, perhaps longer. Please feel free to take pictures, just refrain from using a flash as that disturbs the birds. Approximately 1300 mated pairs of double crested cormorants are nesting on Bird Island this year. This site is protected because only a small percentage of the hatchlings reach maturity, even though each mated pair usually starts with two nestlings."

The young woman paused to clear her throat again and take a sip of water.

"For you landlubbers, mariners refer to the right side of the boat as starboard and the left as port. Those of you on the starboard have the best view of the rookery now. Please remain seated as once I turn around ahead, those of you on the port side will have the better view.

Please keep your hands, arms, cameras and binoculars inside the boat at all times."

"What are those white posts up ahead on the mud flats? They're sticking out at odd angles. I thought they were channel markers, but they don't make any sense," a man near the front of the boat asked.

"You're a little ahead of me, but those are the remains of the houseboat Mr. Andrews set up as an observation station. The hull is buried in the bottom mud. During the fire, the wood beams were charred, but the birds have preserved them by coating them with guano. That's bird droppings for you novices."

An elderly woman sitting near the gangway exit, stood. "I'd like to know your opinion about that bird in the story. Do you believe it was real?"

"If you're asking me if Shoestring was special, I have to say yes. If you want to know if the bird had special powers, that I don't know. I just tell the story. You have to make your own decision about whether you believe it or not."

"Thank you," the woman replied as she returned to her seat.

A second woman wearing a brightly flowered shirt, yellow Bermuda shorts and a wide brimmed straw hat stood up.

"Yes, ma'm. I see you, please sit down."

"I've heard your story. You seem to speak with much conviction. Are you the little girl in the story?"

"You mean Mandy?"

"Yes, you're all grown up now, aren't you?"

"Before I answer, it's time for me to turn the boat around. Everyone please remain seated." As she settled back into a straight course, the young woman answered, "Okay. Let's see. You want to know if I am the little girl in the story. You are very observant, but you missed one thing."

"Ohhh, you aren't Mandy?"

"No, ma'm, I'm not, but you're close. The family picture Talia holds in her arms was taken about twenty years ago. There are two little girls about seven years difference in age. You see, Mandy is my big sister. She lives with her husband and two children in California. I'm the littlest girl in the picture. Talia and Steve are my parents."

"Oh, how wonderful. That is even nicer now that I know the whole story."

"Mandy met her husband here in Key West while he was vacationing. Mandy and I had to make a family decision as to who would remain here to run the tour boat, oversee Bird Island, and take care of our parents. I knew when I was little that one day I would take over my father's job watching out for the birds. Someone has to tell Shoestring's story. Mandy thought it was her story, but I told her she was wrong."

"But it is her story. She knew Shoestring."

"In a way, yes, but you see Mandy only gained a father when Shoestring brought our parents together. If Shoestring had not brought Steve and Talia together, I never would have been born. There are very few people in this world that owe their very existence to a wild bird. That fact makes Shoestring's story a very personal one for me, and more meaningful than if Mandy told the story."

"Oh yes, now I see what you mean. It is such a lovely story. I hope you keep telling it for many years."

The young woman brushed away the wisps of hair that blew into her face as the boat headed back to the dock. She sipped her water and continued her lecture.

"Double crested cormorants are not on the endangered species list. We have many representatives here in the Keys as well as on the mainland as far as Nova Scotia and Alaska, and all along the North American coastline. I hope the story of Shoestring will inspire you to dedicate some of your time to help protect our endangered species. The ever-growing human population is driving many birds and animals to the edge of extinction. I'm fearful that two hundred years from now, the only surviving wild creatures will be those where humans have developed a special bond to save them. Many species need our help today. Please don't forget that extinction is forever."

The diesel throbbed to life as she pushed the throttle forward and the boat responded, speeding back toward the harbor.

"We should arrive back in the Northwest Channel in about fifteen minutes. As we cross the tidal channel, be sure to watch for the shipwreck through the glass observation well. We'll pass directly over the wreck. I'll slow down so you can look closely at the bottom. You will see twenty to thirty pairs of eyes looking back at you. If you look closely you can see the stingrays buried in the sand with only their eyes protruding. For some reason, they have been gathering there in increasing numbers. No one has figured out why, but I have my theory."

"And what is that, dearie?" an older lady asked.

"I think they're just as curious about us as we are of them."

The end...

Other Publications

BOKURU, by Jon C. Hall, edited by Barbara D. Hall, AuthorHouse, Bloomington, Indiana, published June 2005.

ADAM'S EVE A Handbook for the Social Revolution; ECOA and the Story of Adam and Eve©; by Jon C. Hall, J. D., and Barbara D. Hall. AuthorHouse, Bloomington, Indiana, published May 2006. Awarded 1st in the state of New Jersey at NJ Federation of Women's Clubs Achievement Day for the cover design and Foreword Magazine's Silver Award for Book of the Year 2006 for an Independently Published work in Family and Relationships.

SADIE'S SECRET…a real story by Barbara D. Hall and Jon C. Hall. AuthorHouse, Bloomington, Indiana, published December 2007. Awarded 1st for cover design at NJ Federation of Women's Clubs Achievement Day and 1st in state for short story competition for excerpted Sadie's Secret: Sadie.

Visit our website at: www.ournaturematters.net

About the Authors

Jon C. Hall graduated from Purdue University, Lafayette, Indiana, and Indiana University School of Law-Indianapolis. He was admitted to the Indiana Bar, the Illinois Bar, and the Florida Bar. He worked many years in the field of real estate law in Indiana, Illinois and Florida. Due to health reasons, he retired from the active practice of law in 2000. During his retirement years he taught law courses to paralegals at Essex County Community College in New Jersey where he lived with his sister until his death in 2004. He maintained an active interest in nature, environmental issues, and archaeology. He is a former member of the South Florida Archaeological Association, the Florida Anthropological Society and the Roebling Chapter of the National Society for Industrial Archaeology. Jon expanded his natural gift for writing and story telling while recuperating from his health adversities. He was active in The Write Group in Montclair, New Jersey contributing a wealth of professionalism toward the success of the group.

Barbara D. Hall graduated from Wittenberg University in Springfield, Ohio and obtained a Master's degree from The Ohio State University in Columbus, Ohio. She worked many years as a consultant in the pharmaceutical industry, specializing in Food and Drug Law. In addition, she maintained a New Jersey Real Estate License; investing and managing real estate properties. In retirement, she assisted her brother during the last few years of his life writing and editing books, sharing many interests including photography, sailing, nature, archaeology and writing. Barbara is a member of The Write Group in Montclair, New Jersey and the International Woman's Writing Guild.

Printed in the United States
133429LV00006B/14/P

9 781438 90513